The High Window

RAYMOND CHANDLER

VINTAGE BOOKS
A Division of Random House
New York

VINTAGE BOOKS EDITION, September 1976

Copyright © 1942 by Raymond Chandler
Copyright renewed 1970 by Mrs. Helga Greene

Library of Congress Cataloging in Publication Data

Chandler, Raymond, 1888-1959.
  The high window.

  Reprint of the ed. published by Knopf, New York.
  I. Title.
PZ3.C3639.Hi7   [PS3505.H3224]   813'.5'2   76-11807
ISBN 0-394-72141-1

Manufactured in the United States of America

THE HOUSE WAS ON DRESDEN AVENUE IN THE OAK NOLL
section of Pasadena, a big solid cool-looking house with
burgundy brick walls, a terra cotta tile roof, and a white
stone trim. The front windows were leaded downstairs.
Upstairs windows were of the cottage type and had a lot
of rococo imitation stonework trimming around them.
From the front wall and its attendant flowering bushes a
half acre or so of fine green lawn drifted in a gentle slope
down to the street, passing on the way an enormous
deodar around which it flowed like a cool green tide
around a rock. The sidewalk and the parkway were both
very wide and in the parkway were three white acacias
that were worth seeing. There was a heavy scent of
summer on the morning and everything that grew was
perfectly still in the breathless air they get over there on
what they call a nice cool day.

All I knew about the people was that they were a Mrs.
Elizabeth Bright Murdock and family and that she
wanted to hire a nice clean private detective who
wouldn't drop cigar ashes on the floor and never carried
more than one gun. And I knew she was the widow of an
old coot with whiskers named Jasper Murdock who had
made a lot of money helping out the community, and got
his photograph in the Pasadena paper every year on his
anniversary, with the years of his birth and death underneath, and the legend: *His Life Was His Service.*

I left my car on the street and walked over a few
dozen stumble stones set into the green lawn, and rang

the bell in the brick portico under a peaked roof. A low red brick wall ran along the front of the house the short distance from the door to the edge of the driveway. At the end of the walk, on a concrete block, there was a little painted Negro in white riding breeches and a green jacket and a red cap. He was holding a whip, and there was an iron hitching ring in the block at his feet. He looked a little sad, as if he had been waiting there a long time and was getting discouraged. I went over and patted his head while I was waiting for somebody to come to the door. After a while a middle-aged sourpuss in a maid's costume opened the front door about eight inches and gave me the beady eye. "Philip Marlowe," I said. "Calling on Mrs. Murdock. By appointment."

The middle-aged sourpuss ground her teeth, snapped her eyes shut, snapped them open and said in one of those angular hardrock pioneer-type voices: "Which one?"

"Huh?"

"Which Mrs. Murdock?" she almost screamed at me.

"Mrs. Elizabeth Bright Murdock," I said. "I didn't know there was more than one."

"Well, there is," she snapped. "Got a card?"

She still had the door a scant eight inches open. She poked the end of her nose and a thin muscular hand into the opening. I got my wallet out and got one of the cards with just my name on it and put it in the hand. The hand and nose went in and the door slammed in my face. I thought that maybe I ought to have gone to the back door. I went over and patted the little Negro on the head again. "Brother," I said, "you and me both."

Time passed, quite a lot of time. I stuck a cigarette in my mouth but didn't light it. The Good Humor man went by in his little blue and white wagon, playing *Turkey in the Straw* on his music box. A large black and gold butterfly fishtailed in and landed on a hydrangea bush almost at my elbow, moved its wings slowly up and down a few times, then took off heavily and staggered away through the motionless hot scented air. The front door came open again. The sourpuss said: "This way."

I went in. The room beyond was large and square and sunken and cool and had the restful atmosphere of a funeral chapel and something of the same smell. Tapestry on the blank roughened stucco walls, iron grilles imitating balconies outside high side windows, heavy carved chairs with plush seats and tapestry backs and tarnished gilt tassels hanging down their sides. At the back a stained-glass window about the size of a tennis court. Curtained French doors underneath it. An old musty, fusty, narrow-minded, clean and bitter room. It didn't look as if anybody ever sat in it or would ever want to. Marble-topped tables with crooked legs, gilt clocks, pieces of small statuary in two colors of marble. A lot of junk that would take a week to dust. A lot of money, and all wasted. Thirty years before, in the wealthy close-mouthed provincial town Pasadena then was, it must have seemed like quite a room.

We left it and went along a hallway and after a while the sourpuss opened a door and motioned me in. "Mr. Marlowe," she said through the door in a nasty voice, and went away grinding her teeth.

■ 2 ■

IT WAS A SMALL ROOM LOOKING OUT ON THE BACK GARDEN. It had an ugly red and brown carpet and was furnished as an office. It contained what you would expect to find in a small office. A thin fragile-looking blondish girl in shell glasses sat behind a desk with a typewriter on a pulled-out leaf at her left. She had her hands poised on the keys, but she didn't have any paper in the machine. She watched me come into the room with the stiff, half-silly expression of a self-conscious person posing for a snapshot. She had a clear soft voice, asking me to sit down. "I am Miss Davis. Mrs. Murdock's secretary. She wanted me to ask you for a few references."

"References?"

"Certainly. References. Does that surprise you?"

I put my hat on her desk and the unlighted cigarette on the brim of the hat. "You mean she sent for me without knowing anything about me?"

Her lip trembled and she bit it. I didn't know whether she was scared or annoyed or just having trouble being cool and businesslike. But she didn't look happy. "She got your name from the manager of a branch of the California Security Bank. But he doesn't know you personally," she said.

"Get your pencil ready," I said. She held it up and showed me that it was freshly sharpened and ready to go. I said: "First off, one of the vice-presidents of that same bank, George S. Leake. He's in the main office. Then State Senator Huston Oglethorpe. He may be in Sacramento, or he may be at his office in the State Building in L.A. Then Sidney Dreyfus, Jr., of Dreyfus, Turner and Swayne, attorneys in the Title-Insurance Building. Got that?"

She wrote fast and easily. She nodded without looking up. The light danced on her blond hair.

"Oliver Fry of the Fry-Krantz Corporation, Oil Well Tools. They're over on East Ninth, in the industrial district. Then, if you would like a couple of cops, Bernard Ohls of the D.A.'s staff, and Detective-Lieutenant Carl Randall of the Central Homicide Bureau. You think maybe that would be enough?"

"Don't laugh at me," she said. "I'm only doing what I'm told."

"Better not call the last two, unless you know what the job is," I said. "I'm not laughing at you. Hot, isn't it?"

"It's not hot for Pasadena," she said, and hoisted her phone book up on the desk and went to work.

While she was looking up the numbers and telephoning hither and yon I looked her over. She was pale with a sort of natural paleness and she looked healthy enough.

Her coarse-grained coppery blond hair was not ugly in itself, but it was drawn back so tightly over her narrow head that it almost lost the effect of being hair at all. Her eyebrows were thin and unusually straight and were darker than her hair, almost a chestnut color. Her nostrils had the whitish look of an anaemic person. Her chin was too small, too sharp and looked unstable. She wore no makeup except orange-red on her mouth and not much of that. Her eyes behind the glasses were very large, cobalt blue with big irises and a vague expression. Both lids were tight so that the eyes had a slightly oriental look, or as if the skin of her face was naturally so tight that it stretched her eyes at the corners. The whole face had a sort of off-key neurotic charm that only needed some clever makeup to be striking. She wore a one-piece linen dress with short sleeves and no ornament of any kind. Her bare arms had down on them, and a few freckles.

I didn't pay much attention to what she said over the telephone. Whatever was said to her she wrote down in shorthand, with deft easy strokes of the pencil. When she was through she hung the phone book back on a hook and stood up and smoothed the linen dress down over her thighs and said: "If you will just wait a few moments—" and went towards the door.

Halfway there she turned back and pushed a top drawer of her desk shut at the side. She went out. The door closed. There was silence. Outside the window bees buzzed. Far off I heard the whine of a vacuum cleaner. I picked the unlighted cigarette off my hat, put it in my mouth and stood up. I went around the desk and pulled open the drawer she had come back to shut. It wasn't any of my business. I was just curious. It wasn't any of my business that she had a small Colt automatic in the drawer. I shut it and sat down again.

She was gone about four minutes. She opened the door and stayed at it and said: "Mrs. Murdock will see you now."

We went along some more hallway and she opened

half of a double glass door and stood aside. I went in and the door was closed behind me.

It was so dark in there that at first I couldn't see anything but the outdoor light coming through thick bushes and screens. Then I saw that the room was a sort of sun porch that had been allowed to get completely overgrown outside. It was furnished with grass rugs and reed stuff. There was a reed chaise longue over by the window. It had a curved back and enough cushions to stuff an elephant and there was a woman leaning back on it with a wine glass in her hand. I could smell the thick scented alcoholic odor of the wine before I could see her properly. Then my eyes got used to the light and I could see her.

She had a lot of face and chin. She had pewter-colored hair set in a ruthless permanent, a hard beak and large moist eyes with the sympathetic expression of wet stones. There was lace at her throat, but it was the kind of throat that would have looked better in a football sweater. She wore a grayish silk dress. Her thick arms were bare and mottled. There were jet buttons in her ears. There was a low glass-topped table beside her and a bottle of port on the table. She sipped from the glass she was holding and looked at me over it and said nothing.

I stood there. She let me stand while she finished the port in her glass and put the glass down on the table and filled it again. Then she tapped her lips with a handkerchief. Then she spoke. Her voice had a hard baritone quality and sounded as if it didn't want any nonsense. "Sit down, Mr. Marlowe. Please do not light that cigarette. I'm asthmatic."

I sat down in a reed rocker and tucked the still unlighted cigarette down behind the handkerchief in my outside pocket.

"I've never had any dealing with private detectives, Mr. Marlowe. I don't know anything about them. Your references seem satisfactory. What are your charges?"

"To do what, Mrs. Murdock?"

"It's a very confidential matter, naturally. Nothing to

do with the police. If it had to do with the police, I should have called the police."

"I charge twenty-five dollars a day, Mrs. Murdock. And of course expenses."

"It seems high. You must make a great deal of money." She drank some more of her port. I don't like port in hot weather, but it's nice when they let you refuse it.

"No," I said. "It isn't. Of course you can get detective work done at any price—just like legal work. Or dental work. I'm not an organization. I'm just one man and I work at just one case at a time. I take risks, sometimes quite big risks, and I don't work all the time. No, I don't think twenty-five dollars a day is too much."

"I see. And what is the nature of the expenses?"

"Little things that come up here and there. You never know."

"I should prefer to know," she said acidly.

"You'll know," I said. "You'll get it all down in black and white. You'll have a chance to object, if you don't like it."

"And how much retainer would you expect?"

"A hundred dollars would hold me," I said.

"I should hope it would," she said and finished her port and poured the glass full again without even waiting to wipe her lips.

"From people in your position, Mrs. Murdock, I don't necessarily have to have a retainer."

"Mr. Marlowe," she said, "I'm a strong-minded woman. But don't let me scare you. Because if you can be scared by me, you won't be much use to me."

I nodded and let that one drift with the tide.

She laughed suddenly and then she belched. It was a nice light belch, nothing showy, and performed with easy unconcern. "My asthma," she said carelessly. "I drink this wine as medicine. That's why I'm not offering you any."

I swung a leg over my knee. I hoped that wouldn't hurt her asthma.

"Money," she said, "is not really important. A woman in my position is always overcharged and gets to expect it. I hope you will be worth your fee. Here is the situation. Something of considerable value has been stolen from me. I want it back, but I want more than that. I don't want anybody arrested. The thief happens to be a member of my family—by marriage." She turned the wine glass with her thick fingers and smiled faintly in the dim light of the shadowed room. "My daughter-in-law," she said. "A charming girl—and tough as an oak board."

She looked at me with a sudden gleam in her eyes. "I have a damn fool of a son," she said. "But I'm very fond of him. About a year ago he made an idiotic marriage, without my consent. This was foolish of him because he is quite incapable of earning a living and he has no money except what I give him, and I am not generous with money. The lady he chose, or who chose him, was a night club singer. Her name, appropriately enough, was Linda Conquest. They have lived here in this house. We didn't quarrel because I don't allow people to quarrel with me in my own house, but there has not been good feeling between us. I have paid their expenses, given each of them a car, made the lady a sufficient but not gaudy allowance for clothes and so on. No doubt she found the life rather dull. No doubt she found my son dull. I find him dull myself. At any rate she moved out, very abruptly, a week or so ago, without leaving a forwarding address or saying good-by."

She coughed, fumbled for a handkerchief, and blew her nose. "What was taken," she went on, "was a coin. A rare gold coin called a Brasher Doubloon. It was the pride of my husband's collection. I care nothing for such things, but he did. I have kept the collection intact since he died four years ago. It is upstairs, in a locked fireproof room, in a set of fireproof cases. It is insured, but I have not reported the loss yet. I don't want to, if I can help it. I'm quite sure Linda took it. The coin is said to be worth over ten thousand dollars. It's a mint specimen."

"But pretty hard to sell," I said.

"Perhaps. I don't know. I didn't miss the coin until yesterday. I should not have missed it then, as I never go near the collection, except that a man in Los Angeles named Morningstar called up, said he was a dealer, and was the Murdock Brasher, as he called it, for sale? My son happened to take the call. He said he didn't believe it was for sale, it never had been, but that if Mr. Morningstar would call some other time, he could probably talk to me. It was not convenient then, as I was resting. The man said he would do that. My son reported the conversation to Miss Davis, who reported it to me. I had her call the man back. I was faintly curious."

She sipped some more port, flopped her handkerchief about and grunted.

"Why were you curious, Mrs. Murdock?" I asked, just to be saying something.

"If the man was a dealer of any repute, he would know that the coin was not for sale. My husband, Jasper Murdock, provided in his will that no part of his collection might be sold, loaned or hypothecated during my lifetime. Nor removed from this house, except in case of damage to the house necessitating removal, and then only by action of the trustees. My husband—" she smiled grimly— "seemed to feel that I ought to have taken more interest in his little pieces of metal while he was alive."

It was a nice day outside, the sun shining, the flowers blooming, the birds singing. Cars went by on the street with a distant comfortable sound. In the dim room with the hard-faced woman and the winy smell everything seemed a little unreal. I tossed my foot up and down over my knee and waited.

"I spoke to Mr. Morningstar. His full name is Elisha Morningstar and he has offices in the Belfont Building on Ninth Street in downtown Los Angeles. I told him the Murdock collection was not for sale, never had been, and, so far as I was concerned, never would be, and that I was surprised that he didn't know that. He hemmed and hawed and then asked me if he might examine the coin. I said certainly not. He thanked me rather dryly and hung up. He sounded like an old man. So I went upstairs to examine the coin myself, something I had not done in a year. It was gone from its place in one of the locked fireproof cases."

I said nothing. She refilled her glass and played a

tattoo with her thick fingers on the arm of the chaise longue. "What I thought then you can probably guess."

I said: "The part about Mr. Morningstar, maybe. Somebody had offered the coin to him for sale and he had known or suspected where it came from. The coin must be very rare."

"What they call a mint specimen is very rare indeed. Yes, I had the same idea."

"How would it be stolen?" I asked.

"By anyone in this house, very easily. The keys are in my bag, and my bag lies around here and there. It would be a very simple matter to get hold of the keys long enough to unlock a door and a cabinet and then return the keys. Difficult for an outsider, but anybody in the house could have stolen it."

"I see. How do you establish that your daughter-in-law took it, Mrs. Murdock?"

"I don't—in a strictly evidential sense. But I'm quite sure of it. The servants are three women who have been here many, many years—long before I married Mr. Murdock, which was only seven years ago. The gardener never comes in the house. I have no chauffeur, because either my son or my secretary drives me. My son didn't take it, first because he is not the kind of fool that steals from his mother, and secondly, if he had taken it, he could easily have prevented me from speaking to the coin dealer, Morningstar. Miss Davis—ridiculous. Just not the type at all. Too mousy. No, Mr. Marlowe, Linda is the sort of lady who might do it just for spite, if nothing else. And you know what these night club people are."

"All sorts of people—like the rest of us," I said. "No signs of a burglar, I suppose? It would take a pretty smooth worker to lift just one valuable coin, so there wouldn't be. Maybe I had better look the room over, though."

She pushed her jaw at me and muscles in her neck made hard lumps. "I have just told you, Mr. Marlowe, that Mrs. Leslie Murdock, my daughter-in-law, took the Brasher Doubloon."

I stared at her and she stared back. Her eyes were as

hard as the bricks in her front walk. I shrugged the stare off and said: "Assuming that is so, Mrs. Murdock, just what do you want done?"

"In the first place I want the coin back. In the second place I want an uncontested divorce for my son. And I don't intend to buy it. I daresay you know how these things are arranged." She finished the current instalment of port and laughed rudely.

"I may have heard," I said. "You say the lady left no forwarding address. Does that mean you have no idea at all where she went?"

"Exactly that."

"A disappearance then. Your son might have some ideas he hasn't passed along to you. I'll have to see him."

The big gray face hardened into even ruggeder lines. "My son knows nothing. He doesn't even know the doubloon has been stolen. I don't want him to know anything. When the time comes I'll handle him. Until then I want him left alone. He will do exactly what I want him to."

"He hasn't always," I said.

"His marriage," she said nastily, "was a momentary impulse. Afterwards he tried to act like a gentleman. I have no such scruples."

"It takes three days to have that kind of momentary impulse in California, Mrs. Murdock."

"Young man, do you want this job or don't you?"

"I want it if I'm told the facts and allowed to handle the case as I see fit. I don't want it if you're going to make a lot of rules and regulations for me to trip over."

She laughed harshly. "This is a delicate family matter, Mr. Marlowe. And it must be handled with delicacy."

"If you hire me, you'll get all the delicacy I have. If I don't have enough delicacy, maybe you'd better not hire me. For instance, I take it you don't want your daughter-in-law framed. I'm not delicate enough for that."

She turned the color of a cold boiled beet and opened her mouth to yell. Then she thought better of it, lifted her port glass and tucked away some more of her medicine. "You'll do," she said dryly, "I wish I had met you two years ago, before he married her."

I didn't know exactly what this last meant, so I let it ride. She bent over sideways and fumbled with the key on a house telephone and growled into it when she was answered.

There were steps and the little copper-blonde came tripping into the room with her chin low, as if somebody might be going to take a swing at her.

"Make this man a check for two hundred and fifty dollars," the old dragon snarled at her. "And keep your mouth shut about it."

The little girl flushed all the way to her neck. "You know I never talk about your affairs, Mrs. Murdock," she bleated. "You know I don't. I wouldn't dream of it, I—" She turned with her head down and ran out of the room. As she closed the door I looked out at her. Her little lip was trembling but her eyes were mad.

"I'll need a photo of the lady and some information," I said when the door was shut again.

"Look in the desk drawer." Her rings flashed in the dimness as her thick gray finger pointed.

I went over and opened the single drawer of the reed desk and took out the photo that lay all alone in the bottom of the drawer, face up, looking at me with cool dark eyes. I sat down again with the photo and looked it over. Dark hair parted loosely in the middle and drawn back loosely over a solid piece of forehead. A wide cool go-to-hell mouth with very kissable lips. Nice nose, not too small, not too large. Good bone all over the face. The expression of the face lacked something. Once the something might have been called breeding, but these days I didn't know what to call it. The face looked too wise and too guarded for its age. Too many passes had been made at it and it had grown a little too smart in dodging them. And behind this expression of wiseness there was the look of simplicity of the little girl who still believes in Santa Claus.

I nodded over the photo and slipped it into my

pocket, thinking I was getting too much out of it to get out of a mere photo, and in a very poor light at that.

The door opened and the little girl in the linen dress came in with a three-decker check book and a fountain pen and made a desk of her arm for Mrs. Murdock to sign. She straightened up with a strained smile and Mrs. Murdock made a sharp gesture towards me and the little girl tore the check out and gave it to me. She hovered inside the door, waiting. Nothing was said to her, so she went out softly again and closed the door.

I shook the check dry, folded it and sat holding it. "What can you tell me about Linda?"

"Practically nothing. Before she married my son she shared an apartment with a girl named Lois Magic— charming names these people choose for themselves— who is an entertainer of some sort. They worked at a place called the Idle Valley Club, out Ventura Boulevard way. My son Leslie knows it far too well. I know nothing about Linda's family or origins. She said once she was born in Sioux Falls. I suppose she had parents. I was not interested enough to find out."

Like hell she wasn't. I could see her digging with both hands, digging hard, and getting herself a double hand-ful of gravel.

"You don't know Miss Magic's address?"

"No. I never did know."

"Would your son be likely to know—or Miss Davis?"

"I'll ask my son when he comes in. I don't think so. You can ask Miss Davis. I'm sure she doesn't."

"I see. You "don't know of any other friends of Lin-da's?"

"No."

"It's possible that your son is still in touch with her, Mrs. Murdock—without telling you."

She started to get purple again. I held my hand up and dragged a soothing smile over my face. "After all he has been married to her a year," I said. "He must know something about her."

"You leave my son out of this," she snarled.

I shrugged and made a disappointed sound with my

lips. "Very well. She took her car, I suppose. The one you gave her?"

"A steel gray Mercury, 1940 model, a coupé. Miss Davis can give you the license number, if you want that. I don't know whether she took it."

"Would you know what money and clothes and jewels she had with her?"

"Not much money. She might have had a couple of hundred dollars, at most." A fat sneer made deep lines around her nose and mouth. "Unless of course she has found a new friend."

"There's that," I said. "Jewelry?"

"An emerald and diamond ring of no very great value; a platinum Longines watch with rubies in the mounting, a very good cloudy amber necklace which I was foolish enough to give her myself. It has a diamond clasp with twenty-six small diamonds in the shape of a playing card diamond. She had other things, of course. I never paid much attention to them. She dressed well but not strikingly. Thank God for a few small mercies."

She refilled her glass and drank and did some more of her semi-social belching.

"That's all you can tell me, Mrs. Murdock?"

"Isn't it enough?"

"Not nearly enough, but I'll have to be satisfied for the time being. If I find she did not steal the coin, that ends the investigation as far as I'm concerned. Correct?"

"We'll talk it over," she said roughly. "She stole it all right. And I don't intend to let her get away with it. Paste that in your hat, young man. And I hope you are even half as rough as you like to act, because these night club girls are apt to have some very nasty friends."

I was still holding the folded check by one corner down between my knees. I got my wallet out and put it away and stood up, reaching my hat off the floor. "I like them nasty," I said. "The nasty ones have very simple minds. I'll report to you when there is anything to report, Mrs. Murdock. I think I'll tackle this coin dealer first. He sounds like a lead."

She let me get to the door before she growled at my back: "You don't like me very well, do you?"

I turned to grin back at her with my hand on the knob. "Does anybody?"

She threw her head back and opened her mouth wide and roared with laughter. In the middle of the laughter I opened the door and went out and shut the door on the rough mannish sound. I went back along the hall and knocked on the secretary's half open door, then pushed it open and looked in.

She had her arms folded on her desk and her face down on the folded arms. She was sobbing. She screwed her head around and looked up at me with tear-stained eyes. I shut the door and went over beside her and put an arm around her thin shoulders. "Cheer up," I said. "You ought to feel sorry for her. She thinks she's tough and she's breaking her back trying to live up to it."

The little girl jumped erect, away from my arm. "Don't touch me," she said breathlessly. "Please. I never let men touch me. And don't say such awful things about Mrs. Murdock." Her face was all pink and wet from tears. Without her glasses her eyes were very lovely.

I stuck my long-waiting cigarette into my mouth and lit it.

"I—I didn't mean to be rude," she snuffled. "But she does humiliate me so. And I only want to do my best for her." She snuffled some more and got a man's handkerchief out of her desk and shook it out and wiped her eyes with it. I saw on the hanging down corner the initials L. M. embroidered in purple. I stared at it and blew cigarette smoke towards the corner of the room, away from her hair. "Is there something you want?" she asked.

"I want the license number of Mrs. Leslie Murdock's car."

"It's 2X1111, a gray Mercury convertible, 1940 model."

"She told me it was a coupé."

"That's Mr. Leslie's car. They're the same make and year and color. Linda didn't take the car."

"Oh. What do you know about a Miss Lois Magic?"

"I only saw her once. She used to share an apartment with Linda. She came here with a Mr.—a Mr. Vannier."

"Who's he?"

She looked down at her desk. "I—she just came with him. I don't know him."

"Okay, what does Miss Lois Magic look like?"

"She's a tall handsome blond. Very—very appealing."

"You mean sexy?"

"Well—" she blushed furiously, "in a nice well-bred sort of way, if you know what I mean."

"I know what you mean," I said, "but I never got anywhere with it."

"I can believe that," she said tartly.

"Know where Miss Magic lives?"

She shook her head, no. She folded the big handkerchief very carefully and put it in the drawer of her desk, the one where the gun was.

"You can swipe another one when that's dirty," I said.

She leaned back in her chair and put her small neat hands on her desk and looked at me levelly. "I wouldn't carry that tough-guy manner too far, if I were you, Mr. Marlowe. Not with me, at any rate."

"No?"

"No. And I can't answer any more questions without specific instructions. My position here is very confidential."

"I'm not tough," I said. "Just virile."

She picked up a pencil and made a mark on a pad. She smiled faintly up at me, all composure again. "Perhaps I don't like virile men," she said.

"You're a screwball," I said, "if ever I met one. Goodby."

I went out of her office, shut the door firmly, and walked back along the empty halls through the big silent sunken funereal living room and out of the front door. The sun danced on the warm lawn outside. I put my dark glasses on and went over and patted the little Negro on the head again. "Brother, it's even worse than I expected," I told him.

The stumble stones were hot through the soles of my

shoes. I got into the car and started it and pulled away from the curb. A small sand-colored coupé pulled away from the curb behind me. I didn't think anything of it. The man driving it wore a dark porkpie type straw hat with a gay print band and dark glasses were over his eyes, as over mine.

I drove back towards the city. A dozen blocks later at a traffic stop, the sand-colored coupé was still behind me. I shrugged and just for the fun of it circled a few blocks. The coupé held its position. I swung into a street lined with immense pepper trees, dragged my heap around in a fast U-turn and stopped against the curbing.

The coupé came carefully around the corner. The blond head under the cocoa straw hat with the tropical print band didn't even turn my way. The coupé sailed on and I drove back to the Arroyo Seco and on towards Hollywood. I looked carefully several times, but I didn't spot the coupé again.

■ 3 ■

I HAD AN OFFICE IN THE CAHUENGA BUILDING, SIXTH FLOOR, two small rooms at the back. One I left open for a patient client to sit in, if I had a patient client. There was a buzzer on the door which I could switch on and off from my private thinking parlor.

I looked into the reception room. It was empty of everything but the smell of dust. I threw up another window, unlocked the communicating door and went into the room beyond. Three hard chairs and a swivel chair, flat desk with a glass top, five green filing cases, three of them full of nothing, a calendar and a framed license bond on the wall, a phone, a washbowl in a stained wood cupboard, a hatrack, a carpet that was just something on the floor, and two open windows with net curtains that puckered in and out like the lips of a toothless old man sleeping. The same stuff I had had last year, and the year before that. Not beautiful, not gay, but better than a tent on the beach.

I hung my hat and coat on the hatrack, washed my face and hands in cold water, lit a cigarette and hoisted the phone book onto the desk. Elisha Morningstar was listed at 824 Belfont Building, 422 West Ninth Street. I wrote that down and the phone number that went with it and had my hand on the instrument when I remembered that I hadn't switched on the buzzer for the reception room. I reached over the side of the desk and clicked it on and caught it right in stride. Somebody had just opened the door of the outer office.

I turned my pad face down on the desk and went over to see who it was. It was a slim tall self-satisfied looking number in a tropical worsted suit of slate blue, black and white shoes, a dull ivory-colored shirt and a tie and display handkerchief the color of jacaranda bloom. He was holding a long black cigarette-holder in a peeled back white pigskin glove and he was wrinkling his nose at the dead magazines on the library table and the chairs and the rusty floor covering and the general air of not much money being made.

As I opened the communicating door he made a quarter turn and stared at me out of a pair of rather dreamy pale eyes set close to a narrow nose. His skin was sun-flushed, his reddish hair was brushed back hard over a narrow skull, and the thin line of his mustache was much redder than his hair. He looked me over without haste and without much pleasure. He blew some smoke delicately and spoke through it with a faint sneer.

"You're Marlowe?"

I nodded.

"I'm a little disappointed," he said. "I rather expected something with dirty fingernails."

"Come inside," I said, "and you can be witty sitting down."

I held the door for him and he strolled past me flicking

cigarette ash on the floor with the middle nail of his free hand. He sat down on the customer's side of the desk, took off the glove from his right hand and folded this with the other already off and laid them on the desk. He tapped the cigarette end out of the long black holder, prodded the coal with a match until it stopped smoking, fitted another cigarette and lit it with a broad mahogany-colored match. He leaned back in his chair with the smile of a bored aristocrat.

"All set?" I enquired. "Pulse and respiration normal? You wouldn't like a cold towel on your head or anything?"

He didn't curl his lip because it had been curled when he came in. "A private detective," he said. "I never met one. A shifty business, one gathers. Keyhole peeping, raking up scandal, that sort of thing."

"You here on business," I asked him, "or just slumming?"

His smile was as faint as a fat lady at a fireman's ball.

"The name is Murdock. That probably means a little something to you."

"You certainly made nice time over here," I said, and started to fill a pipe.

He watched me fill the pipe. He said slowly: "I understand my mother has employed you on a job of some sort. She has given you a check."

I finished filling the pipe, put a match to it, got it drawing and leaned back to blow smoke over my right shoulder towards the open window. I didn't say anything.

He leaned forward a little more and said earnestly: "I know being cagey is all part of your trade, but I am not guessing. A little worm told me, a simple garden worm, often trodden on, but still somehow surviving—like myself. I happened to be not far behind you. Does that help to clear things up?"

"Yeah," I said. "Supposing it made any difference to me."

"You are hired to find my wife, I gather."

I made a snorting sound and grinned at him over the pipe bowl.

"Marlowe," he said, even more earnestly, "I'll try hard, but I don't think I am going to like you."

"I'm screaming," I said. "With rage and pain."

"And if you will pardon a homely phrase, your tough guy act stinks."

"Coming from you, that's bitter."

He leaned back again and brooded at me with pale eyes. He fussed around in the chair, trying to get comfortable. A lot of people had tried to get comfortable in that chair. I ought to try it myself sometime. Maybe it was losing business for me.

"Why should my mother want Linda found?" he asked slowly. "She hated her guts. I mean my mother hated Linda's guts. Linda was quite decent to my mother. What do you think of her?"

"Your mother?"

"Of course. You haven't met Linda, have you?"

"That secretary of your mother's has her job hanging by a frayed thread. She talks out of turn."

He shook his head sharply. "Mother won't know. Anyhow, Mother couldn't do without Merle. She has to have somebody to bully. She might yell at her or even slap her face, but she couldn't do without her. What do you think of her?"

"Kind of cute—in an old world sort of way."

He frowned. "I mean Mother. Merle's just a simple little girl, I know."

"Your powers of observation startle me," I said.

He looked surprised. He almost forgot to fingernail the ash of his cigarette. But not quite. He was careful not to get any of it in the ashtray, however. "About my mother," he said patiently.

"A grand old warhorse," I said. "A heart of gold, and the gold buried good and deep."

"But why does she want Linda found? I can't understand it. Spending money on it too. My mother hates to spend money. She thinks money is part of her skin. Why does she want Linda found?"

"Search me," I said. "Who said she did?"

"Why, you implied so. And Merle—"

"Merle's just romantic. She made it up. Hell, she blows her nose in a man's handkerchief. Probably one of yours."

He blushed. "That's silly. Look, Marlowe. Please, be reasonable and give me an idea what it's all about. I haven't much money, I'm afraid, but would a couple of hundred—"

"I ought to bop you," I said. "Besides I'm not supposed to talk to you. Orders."

"Why, for heaven's sake?"

"Don't ask me things I don't know. I can't tell you the answers. And don't ask me things I do know, because I won't tell you the answers. Where have you been all your life? If a man in my line of work is handed a job, does he go around answering questions about it to anyone that gets curious?"

"There must be a lot of electricity in the air," he said nastily, "for a man in your line of work to turn down two hundred dollars."

There was nothing in that for me either. I picked his broad mahogany match out of the tray and looked at it. It had thin yellow edges and there was white printing on it. ROSEMONT. H. RICHARDS '3—the rest was burnt off. I doubled the match and squeezed the halves together and tossed it in the waste basket.

"I love my wife," he said suddenly and showed me the hard white edges of his teeth. "A corny touch, but it's true."

"The Lombardos are still doing all right."

He kept his lips pulled back from his teeth and talked through them at me. "She doesn't love me. I know of no particular reason why she should. Things have been strained between us. She was used to a fast moving sort of life. With us, well, it has been pretty dull. We haven't quarreled. Linda's the cool type. But she hasn't really had a lot of fun being married to me."

"You're just too modest," I said.

His eyes glinted, but he kept his smooth manner pretty well in place. "Not good, Marlowe. Not even fresh. Look, you have the air of a decent sort of guy. I know my mother is not putting out two hundred and fifty bucks just to be breezy. Maybe it's not Linda. Maybe it's something else. Maybe—" he stopped and then said this very slowly, watching my eyes, "maybe it's Morny."

"Maybe it is," I said cheerfully.

He picked his gloves up and slapped the desk with them and put them down again. "I'm in a spot there all right," he said. "But I didn't think she knew about it. Morny must have called her up. He promised not to."

This was easy. I said: "How much are you into him for?"

It wasn't so easy. He got suspicious again. "If he called her up, he would have told her. And she would have told you," he said thinly.

"Maybe it isn't Morny," I said, beginning to want a drink very badly. "Maybe the cook is with child by the iceman. But if it was Morny, how much?"

"Twelve thousand," he said, looking down and flushing.

"Threats?"

He nodded.

"Tell him to go fly a kite," I said. "What kind of lad is he? Tough?"

He looked up again, his face being brave. "I suppose he is. I suppose they all are. He used to be a screen heavy. Good looking in a flashy way, a chaser. But don't get any ideas. Linda just worked there, like the waiters and the band. And if you are looking for her, you'll have a hard time finding her."

I sneered at him politely. "Why would I have a hard time finding her? She's not buried in the back yard, I hope."

He stood up with a flash of anger in his pale eyes. Standing there leaning over the desk a little he whipped his right hand up in a neat enough gesture and brought out a small automatic, about .25 caliber with a walnut grip. It looked like the brother of the one I had seen in the drawer of Merle's desk. The muzzle looked vicious enough pointing at me. I didn't move.

"If anybody tries to push Linda around, he'll have to push me around first," he said tightly.

"That oughtn't to be too hard. Better get more gun—unless you're just thinking of bees."

He put the little gun back in his inside pocket. He gave me a straight hard look and picked his gloves up and started for the door. "It's a waste of time talking to you," he said. "All you do is crack wise."

I said: "Wait a minute," and got up and went around the desk. "It might be a good idea for you not to mention this interview to your mother, if only for the little girl's sake."

He nodded. "For the amount of information I got, it doesn't seem worth mentioning."

"That straight goods about your owing Morny twelve grand?"

He looked down, then up, then down again. He said: "Anybody who could get into Alex Morny for twelve grand would have to be a lot smarter than I am."

I was quite close to him. I said: "As a matter of fact I don't even think you are worried about your wife. I think you know where she is. She didn't run away from you at all. She just ran away from your mother."

He lifted his eyes and drew one glove on. He didn't say anything.

"Perhaps she'll get a job," I said. "And make enough money to support you."

He looked down at the floor again, turned his body to the right a little and the gloved fist made a tight unrelaxed arc through the air upwards. I moved my jaw out of the way and caught his wrist and pushed it slowly back against his chest, leaning on it. He slid a foot back on the floor and began to breathe hard. It was a slender wrist. My fingers went around it and met.

We stood there looking into each other's eyes. He was breathing like a drunk, his mouth open and his lips pulled back. Small round spots of bright red flamed on his cheeks. He tried to jerk his wrist away, but I put so much weight on him that he had to take another short step back to brace himself. Our faces were now only inches apart.

"How come your old man didn't leave you some money?" I sneered. "Or did you blow it all?"

He spoke between his teeth, still trying to jerk loose. "If it's any of your rotten business and you mean Jasper Murdock, he wasn't my father. He didn't like me and he didn't leave me a cent. My father was a man named Horace Bright who lost his money in the crash and jumped out of his office window."

"You milk easy," I said, "but you give pretty thin milk. I'm sorry for what I said about your wife supporting you. I just wanted to get your goat."

I dropped his wrist and stepped back. He still breathed hard and heavily. His eyes on mine were very angry, but he kept his voice down. "Well, you got it. If you're satisfied, I'll be on my way."

"I was doing you a favor," I said. "A gun toter oughtn't to insult so easily. Better ditch it."

"That's my business," he said. "I'm sorry I took a swing at you. It probably wouldn't have hurt much, if it had connected."

"That's all right."

He opened the door and went on out. His steps died along the corridor. Another screwball. I tapped my teeth with a knuckle in time to the sound of his steps as long as I could hear them. Then I went back to the desk, looked at my pad, and lifted the phone.

■ 4 ■

AFTER THE BELL HAD RUNG THREE TIMES AT THE OTHER end of the line a light childish sort of girl's voice filtered itself through a hunk of gum and said: "Good morning. Mr. Morningstar's office."

"Is the old gentleman in?"

"Who is calling, please?"

"Marlowe."

"Does he know you, Mr. Marlowe?"

"Ask him if he wants to buy any early American gold coins."

"Just a minute, please."

There was a pause suitable to an elderly party in an inner office having his attention called to the fact that somebody on the telephone wanted to talk to him. Then the phone clicked and a man spoke. He had a dry voice. You might even call it parched. "This is Mr. Morningstar."

"I'm told you called Mrs. Murdock in Pasadena, Mr. Morningstar. About a certain coin."

"About a certain coin," he repeated. "Indeed. Well?"

"My understanding is that you wished to buy the coin in question from the Murdock collection."

"Indeed? And who are you, sir?"

"Philip Marlowe. A private detective. I'm working for Mrs. Murdock."

"Indeed," he said for the third time. He cleared his throat carefully. "And what did you wish to talk to me about, Mr. Marlowe?"

"About this coin."

"But I was informed it was not for sale."

"I still want to talk to you about it. In person."

"Do you mean she has changed her mind about selling?"

"No."

"Then I'm afraid I don't understand what you want, Mr. Marlowe. What have we to talk about?" He sounded sly now.

I took the ace out of my sleeve and played it with a languid grace. "The point is, Mr. Morningstar, that at the time you called up you already knew the coin wasn't for sale."

"Interesting," he said slowly. "How?"

"You're in the business, you couldn't help knowing. It's

a matter of public record that the Murdock collection cannot be sold during Mrs. Murdock's lifetime."

"Ah," he said. "Ah." There was a silence. Then, "At three o'clock," he said, not sharp, but quick. "I shall be glad to see you here in my office. You probably know where it is. Will that suit you?"

"I'll be there," I said.

I hung up and lit my pipe again and sat there looking at the wall. My face was stiff with thought, or with something that made my face stiff. I took Linda Murdock's photo out of my pocket, stared at it for a while, decided that the face was pretty commonplace after all, locked the photo away in my desk. I picked Murdock's second match out of my ashtray and looked it over. The lettering on this one read: TOP ROW W. D. WRIGHT '36. I dropped it back in the tray, wondering what made this important. Maybe it was a clue.

I got Mrs. Murdock's check out of my wallet, endorsed it, made out a deposit slip and a check for cash, got my bank book out of the desk, and folded the lot under a rubber band and put them in my pocket.

Lois Magic was not listed in the phone book. I got the classified section up on the desk and made a list of the half dozen theatrical agencies that showed in the largest type and called them. They all had bright cheerful voices and wanted to ask a lot of questions, but they either didn't know or didn't care to tell me anything about a Miss Lois Magic, said to be an entertainer.

I threw the list in the waste basket and called Kenny Haste, a crime reporter on the Chronicle. "What do you know about Alex Morny?" I asked him when we were through cracking wise at each other.

"Runs a plushy night club and gambling joint in Idle Valley, about two miles off the highway back towards the hills. Used to be in pictures. Lousy actor. Seems to have plenty of protection. I never heard of him shooting anybody on the public square at high noon. Or at any other time for that matter. But I wouldn't like to bet on it."

"Dangerous?"

"I'd say he might be, if necessary. All those boys have been to picture shows and know how night club bosses are supposed to act. He has a bodyguard who is quite a character. His name's Eddie Prue, he's about six feet five inches tall and thin as an honest alibi. He has a frozen eye, the result of a war wound."

"Is Morny dangerous to women?"

"Don't be Victorian, old top. Women don't call it danger."

"Do you know a girl named Lois Magic, said to be an entertainer? A tall gaudy blond, I hear."

"No. Sounds as though I might like to."

"Don't be cute. Do you know anybody named Vannier? None of these people are in the phone book."

"Nope. But I could ask Gertie Arbogast, if you want to call back. He knows all the night club aristocrats. And heels."

"Thanks, Kenny. I'll do that. Half an hour?"

He said that would be fine, and we hung up. I locked the office and left.

At the end of the corridor, in the angle of the wall, a youngish blond man in a brown suit and a cocoa-colored straw hat with a brown and yellow tropical print band was reading the evening paper with his back to the wall. As I passed him he yawned and tucked the paper under his arm and straightened up. He got into the elevator with me. He could hardly keep his eyes open he was so tired. I went out on the street and walked a block to the bank to deposit my check and draw out a little folding money for expenses. From there I went to the Tigertail Lounge and sat in a shallow booth and drank a martini and ate a sandwich. The man in the brown suit posted himself at the end of the bar and drank coca colas and looked bored and piled pennies in front of him, carefully smoothing the edges. He had his dark glasses on again. That made him invisible.

I dragged my sandwich out as long as I could and then strolled back to the telephone booth at the inner end of the bar. The man in the brown suit turned his head quickly and then covered the motion by lifting his glass. I dialed the Chronicle office again.

"Okay," Kenny Haste said. "Gertie Arbogast says Morny married your gaudy blond not very long ago. Lois Magic. He doesn't know Vannier. He says Morny bought a place out beyond Bel-Air, a white house on Stillwood Crescent Drive, about five blocks north of Sunset. Gertie says Morny took it over from a busted flush named Arthur Blake Popham who got caught in a mail fraud rap. Popham's initials are still on the gates. And probably on the toilet paper, Gertie says. He was that kind of a guy. That's all we seem to know."

"Nobody could ask more. Many thanks, Kenny."

I hung up, stepped out of the booth, met the dark glasses above the brown suit under the cocoa straw hat and watched them turn quickly away. I spun around and went back through a swing door into the kitchen and through that to the alley and along the alley a quarter block to the back of the parking lot where I had put my car.

No sand-colored coupé succeeded in getting behind me as I drove off, in the general direction of Bel-Air.

■ 5 ■

STILLWOOD CRESCENT DRIVE CURVED LEISURELY NORTH from Sunset Boulevard, well beyond the Bel-Air Country Club golf course. The road was lined with walled and fenced estates. Some had high walls, some had low walls, some had ornamental iron fences, some were a bit old-fashioned and got along with tall hedges. The street had no sidewalk. Nobody walked in that neighborhood, not even the mailman.

The afternoon was hot, but not hot like Pasadena. There was a drowsy smell of flowers and sun, a swishing of lawn sprinklers gentle behind hedges and walls, the clear ratchety sound of lawn mowers moving delicately over serene and confident lawns.

I drove up the hill slowly, looking for monograms on gates. Arthur Blake Popham was the name. ABP would be the initials. I found them almost at the top, gilt on a black shield, the gates folded back on a black composition driveway.

It was a glaring white house that had the air of being brand new, but the landscaping was well advanced. It was modest enough for the neighborhood, not more than fourteen rooms and probably only one swimming pool. Its wall was low, made of brick with the concrete all oozed out between and set that way and painted over white. On top of the wall a low iron railing painted black. The name A. P. Morny was stencilled on the large silver-colored mailbox at the service entrance.

I parked my crate on the street and walked up the black driveway to a side door of glittering white paint shot with patches of color from the stained glass canopy over it. I hammered on a large brass knocker. Back along the side of the house a chauffeur was washing off a Cadillac.

The door opened and a hard-eyed Filipino in a white coat curled his lip at me. I gave him a card. "Mrs. Morny," I said.

He shut the door. Time passed, as it always does when I go calling. The swish of water on the Cadillac had a cool sound. The chauffeur was a little runt in breeches and leggings and a sweat-stained shirt. He looked like an overgrown jockey and he made the same kind of hissing noise as he worked on the car that a groom makes rubbing down a horse.

A red-throated hummingbird went into a scarlet bush beside the door, shook the long tubular blooms around a little, and zoomed off so fast he simply disappeared in the air.

The door opened, the Filipino poked my card at me. I didn't take it. "What you want?" It was a tight crackling voice, like someone tiptoeing across a lot of eggshells.

"Want to see Mrs. Morny."

"She not at home."

"Didn't you know that when I gave you the card?"

He opened his fingers and let the card flutter to the ground. He grinned, showing me a lot of cut-rate dental work. "I know when she tell me." He shut the door in my face, not gently.

I picked the card up and walked along the side of the house to where the chauffeur was squirting water on the Cadillac sedan and rubbing the dirt off with a big sponge. He had red-rimmed eyes and a bang of corn-colored hair. A cigarette hung exhausted at the corner of his lower lip. He gave me the quick side glance of a man who is minding his own business with difficulty. I said: "Where's the boss?"

The cigarette jiggled in his mouth. The water went on swishing gently on the paint. "Ask at the house, Jack."

"I done asked. They done shut the door in mah face."

"You're breaking my heart, Jack."

"How about Mrs. Morny?"

"Same answer, Jack. I just work here. Selling something?"

I held my card so that he could read it. It was a business card this time. He put the sponge down on the running board, and the hose on the cement. He stepped around the water to wipe his hands on a towel that hung at the side of the garage doors. He fished a match out of his pants, struck it and tilted his head back to light the dead butt that was stuck in his face. His foxy little eyes flicked around this way and that and he moved behind the car, with a jerk of the head. I went over near him. "How's the little old expense account?" he asked in a small careful voice.

"Fat with inactivity."

"For five I could start thinking."

"I wouldn't want to make it that tough for you."

"For ten I could sing like four canaries and a steel guitar."

"I don't like these plushy orchestrations," I said.

He cocked his head sideways. "Talk English, Jack."

"I don't want you to lose your job, son. All I want to

know is whether Mrs. Morny is home. Does that rate more than a buck?"

"Don't worry about my job, Jack. I'm solid."

"With Morny—or somebody else?"

"You want that for the same buck?"

"Two bucks."

He eyed me over. "You ain't working for him, are you?"

"Sure."

"You're a liar."

"Sure."

"Gimme the two bucks," he snapped.

I gave him two dollars.

"She's in the backyard with a friend," he said. "A nice friend. You got a friend that don't work and a husband that works, you're all set, see?" He leered.

"You'll be all set in an irrigation ditch one of these days."

"Not me, Jack. I'm wise. I know how to play 'em. I monkeyed around these kind of people all my life."

He rubbed the two dollar bills between his palms, blew on them, folded them longways and wideways and tucked them in the watch pocket of his breeches.

"That was just the soup," he said. "Now for five more—"

A rather large blond cocker spaniel tore around the Cadillac, skidded a little on the wet concrete, took off neatly, hit me in the stomach and thighs with all four paws, licked my face, dropped to the ground, ran around my legs, sat down between them, let his tongue out all the way and started to pant. I stepped over him and braced myself against the side of the car and got my handkerchief out.

A male voice called: "Here, Heathcliff. Here, Heathcliff." Steps sounded on a hard walk.

"That's Heathcliff," the chauffeur said sourly.

"Heathcliff?"

"Cripes, that's what they call the dog, Jack."

"*Wuthering Heights?*" I asked.

"Now you're double-talking again," he sneered. "Look

out—company." He picked up the sponge and the hose and went back to washing the car. I moved away from him. The cocker spaniel immediately moved between my legs again, almost tripping me.

"Here, Heathcliff," the male voice called out louder, and a man came into view through the opening of a latticed tunnel covered with climbing roses.

Tall, dark, with a clear olive skin, brilliant black eyes, gleaming white teeth. Sideburns. A narrow black mustache. Sideburns too long, much too long. White shirt with embroidered initials on the pocket, white slacks, white shoes. A wrist watch that curved halfway around a lean dark wrist, held on by a gold chain. A yellow scarf around a bronzed slender neck. He saw the dog squatted between my legs and didn't like it. He snapped long fingers and snapped a clear hard voice: "Here, Heathcliff. Come here at once!"

The dog breathed hard and didn't move, except to lean a little closer to my right leg.

"Who are you?" the man asked, staring me down.

I held out my card. Olive fingers took the card. The dog quietly backed out from between my legs, edged around the front end of the car, and faded silently into the distance.

"Marlowe," the man said. "Marlowe, eh? What's this? A detective? What do you want?"

"Want to see Mrs. Morny."

He looked me up and down, brilliant black eyes sweeping slowly and the silky fringes of long eyelashes following them. "Weren't you told she was not in?"

"Yeah, but I didn't believe it. Are you Mr. Morny?"

"No."

"That's Mr. Vannier," the chauffeur said behind my back, in the drawled, over-polite voice of deliberate insolence. "Mr. Vannier's a friend of the family. He comes here quite a lot."

Vannier looked past my shoulder, his eyes furious. The chauffeur came around the car and spit the cigarette stub out of his mouth with casual contempt. "I told the shamus the boss wasn't here, Mr. Vannier."

"I see."

"I told him Mrs. Morny and you was here. Did I do wrong?"

Vannier said: "You could have minded your own business."

The chauffeur said: "I wonder why the hell I didn't think of that."

Vannier said: "Get out before I break your dirty little neck for you."

The chauffeur eyed him quietly and then went back into the gloom of the garage and started to whistle. Vannier moved his hot angry eyes over to me and snapped: "You were told Mrs. Morny was not in, but it didn't take. Is that it? In other words the information failed to satisfy you."

"If we have to have other words," I said, "those might do."

"I see. Could you bring yourself to say what point you wish to discuss with Mrs. Morny?"

"I'd prefer to explain that to Mrs. Morny herself."

"The implication is that she doesn't care to see you."

Behind the car the chauffeur said: "Watch his right, Jack. It might have a knife in it."

Vannier's olive skin turned the color of dried seaweed. He turned on his heel and rapped at me in a stifled voice: "Follow me."

He went along the brick path under the tunnel of roses and through a white gate at the end. Beyond was a walled-in garden containing flowerbeds crammed with showy annuals, a badminton court, a nice stretch of greensward, and a small tiled pool glittering angrily in the sun. Beside the pool there was a flagged space set with blue and white garden furniture, low tables with composition tops, reclining chairs with foot-rests and enormous cushions, and over all a blue and white umbrella as big as a small tent.

A long-limbed languorous type of showgirl blond lay at her ease in one of the chairs, with her feet raised on a padded rest and a tall misted glass at her elbow, near a silver ice bucket and a Scotch bottle. She looked at us lazily as we came over the grass. From thirty feet away she looked like a lot of class. From ten feet away she looked like something made up to be seen from thirty feet away. Her mouth was too wide, her eyes were too blue, her makeup was too vivid, the thin arch of her eyebrows was almost fantastic in its curve and spread, and the mascara was so thick on her eyelashes that they looked like miniature iron railings.

She wore white duck slacks, blue and white open-toed sandals over bare feet and crimson toenails, a white silk blouse and a necklace of green stones that were not square cut emeralds. Her hair was as artificial as a night club lobby.

On the chair beside her there was a white straw garden hat with a brim the size of a spare tire and a white satin chin strap. On the brim of the hat lay a pair of green sun glasses with lenses the size of doughnuts.

Vannier marched over to her and snapped out: "You've got to can that nasty little red-eyed driver of yours, but quick. Otherwise I'm liable to break his neck any minute. I can't go near him without getting insulted."

The blond coughed lightly, flicked a handkerchief around without doing anything with it, and said: "Sit down and rest your sex appeal. Who's your friend?"

Vannier looked for my card, found he was holding it in his hand and threw it on her lap. She picked it up languidly, ran her eyes over it, ran them over me, sighed and tapped her teeth with her fingernails. "Big, isn't he? Too much for you to handle, I guess."

Vannier looked at me nastily. "All right, get it over with, whatever it is."

"Do I talk to her?" I asked. "Or do I talk to you and have you put it in English?"

The blond laughed. A silvery ripple of laughter that held the unspoiled naturalness of a bubble dance. A small tongue played roguishly along her lips.

Vannier sat down and lit a gold-tipped cigarette and I stood there looking at them.

I said: "I'm looking for a friend of yours, Mrs. Morny. I

understand that she shared an apartment with you about a year ago. Her name is Linda Conquest."

Vannier flicked his eyes up, down, up, down. He turned his head and looked across the pool. The cocker spaniel named Heathcliff sat over there looking at us with the white of one eye. Vannier snapped his fingers. "Here, Heathcliff! Here, Heathcliff! Come here, sir!"

The blond said: "Shut up. The dog hates your guts. Give your vanity a rest, for heaven's sake."

Vannier snapped: "Don't talk like that to me."

The blond giggled and petted his face with her eyes.

I said: "I'm looking for a girl named Linda Conquest, Mrs. Morny."

The blond looked at me and said: "So you said. I was just thinking. I don't think I've seen her in six months. She got married."

"You haven't seen her in six months?"

"That's what I said, big boy. What do you want to know for?"

"Just a private enquiry I'm making."

"About what?"

"About a confidential matter," I said.

"Just think," the blond said brightly. "He's making a private enquiry about a confidential matter. You hear that, Lou? Busting in on total strangers that don't want to see him is quite all right, though, isn't it, Lou? On account of he's making a private enquiry about a confidential matter."

"Then you don't know where she is, Mrs. Morny?"

"Didn't I say so?" Her voice rose a couple of notches.

"No. You said you didn't think you had seen her in six months. Not quite the same thing."

"Who told you I shared an apartment with her?" the blond snapped.

"I never reveal a source of information, Mrs. Morny."

"Sweetheart, you're fussy enough to be a dance director. I should tell you everything, you should tell me nothing."

"The position is quite different," I said. "I'm a hired

hand obeying instructions. The lady has no reason to hide out, has she?"

"Who's looking for her?"

"Her folks."

"Guess again. She doesn't have any folks."

"You must know her pretty well, if you know that," I said.

"Maybe I did once. That don't prove I do now."

"Okay," I said. "The answer is you know, but you won't tell."

"The answer," Vannier said suddenly, "is that you're not wanted here and the sooner you get out, the better we like it."

I kept on looking at Mrs. Morny. She winked at me and said to Vannier: "Don't get so hostile, darling. You have a lot of charm, but you have small bones. You're not built for the rough work. That right, big boy?"

I said: "I hadn't thought about it, Mrs. Morny. Do you think Mr. Morny could help me—or would?"

She shook her head. "How would I know? You could try. If he don't like you, he has guys around that can bounce you."

"I think you could tell me yourself, if you wanted to."

"How are you going to make me want to?" Her eyes were inviting.

"With all these people around," I said, "how can I?"

"That's a thought," she said, and sipped from her glass, watching me over it.

Vannier stood up very slowly. His face was white. He put his hand inside his shirt and said slowly, between his teeth: "Get out, mug. While you can still walk."

I looked at him in surprise. "Where's your refinement?" I asked him. "And don't tell me you wear a gun with your garden clothes."

The blond laughed, showing a fine strong set of teeth. Vannier thrust his hand under his left arm inside the shirt and set his lips. His black eyes were sharp and blank at the same time, like a snake's eyes. "You heard me," he said, almost softly. "And don't write me off too quickly. I'd plug you as soon as I'd strike a match. And fix it afterwards."

I looked at the blond. Her eyes were bright and her mouth looked sensual and eager, watching us. I turned and walked away across the grass. About halfway across it I looked back at them. Vannier stood in exactly the same position, his hand inside his shirt. The blond's eyes were still wide and her lips parted, but the shadow of the umbrella had dimmed her expression and at that distance it might have been either fear or pleased anticipation.

I went on over the grass, through the white gate and along the brick path under the rose arbor. I reached the end of it, turned, walked quietly back to the gate and took another look at them. I didn't know what there would be to see or what I cared about it when I saw it. What I saw was Vannier practically sprawled on top of the blond, kissing her.

I shook my head and went back along the walk.

The red-eyed chauffeur was still at work on the Cadillac. He had finished the wash job and was wiping off the glass and nickel with a large chamois. I went around and stood beside him.

"How you come out?" he asked me out of the side of his mouth.

"Badly. They tramped all over me," I said.

He nodded and went on making the hissing noise of a groom rubbing down a horse. "You better watch your step. The guy's heeled," I said. "Or pretends to be."

The chauffeur laughed shortly. "Under that suit? Nix."

"Who is this guy Vannier? What does he do?"

The chauffeur straightened up, put the chamois over the sill of a window and wiped his hands on the towel that was now stuck in his waistband. "Women, my guess would be," he said.

"Isn't it a bit dangerous—playing with this particular woman?"

"I'd say it was," he agreed. "Different guys got different ideas of danger. It would scare me."

"Where does he live?"

"Sherman Oaks. She goes over there. She'll go once too often."

"Ever run across a girl named Linda Conquest? Tall, dark, handsome, used to be a singer with a band?"

"For two bucks, Jack, you expect a lot of service."

"I could build it up to five."

He shook his head. "I don't know the party. Not by that name. All kinds of dames come here, mostly pretty flashy. I don't get introduced." He grinned.

I got my wallet out and put three ones in his little damp paw. I added a business card. "I like small close-built men," I said. "They never seem to be afraid of anything. Come and see me some time."

"I might at that, Jack. Thanks. Linda Conquest, huh? I'll keep my ear flaps off."

"So long," I said. "The name?"

"They call me Shifty. I never knew why."

"So long, Shifty."

"So long. Gat under his arm—in them clothes? Not a chance."

"I don't know," I said. "He made the motion. I'm not hired to gunfight with strangers."

"Hell, that shirt he's wearing only got two buttons at the top. I noticed. Take him a week to pull a rod from under that." But he sounded faintly worried.

"I guess he was just bluffing," I agreed. "If you hear mention of Linda Conquest, I'll be glad to talk business with you."

"Okay, Jack."

I went back along the black driveway. He stood there scratching his chin.

■ 6 ■

I DROVE ALONG THE BLOCK LOOKING FOR A PLACE TO PARK so that I could run up to the office for a moment before going on downtown. A chauffeur-driven Packard edged out from the curb in front of a cigar store about thirty feet from the entrance to my building. I slid into the space, locked the car and stepped out. It was only then that I noticed the car in front of which I had parked was a familiar-looking sand-colored coupé. It didn't have to be the same one. There were thousands of them. Nobody was in it. Nobody was near it that wore a cocoa straw hat with a brown and yellow band.

I went around to the street side and looked at the steering post. No license holder. I wrote the license plate number down on the back of an envelope, just in case, and went on into my building. He wasn't in the lobby, or in the corridor upstairs.

I went into the office, looked on the floor for mail, didn't find any, bought myself a short drink out of the office bottle and left. I didn't have any time to spare to get downtown before three o'clock. The sand-colored coupé was still parked, still empty. I got into mine and started up and moved out into the traffic stream.

I was below Sunset on Vine before he picked me up. I kept on going, grinning, and wondering where he had hid. Perhaps in the car parked behind his own. I hadn't thought of that.

I drove south to Third and all the way downtown on Third. The sand-colored coupé kept half a block behind me all the way. I moved over to Seventh and Grand, parked near Seventh and Olive, stopped to buy cigarettes I didn't need, and then walked east along Seventh without looking behind me. At Spring I went into the Hotel Metropole, strolled over to the big horseshoe cigar counter to light one of my cigarettes and then sat down in one of the old brown leather chairs in the lobby.

A blond man in a brown suit, dark glasses and the now familiar hat came into the lobby and moved unobtrusively among the potted palms and the stucco arches to the cigar counter. He bought a package of cigarettes and broke it open standing there, using the time to lean his back against the counter and give the lobby the benefit of his eagle eye.

He picked up his change and went over and sat down with his back to a pillar. He tipped his hat down over his dark glasses and seemed to go to sleep with an unlighted cigarette between his lips.

I got up and wandered over and dropped into the chair beside him. I looked at him sideways. He didn't move. Seen at close quarters his face seemed young and pink and plump and the blond beard on his chin was very carelessly shaved. Behind the dark glasses his eyelashes flicked up and down rapidly. A hand on his knee tightened and pulled the cloth into wrinkles. There was a wart on his cheek just below the right eyelid.

I struck a match and held the flame to his cigarette. "Light?"

"Oh—thanks," he said, very surprised. He drew breath in until the cigarette tip glowed. I shook the match out, tossed it into the sand jar at my elbow and waited. He looked at me sideways several times before he spoke. "Haven't I seen you somewhere before?"

"Over on Dresden Avenue in Pasadena. This morning."

I could see his cheeks get pinker than they had been. He sighed. "I must be lousy," he said.

"Boy, you stink," I agreed.

"Maybe it's the hat," he said.

"The hat helps," I said. "But you don't really need it."

"It's a pretty tough dollar in this town," he said sadly. "You can't do it on foot, you ruin yourself with taxi fares if you use taxis, and if you use your own car, it's always where you can't get to it fast enough. You have to stay too close."

"But you don't have to climb in a guy's pocket," I said. "Did you want something with me or are you just practicing?"

"I figured I'd find out if you were smart enough to be worth talking to."

"I'm very smart," I said. "It would be a shame not to talk to me."

He looked carefully around back of his chair and on both sides of where we were sitting and then drew a small, pigskin wallet out. He handed me a nice fresh card from it. It read: George Anson Phillips. Confidential Investigations. 212 Senger Building, 1924 North Wilcox Avenue, Hollywood. A Glenview telephone number. In the upper left hand corner there was an open eye with an eyebrow arched in surprise and very long lashes.

"You can't do that," I said, pointing to the eye. "That's the Pinkertons'. You'll be stealing their business."

"Oh hell," he said, "what little I get wouldn't bother them."

I snapped the card on my fingernail and bit down hard on my teeth and slipped the card into my pocket. "You want one of mine—or have you completed your file on me?"

"Oh, I know all about you," he said. "I was a deputy at Ventura the time you were working on the Gregson case."

Gregson was a con man from Oklahoma City who was followed all over the United States for two years by one of his victims until he got so jittery that he shot up a service station attendant who mistook him for an acquaintance. It seemed a long time ago to me. I said: "Go on from there."

"I remembered your name when I saw it on your registration this a.m. So when I lost you on the way into town I just looked you up. I was going to come in and talk, but it would have been a violation of confidence. This way I kind of can't help myself."

Another screwball. That made three in one day, not counting Mrs. Murdock, who might turn out to be a screwball too. I waited while he took his dark glasses off and polished them and put them on again and gave the neighborhood the once over again. Then he said: "I figured we could maybe make a deal. Pool our resources, as they say. I saw the guy go into your office, so I figured he had hired you."

"You knew who he was?"

"I'm working on him," he said, and his voice sounded flat and discouraged. "And where I am getting is no place at all."

"What did he do to you?"

"Well, I'm working for his wife."

"Divorce?"

He looked all around him carefully and said in a small voice: "So she says. But I wonder."

"They both want one," I said. "Each trying to get something on the other. Comical, isn't it?"

"My end I don't like so well. A guy is tailing me around some of the time. A very tall guy with a funny eye. I shake him but after a while I see him again. A very tall guy. Like a lamppost."

A very tall man with a funny eye. I smoked thoughtfully.

"Anything to do with you?" the blond man asked me a little anxiously.

I shook my head and threw my cigarette into the sand jar. "Never saw him that I know of." I looked at my strap watch. "We better get together and talk this thing over properly, but I can't do it now. I have an appointment."

"I'd like to," he said. "Very much."

"Let's then. My office, my apartment, or your office, or where?"

He scratched his badly shaved chin with a well-chewed thumbnail. "My apartment," he said at last. "It's not in the phone book. Give me that card a minute."

He turned it over on his palm when I gave it to him

and wrote slowly with a small metal pencil, moving his tongue along his lips. He was getting younger every minute. He didn't seem much more than twenty by now, but he had to be, because the Gregson case had been six years back.

He put his pencil away and handed me back the card. The address he had written on it was 204 Florence Apartments, 128 Court Street.

I looked at him curiously. "Court Street on Bunker Hill?"

He nodded, flushing all over his blond skin. "Not too good," he said quickly. "I haven't been in the chips lately. Do you mind?"

"No, why would I?" I stood up and held a hand out. He shook it and dropped it and I pushed it down into my hip pocket and rubbed the palm against the handkerchief I had there. Looking at his face more closely I saw that there was a line of moisture across his upper lip and more of it along the side of his nose. It was not as hot as all that. I started to move off and then I turned back to lean down close to his face and say: "Almost anybody can pull my leg, but just to make sure, she's a tall blond with careless eyes, huh?"

"I wouldn't call them careless," he said.

I held my face together while I said: "And just between the two of us this divorce stuff is a lot of hooey. It's something else entirely, isn't it?"

"Yes," he said softly, "and something I don't like more every minute I think about it. Here." He pulled something out of his pocket and dropped it into my hand. It was a flat key. "No need for you to wait around in the hall, if I happen to be out. I have two of them. What time would you think you would come?"

"About four-thirty, the way it looks now. You sure you want to give me this key?"

"Why, we're in the same racket," he said, looking up at me innocently, or as innocently as he could look through a pair of dark glasses.

At the edge of the lobby I looked back. He sat there peacefully, with a half-smoked cigarette dead between his lips and the gaudy brown and yellow band on his hat looking as quiet as a cigarette ad on the back page of the *Saturday Evening Post.*

We were in the same racket. So I wouldn't chisel him. Just like that. I could have the key to his apartment and go in and make myself at home. I could wear his slippers and drink his liquor and lift up his carpet and count the thousand dollar bills under it. We were in the same racket.

■ 7 ■

THE BELFONT BUILDING WAS EIGHT STORIES OF NOTHING in particular that had got itself pinched off between a large green and chromium cut rate suit emporium and a three-story and basement garage that made a noise like lion cages at feeding time. The small dark narrow lobby was as dirty as a chicken yard. The building directory had a lot of vacant space on it. Only one of the names meant anything to me and I knew that one already. Opposite the directory a large sign tilted against the fake marble wall said: *Space for Renting Suitable for Cigar Stand. Apply Room 316.*

There were two open-grill elevators but only one seemed to be running and that not busy. An old man sat inside it slack-jawed and watery-eyed on a piece of folded burlap on top of a wooden stool. He looked as if he had been sitting there since the Civil War and had come out of that badly. I got in with him and said eight, and he wrestled the doors shut and cranked his buggy and we dragged upwards lurching. The old man breathed hard, as if he was carrying the elevator on his back.

I got out at my floor and started along the hallway and

behind me the old man leaned out of the car and blew his nose with his fingers into a carton full of floor sweepings.

Elisha Morningstar's office was at the back, opposite the firedoor. Two rooms, both lettered in flaked black paint on pebbled glass. *Elisha Morningstar. Numismatist.* The one farthest back said: *Entrance.*

I turned the knob and went into a small narrow room with two windows, a shabby little typewriter desk, closed, a number of wall cases of tarnished coins in tilted slots with yellowed typewritten labels under them, two brown filing cases at the back against the wall, no curtains at the windows, and a dust gray floor carpet so threadbare that you wouldn't notice the rips in it unless you tripped over one. An inner wooden door was open at the back across from the filing cases, behind the little typewriter desk. Through the door came the small sounds a man makes when he isn't doing anything at all. Then the dry voice of Elisha Morningstar called out: "Come in, please. Come in."

I went along and in. The inner office was just as small but had a lot more stuff in it. A green safe almost blocked off the front half. Beyond this a heavy old mahogany table against the entrance door held some dark books, some flabby old magazines, and a lot of dust. In the back wall a window was open a few inches, without effect on the musty smell. There was a hat rack with a greasy black felt hat on it. There were three long-legged tables with glass tops and more coins under the glass tops. There was a heavy dark leather-topped desk midway of the room. It had the usual desk stuff on it, and in addition a pair of jeweller's scales under a glass dome and two large nickel-framed magnifying glasses and a jeweller's eyepiece lying on a buff scratch pad, beside a cracked yellow silk handkerchief spotted with ink.

In the swivel chair at the desk sat an elderly party in a dark gray suit with high lapels and too many buttons down the front. He had some stringy white hair that grew long enough to tickle his ears. A pale gray bald patch loomed high up in the middle of it, like a rock

above timberline. Fuzz grew out of his ears, far enough
to catch a moth. He had sharp black eyes with a pair of
pouches under each eye, brownish purple in color and
traced with a network of wrinkles and veins. His cheeks
were shiny and his short sharp nose looked as if it had
hung over a lot of quick ones in its time. A Hoover collar
which no decent laundry would have allowed on the
premises nudged his Adam's apple and a black string tie
poked a small hard knot out at the bottom of the collar,
like a mouse getting ready to come out of a mousehole.
He said: "My young lady had to go to the dentist. You
are Mr. Marlowe?"

I nodded.

"Pray, be seated." He waved a thin hand at the chair
across the desk. I sat down. "You have some identification, I presume?"

I showed it to him. While he read it I smelled him
from across the desk. He had a sort of dry musty smell,
like a fairly clean Chinaman.

He placed my card face down on top of his desk and
folded his hands on it. His sharp black eyes didn't miss
anything in my face. "Well, Mr. Marlowe, what can I do
for you?"

"Tell me about the Brasher Doubloon."

"Ah, yes," he said. "The Brasher Doubloon. An interesting coin." He lifted his hands off the desk and made a
steeple of the fingers, like an old time family lawyer
getting set for a little tangled grammar. "In some ways
the most interesting and valuable of all early American
coins. As no doubt you know."

"What I don't know about early American coins you
could almost crowd into the Rose Bowl."

"Is that so?" he said. "Is that so? Do you want me to
tell you?"

"What I'm here for, Mr. Morningstar."

"It is a gold coin, roughly equivalent to a twenty-dollar
gold piece, and about the size of a half dollar. Almost
exactly. It was made for the State of New York in the
year 1787. It was not minted. There were no mints until
1793, when the first mint was opened in Philadelphia.

The Brasher Doubloon was coined probably by the pressure molding process and its maker was a private goldsmith named Ephraim Brasher, or Brashear. Where the name survives it is usually spelled Brashear, but not on the coin. I don't know why."

I got a cigarette into my mouth and lit it. I thought it might do something to the musty smell. "What's the pressure molding process?"

"The two halves of the mold were engraved in steel, in intaglio, of course. These halves were then mounted in lead. Gold blanks were pressed between them in a coin press. Then the edges were trimmed for weight and smoothed. The coin was not milled. There were no milling machines in 1787."

"Kind of a slow process," I said.

He nodded his peaked white head. "Quite. And, since the surface hardening of steel without distortion could not be accomplished at that time, the dies wore and had to be remade from time to time. With consequent slight variations in design which would be visible under strong magnification. In fact it would be safe to say no two of the coins would be identical, judged by modern methods of microscopic examination. Am I clear?"

"Yeah," I said. "Up to a point. How many of these coins are there and what are they worth?"

He undid the steeple of fingers and put his hands back on the desk top and patted them gently up and down. "I don't know how many there are. Nobody knows. A few hundred, a thousand, perhaps more. But of these very few indeed are uncirculated specimens in what is called mint condition. The value varies from a couple of thousand on up. I should say that at the present time, since the devaluation of the dollar, an uncirculated specimen, carefully handled by a reputable dealer, might easily bring ten thousand dollars, or even more. It would have to have a history, of course."

I said: "Ah," and let smoke out of my lungs slowly and waved it away with the flat of my hand, away from the old party across the desk from me. He looked like a non-smoker. "And without a history and not so carefully handled—how much?"

He shrugged. "There would be the implication that the coin was illegally acquired. Stolen, or obtained by fraud. Of course it might not be so. Rare coins do turn up in odd places at odd times. In old strong boxes, in the secret drawers of desks in old New England houses. Not often, I grant you. But it happens. I know of a very valuable coin that fell out of the stuffing of a horsehair sofa which was being restored by an antique dealer. The sofa had been in the same room in the same house in Fall River, Massachusetts, for ninety years. Nobody knew how the coin got there. But generally speaking, the implication of theft would be strong. Particularly in this part of the country."

He looked at the corner of the ceiling with an absent stare. I looked at him with a not so absent stare. He looked like a man who could be trusted with a secret—if it was his own secret.

He brought his eyes down to my level slowly and said: "Five dollars, please."

I said: "Huh?"

"Five dollars, please."

"What for?"

"Don't be absurd, Mr. Marlowe. Everything I have told you is available in the public library. In Fosdyke's Register, in particular. You choose to come here and take up my time relating it to you. For this my charge is five dollars."

"And suppose I don't pay it," I said.

He leaned back and closed his eyes. A very faint smile twitched at the corners of his lips. "You will pay it," he said.

I paid it. I took the five out of my wallet and got up to lean over the desk and spread it out right in front of him, carefully. I stroked the bill with my fingertips, as if it were a kitten.

"Five dollars, Mr. Morningstar," I said. He opened his eyes and looked at the bill. He smiled. "And now," I said, let's talk about the Brasher Doubloon that somebody tried to sell you."

He opened his eyes a little wider. "Oh, did somebody try to sell me a Brasher Doubloon? Now why would they do that?"

"They needed the money," I said. "And they didn't want too many questions asked. They knew or found out that you were in the business and that the building where you had your office was a shabby dump where anything could happen. They knew an elderly man who would probably not make any false moves—out of regard for your health."

"They seem to have known a great deal," Elisha Morningstar said dryly.

"Thay knew what they had to know in order to transact their business. Just like you and me. And none of it was hard to find out."

He stuck his little finger in his ear and worked it around and brought it out with a little dark wax on it. He wiped it off casually on his coat. "And you assume all this from the mere fact that I called up Mrs. Murdock and asked if her Brasher Doubloon was for sale?"

"Sure. She had the same idea herself. It's reasonable. Like I said over the phone to you, you would know that coin was not for sale. If you knew anything about the business at all. And I can see that you do."

He bowed, about one inch. He didn't quite smile but he looked about as pleased as a man in a Hoover collar ever looks.

"You would be offered this coin for sale," I said, "in suspicious circumstances. You would want to buy it, if you could get it cheap and had the money to handle it. But you would want to know where it came from. And even if you were quite sure it was stolen, you could still buy it, if you could get it cheap enough."

"Oh, I could, could I?" He looked amused, but not in a large way.

"Sure you could—if you are a reputable dealer. I'll assume you are. By buying the coin—cheap—you would be protecting the owner or his insurance carrier from

complete loss. They'd be glad to pay you back you
outlay. It's done all the time."

"Then the Murdock Brasher has been stolen," he said
abruptly.

"Don't quote me," I said. "It's a secret."

He almost picked his nose this time. He just caught
himself. He picked a hair out of one nostril instead, with
a quick jerk and a wince. He held it up and looked at it
Looking at me past it he said: "And how much will your
principal pay for the return of the coin?"

I leaned over the desk and gave him my shady leer.
"One grand. What did you pay?"

"I think you are a very smart young man," he said
Then he screwed his face up and his chin wobbled and
his chest began to bounce in and out and a sound came
out of him like a convalescent rooster learning to crow
again after a long illness. He was laughing.

It stopped after a while. His face came all smooth
again and his eyes opened, black and sharp and shrewd
"Eight hundred dollars," he said. "Eight hundred dollars
for an uncirculated specimen of the Brasher Doubloon."
He chortled.

"Fine. Got it with you? That leaves you two hundred
Fair enough. A quick turnover, a reasonable profit and
no trouble for anybody."

"It is not in my office," he said. "Do you take me for a
fool?" He reached an ancient silver watch out of his vest
on a black fob. He screwed up his eyes to look at it. "Let
us say eleven in the morning," he said. "Come back with
your money. The coin may or may not be here, but if I
am satisfied with your behavior, I will arrange matters."

"That is satisfactory," I said, and stood up. "I have to
get the money anyhow."

"Have it in used bills," he said almost dreamily. "Used
twenties will do. An occasional fifty will do no harm."

I grinned and started for the door. Halfway there I
turned around and went back to lean both hands on the
desk and push my face over it. "What did she look like?"

He looked blank.

"The girl that sold you the coin."

He looked blanker.

"Okay," I said. "It wasn't a girl. She had help. It was a man. What did the man look like?"

He pursed his lips and made another steeple with his fingers. "He was a middle-aged man, heavy set, about five feet seven inches tall and weighing around one hundred and seventy pounds. He said his name was Smith. He wore a blue suit, black shoes, a green tie and shirt, no hat. There was a brown bordered handkerchief in his outer pocket. His hair was dark brown sprinkled with gray. There was a bald patch about the size of a dollar on the crown of his head and a scar about two inches long running down the side of his jaw. On the left side, I think. Yes, on the left side."

"Not bad," I said. "What about the hole in his right sock?"

"I omitted to take his shoes off."

"Darn careless of you," I said.

He didn't say anything. We just stared at each other, half curious, half hostile, like new neighbors. Then suddenly he went into his laugh again.

The five dollar bill I had given him was still lying on his side of the desk. I flicked a hand across and took it. "You won't want this now," I said. "Since we started talking in thousands."

He stopped laughing very suddenly. Then he shrugged. "At eleven a.m.," he said. "And no tricks, Mr. Marlowe. Don't think I don't know how to protect myself."

"I hope you do," I said, "because what you are handling is dynamite."

I left him and tramped across the empty outer office and opened the door and let it shut, staying inside. There ought to be footsteps outside in the corridor, but his transom was closed and I hadn't made much noise coming on crepe rubber soles. I hoped he would remember that. I sneaked back across the threadbare carpet and edged in behind the door, between the door and the little closed typewriter desk. A kid trick, but once in a while it will work, especially after a lot of smart conver-

sation, full of worldliness and sly wit. Like a sucker play
in football. And if it didn't work this time, we would just
be there sneering at each other again.

It worked. Nothing happened for a while except that a
nose was blown. Then all by himself in there he went
into his sick rooster laugh again. Then a throat was
cleared. Then a swivel chair squeaked, and feet walked.

A dingy white head poked into the room, about two
inches past the end of the door. It hung there suspended
and I went into a state of suspended animation. Then the
head was drawn back and four unclean fingernails came
around the edge of the door and pulled. The door closed,
clicked, was shut. I started breathing again and put my
ear to the wooden panel.

The swivel chair squeaked once more. The threshing
sound of a telephone being dialed. I lunged across to the
instrument on the little typewriter desk and lifted it. At
the other end of the line the bell had started to ring. It
rang six times. Then a man's voice said: "Yeah?"

"The Florence Apartments?"

"Yeah."

"I'd like to speak to Mr. Anson in Apartment two-o-
four."

"Hold the wire. I'll see if he's in."

Mr. Morningstar and I held the wire. Noise came over
it, the blaring sound of a loud radio broadcasting a
baseball game. It was not close to the telephone, but it
was noisy enough. Then I could hear the hollow sound of
steps coming nearer and the harsh rattle of the telephone
receiver being picked up and the voice said: "Not in.
Any message?"

"I'll call later," Mr. Morningstar said.

I hung up fast and did a rapid glide across the floor to
the entrance door and opened it very silently, like snow
falling, and let it close the same way, taking its weight at
the last moment, so that the click of the catch would not
have been heard three feet away.

I breathed hard and tight going down the hall, listening to myself. I pushed the elevator button. Then I got
out the card which Mr. George Anson Phillips had given

me in the lobby of the Hotel Metropole. I didn't look at it
in any real sense. I didn't have to look at it to recall that
it referred to Apartment 204, Florence Apartments, 128
Court Street. I just stood there flicking it with a fingernail while the old elevator came heaving up in the shaft,
straining like a gravel truck on a hairpin turn.

The time was three-fifty.

■ 8 ■

BUNKER HILL IS OLD TOWN, LOST TOWN, SHABBY TOWN,
crook town. Once, very long ago, it was the choice
residential district of the city, and there are still standing
a few of the jigsaw Gothic mansions with wide porches
and walls covered with round-end shingles and full corner bay windows with spindle turrets. They are all room-
ing houses now, their parquetry floors are scratched and
worn through the once glossy finish and the wide sweeping staircases are dark with time and with cheap varnish
laid on over generations of dirt. In the tall rooms haggard
landladies bicker with shifty tenants. On the wide cool
front porches, reaching their cracked shoes into the sun,
and staring at nothing, sit the old men with faces like lost
battles.

In and around the old houses there are flyblown restaurants and Italian fruitstands and cheap apartment
houses and little candy stores where you can buy even
nastier things than their candy. And there are ratty
hotels where nobody except people named Smith and
Jones sign the register and where the night clerk is half
watchdog and half pander.

Out of the apartment houses come women who should
be young but have faces like stale beer; men with pulled-
down hats and quick eyes that look the street over

behind the cupped hand that shields the match flame; worn intellectuals with cigarette coughs and no money in the bank; fly cops with granite faces and unwavering eyes; cokies and coke peddlers; people who look like nothing in particular and know it, and once in a while even men that actually go to work. But they come out early, when the wide cracked sidewalks are empty and still have dew on them.

I was earlier than four-thirty getting over there, but not much. I parked at the end of the street, where the funicular railway comes struggling up the yellow clay bank from Hill Street, and walked along Court Street to the Florence Apartments. It was dark brick in front, three stories, the lower windows at sidewalk level and masked by rusted screens and dingy net curtains. The entrance door had a glass panel and enough of the name left to be read. I opened it and went down three brass bound steps into a hallway you could touch on both sides without stretching. Dim doors painted with numbers in dim paint. An alcove at the foot of the stairs with a pay telephone. A sign: *Manager, Apt. 106.* At the back of the hallway a screen door and in the alley beyond it four tall battered garbage pails in a line, with a dance of flies in the sunlit air above them.

I went up the stairs. The radio I had heard over the telephone was still blatting the baseball game. I read numbers and went up front. Apartment 204 was on the right side and the baseball game was right across the hall from it. I knocked, got no answer and knocked louder. Behind my back three Dodgers struck out against a welter of synthetic crowd noise. I knocked a third time and looked out of the front hall window while I felt in my pocket for the key George Anson Phillips had given me.

Across the street was an Italian funeral home, neat and quiet and reticent, white painted brick, flush with the sidewalk. Pietro Palermo Funeral Parlors. The thin green script of a neon sign lay across its façade, with a chaste air. A tall man in dark clothes came out of the front door and leaned against the white wall. He looked very handsome. He had dark skin and a handsome head of iron-gray hair brushed back from his forehead. He got out what looked at that distance to be a silver or platinum and black enamel cigarette case, opened it languidly with two long brown fingers and selected a gold-tipped cigarette. He put the case away and lit the cigarette with a pocket lighter that seemed to match the case. He put that away and folded his arms and stared at nothing with half-closed eyes. From the tip of his motionless cigarette a thin wisp of smoke rose straight up past his face, as thin and straight as the smoke of a dying campfire at dawn.

Another batter struck out or flied out behind my back in the recreated ball game. I turned from watching the tall Italian, put the key into the door of Apartment 204 and went in. A square room with a brown carpet, very little furniture and that not inviting. The wall bed with the usual distorting mirror faced me as I opened the door and made me look like a two-time loser sneaking home from a reefer party. There was a birchwood easy chair with some hard looking upholstery beside it in the form of a davenport. A table before the window held a lamp with a shirred paper shade. There was a door on either side of the bed.

The door to the left led into a small kitchenette with a brown woodstone sink and a three-burner stove and an old electric icebox that clicked and began to throb in torment just as I pushed the door open. On the woodstone drain board stood the remains of somebody's breakfast, mud at the bottom of a cup, a burnt crust of bread, crumbs on a board, a yellow slime of melted butter down the slope of a saucer, a smeared knife and a granite coffee pot that smelled like sacks in a hot barn.

I went back around the wall bed and through the other door. It gave on a short hallway with an open space for clothes and a built-in dresser. On the dresser was a comb and a black brush with a few blond hairs in its black bristles. Also a can of talcum, a small flashlight with a cracked lens, a pad of writing paper, a bank pen, a bottle of ink on a blotter, cigarettes and matches in a glass ashtray that contained half a dozen stubs. In the drawers of the dresser were about what one suitcase would hold in the way of socks and underclothes and handkerchiefs. There was a dark gray suit on a hanger, not new but still good, and a pair of rather dusty black brogues on the floor under it.

I pushed the bathroom door. It opened about a foot and then stuck. My nose twitched and I could feel my lips stiffen and I smelled the harsh sharp bitter smell from beyond the door. I leaned against it. It gave a little, but came back, as though somebody was holding it against me. I poked my head through the opening.

The floor of the bathroom was too short for him, so his knees were poked up and hung outwards slackly and his head was pressed against the woodstone baseboard at the other end, not tilted up, but jammed tight. His brown suit was rumpled a little and his dark glasses stuck out of his breast pocket at an unsafe angle. As if that mattered. His right hand was thrown across his stomach, his left hand lay on the floor, palm up, the fingers curled a little. There was a blood-caked bruise on the right side of his head, in the blond hair. His open mouth was full of shiny crimson blood.

The door was stopped by his leg. I pushed hard and edged around it and got in. I bent down to push two fingers into the side of his neck against the big artery. No artery throbbed there, or even whispered. Nothing at all. The skin was icy. It couldn't have been icy. I just thought it was. I straightened up and leaned my back against the door and made hard fists in my pockets and smelled the cordite fumes. The baseball game was still going on, but through two closed doors it sounded remote.

I stood and looked down at him. Nothing in that, Marlowe, nothing at all. Nothing for you here, nothing. You didn't even know him. Get out, get out fast.

I pulled away from the door and pulled it open and went back through the hall into the living room. A face in the mirror looked at me. A strained, leering face. I turned away from it quickly and took out the flat key George Anson Phillips had given me and rubbed it between my moist palms and laid it down beside the lamp.

I smeared the doorknob opening the door and the outside knob closing the door. The Dodgers were ahead seven to three, the first half of the eighth. A lady who sounded well on with her drinking was singing Frankie and Johnny, the roundhouse version, in a voice that even whiskey had failed to improve. A deep man's voice growled at her to shut up and she kept on singing and there was a hard quick movement across the floor and a smack and a yelp and she stopped singing and the baseball game went right on.

I put the cigarette in my mouth and lit it and went back down the stairs and stood in the half dark of the hall angle looking at the little sign that read: *Manager, Apt. 106.* I was a fool even to look at it. I looked at it for a long minute, biting the cigarette hard between my teeth. I turned and walked down the hallway towards the back. A small enameled plate on a door said: *Manager.* I knocked on the door.

■ **9** ■

A CHAIR WAS PUSHED BACK, FEET SHUFFLED, THE DOOR opened.

"You the manager?"

"Yeah." It was the same voice I had heard over the telephone. Talking to Elisha Morningstar.

He held an empty smeared glass in his hand. It looked as if somebody had been keeping goldfish in it. He was a lanky man with carroty short hair growing down to a point on his forehead. He had a long narrow head packed with shabby cunning. Greenish eyes stared under orange eyebrows. His ears were large and might have flapped in a high wind. He had a long nose that would be into things. The whole face was a trained face, a face that would know how to keep a secret, a face that held the effortless composure of a corpse in the morgue. He wore his vest open, no coat, a woven hair watchguard, and round blue sleeve garters with metal clasps.

I said: "Mr. Anson?"

"Two-o-four."

"He's not in."

"What should I do—lay an egg?"

"Neat," I said. "You have them all the time, or is this your birthday?"

"Beat it," he said. "Drift." He started to close the door. He opened it again to say: "Take the air. Scram. Push off." Having made his meaning clear he started to close the door again.

I leaned against the door. He leaned against it on his side. That brought our faces close together. "Five bucks," I said. It rocked him. He opened the door very suddenly and I had to take a quick step forward in order not to butt his chin with my head.

"Come in," he said.

A living room with a wall bed, everything strictly to specifications, even to the shirred paper lampshade and the glass ashtray. This room was painted egg-yolk yellow. All it needed was a few black spiders painted on the yellow to be anybody's bilious attack.

"Sit down," he said, shutting the door.

I sat down. We looked at each other with the clear innocent eyes of a couple of used car salesmen.

"Beer?" he said.

"Thanks."

He opened two cans, filled the smeared glass he had been holding, and reached for another like it. I said I would drink out of the can. He handed me the can. "A dime," he said.

I gave him a dime. He dropped it into his vest and went on looking at me. He pulled a chair over and sat in it and spread his bony upjutting knees and let his empty hand droop between them. "I ain't interested in your five bucks," he said.

"That's fine," I said. "I wasn't really thinking of giving it to you."

"A wisey," he said. "What gives? We run a nice respectable place here. No funny stuff gets pulled."

"Quiet too," I said. "Upstairs you could almost hear an eagle scream."

His smile was wide, about three quarters of an inch. "I don't amuse easy," he said.

"Just like Queen Victoria," I said.

"I don't get it."

"I don't expect miracles," I said. The meaningless talk had a sort of cold bracing effect on me, making a mood with a hard gritty edge.

I got my wallet out and selected a card from it. It wasn't my card. It read: *James B. Pollock, Reliance Indemnity Company, Field Agent.* I tried to remember what James B. Pollock looked like and where I had met him. I couldn't. I handed the carroty man the card.

He read it and scratched the end of his nose with one of the corners. "Wrong john?" he asked, keeping his green eyes plastered to my face.

"Jewelry," I said and waved a hand.

He thought this over. While he thought it over I tried to make up my mind whether it worried him at all. It didn't seem to. "We get one once in a while," he conceded. "You can't help it. He didn't look like it to me, though. Soft looking."

"Maybe I got a bum steer," I said. I described George Anson Phillips to him, George Anson Phillips alive, in his brown suit and his dark glasses and his cocoa straw hat with the brown and yellow print band. I wondered what had happened to the hat. It hadn't been up there. He must have got rid of it, thinking it was too conspicuous. His blond head was almost, but not quite, as bad.

"That sounds like him?"

The carroty man took his time making up his mind. Finally he nodded yes, green eyes watching me carefully, lean hard hand holding the card up to his mouth and running the card along his teeth like a stick along the palings of a picket fence.

"I didn't figure him for no crook," he said. "But hell, they come all sizes and shapes. Only been here a month. If he looked like a wrong gee, wouldn't have been here at all."

I did a good job of not laughing in his face. "What say we frisk the apartment while he's out?"

He shook his head. "Mr. Palermo wouldn't like it."

"Mr. Palermo?"

"He's the owner. Across the street. Owns the funeral parlors. Owns this building and a lot of other buildings. Practically owns the district, if you know what I mean." He gave me a twitch of the lip and a flutter of the right eyelid. "Gets the vote out. Not a guy to crowd."

"Well, while he's getting the vote out or playing with a stiff or whatever he's doing at the moment, let's go up and frisk the apartment."

"Don't get me sore at you," the carroty man said briefly.

"That would bother me like two per cent of nothing at all," I said. "Let's go up and frisk the apartment." I threw my empty beer can at the wastebasket and watched it bounce back and roll halfway across the room.

The carroty man stood up suddenly and spread his feet apart and dusted his hands together and took hold of his lower lip with his teeth. "You said something about five," he shrugged.

"That was hours ago," I said. "I thought better of it. Let's go up and frisk the apartment."

"Say that just once more—" his right hand slid towards his hip.

"If you're thinking of pulling a gun, Mr. Palermo wouldn't like it," I said.

"To hell with Mr. Palermo," he snarled, in a voice suddenly furious, out of a face suddenly charged with dark blood.

"Mr. Palermo will be glad to know that's how you feel about him," I said.

"Look," the carroty man said very slowly, dropping his

hand to his side and leaning forward from the hips and pushing his face at me as hard as he could. "Look. I was sitting here having myself a beer or two. Maybe three. Maybe nine. What the hell? I wasn't bothering anybody. It was a nice day. It looked like it might be a nice evening— Then you come in." He waved a hand violently.

"Let's go up and frisk the apartment," I said.

He threw both fists forward in tight lumps. At the end of the motion he threw his hands wide open, straining the fingers as far as they would go. His nose twitched sharply. "If it wasn't for the job," he said.

I opened my mouth. "Don't say it!" he yelled.

He put a hat on, but no coat, opened a drawer and took out a bunch of keys, walked past me to open the door and stood in it, jerking his chin at me. His face still looked a little wild.

We went out into the hall and along it and up the stairs. The ball game was over and dance music had taken its place. Very loud dance music. The carroty man selected one of his keys and put it in the lock of Apartment 204. Against the booming of the dance band behind us in the apartment across the way a woman's voice suddenly screamed hysterically.

The carroty man withdrew the key and bared his teeth at me. He walked across the narrow hallway and banged on the opposite door. He had to knock hard and long before any attention was paid. Then the door was jerked open and a sharp-faced blond in scarlet slacks and a green pullover stared out with sultry eyes, one of which was puffed and the other had been socked several days ago. She also had a bruise on her throat and her hand held a tall cool glass of amber fluid. "Pipe down, but soon," the carroty man said. "Too much racket. I don't aim to ask you again. Next time I call some law."

The girl looked back over her shoulder and screamed against the noise of the radio: "Hey, Dell The guy says to pipe down! You wanna sock him?"

A chair squeaked, the radio noise died abruptly and a thick bitter-eyed dark man appeared behind the blond, yanked her out of the way with one hand and pushed his face at us. He needed a shave. He was wearing pants, street shoes and an undershirt. He settled his feet in the doorway, whistled a little breath in through his nose and said: "Buzz off. I just come in from lunch. I had a lousy lunch. I wouldn't want nobody to push muscle at me." He was very drunk, but in a hard practised sort of way.

The carroty man said: "You heard me, Mr. Hench. Dim that radio and stop the roughhouse in here. And make it sudden."

The man addressed as Hench said: "Listen, pickle-puss—" and heaved forward with his right foot in a hard stamp.

The carroty man's left foot didn't wait to be stamped on. The lean body moved quickly and the thrown bunch of keys hit the floor behind, and clanked against the door of Apartment 204. The carroty man's right hand made a sweeping movement and came up with a woven leather blackjack.

Hench said: "Yah!" and took two big handfuls of air in his two hairy hands, closed the hands into fists and swung hard at nothing.

The carroty man hit him on the top of his head and the girl screamed again and threw a glass of liquor in her boy friend's face. Whether because it was safe to do it now or because she made an honest mistake, I couldn't tell.

Hench turned blindly with his face dripping, stumbled and ran across the floor in a lurch that threatened to land him on his nose at every step. The bed was down and tumbled. Hench made the bed on one knee and plunged a hand under the pillow.

I said: "Look out—gun."

"I can fade that too," the carroty man said between his teeth and slid his right hand, empty now, under his open vest.

Hench was down on both knees. He came up on one and turned and there was a short black gun in his right hand and he was staring down at it, not holding it by the grip at all, holding it flat on his palm.

"Drop it!" the carroty man's voice said tightly and he went on into the room.

The blond promptly jumped on his back and wound her long green arms around his neck, yelling lustily. The carroty man staggered and swore and waved his gun around.

"Get him, Dell!" the blond screamed. "Get him good!"

Hench, one hand on the bed and one foot on the floor, both knees doubled, right hand holding the black gun flat on his palm, eyes staring down at it, pushed himself slowly to his feet and growled deep in his throat: "This ain't my gun."

I relieved the carroty man of the gun that was not doing him any good and stepped around him, leaving him to shake the blond off his back as best he could. A door banged down the hallway and steps came along toward us.

I said: "Drop it, Hench."

He looked up at me, puzzled dark eyes suddenly sober. "It ain't my gun," he said and held it out flat. "Mine's a Colt .32—belly gun."

I took the gun off his hand. He made no effort to stop me. He sat down on the bed, rubbed the top of his head slowly, and screwed his face up in difficult thought. "Where the hell—" his voice trailed off and he shook his head and winced.

I sniffed the gun. It had been fired. I sprang the magazine out and counted the bullets through the small holes in the side. There were six. With one in the magazine, that made seven. The gun was a Colt .32, automatic, eight shot. It had been fired. If it had not been reloaded, one shot had been fired from it.

The carroty man had the blond off his back now. He had thrown her into a chair and was wiping a scratch on his cheek. His green eyes were baleful.

"Better get some law," I said. "A shot has been fired from this gun and it's about time you found out there's a dead man in the apartment across the hall."

Hench looked up at me stupidly and said in a quiet, reasonable voice: "Brother, that simply ain't my gun."

The blond sobbed in a rather theatrical manner and showed me an open mouth twisted with misery and ham acting. The carroty man went softly out of the door.

■ **10** ■

"SHOT IN THE THROAT WITH A MEDIUM CALIBER GUN AND a soft-nosed bullet," Detective-Lieutenant Jesse Breeze said. "A gun like this and bullets like is in here." He danced the gun on his hand, the gun Hench had said was not his gun. "Bullet ranged upwards and probably hit the back of the skull. Still inside his head. The man's dead about two hours. Hands and face cold, but body still warm. No rigor. Was sapped with something hard before being shot. Likely with a gun butt. All that mean anything to you boys and girls?"

The newspaper he was sitting on rustled. He took his hat off and mopped his face and the top of his almost bald head. A fringe of light colored hair around the crown was damp and dark with sweat. He put his hat back on, a flat-crowned panama, burned dark by the sun. Not this year's hat, and probably not last year's.

He was a big man, rather paunchy, wearing brown and white shoes and sloppy socks and white trousers with thin black stripes, an open neck shirt showing some ginger-colored hair at the top of his chest, and a rough sky-blue sports coat not wider at the shoulders than a two-car garage. He would be about 50 years old and the only thing about him that very much suggested cop was the calm, unwinking unwavering stare of his prominent pale blue eyes, a stare that had no thought of being rude, but that anybody but a cop would feel to be rude. Below his eyes across the top of his cheeks and the bridge of his nose there was a wide path of freckles, like a mine field on a war map.

We were sitting in Hench's apartment and the door was shut. Hench had his shirt on and he was absently tying a tie with thick blunt fingers that trembled. The girl was lying on the bed. She had a green wrap-around thing twisted about her head, a purse by her side and a short squirrel coat across her feet. Her mouth was a little open and her face was drained and shocked.

Hench said thickly: "If the idea is the guy was shot with the gun under the pillow, okay. Seems like he might have been. It ain't my gun and nothing you boys can think up is going to make me say it's my gun."

"Assuming that to be so," Breeze said, "how come? Somebody swiped your gun and left this one. When, how, what kind of gun was yours?"

"We went out about three-thirty or so to get something to eat at the hashhouse around the corner," Hench said. "You can check that. We must have left the door unlocked. We were kind of hitting the bottle a little. I guess we were pretty noisy. We had the ball game going on the radio. I guess we shut it off when we went out. I'm not sure. You remember?" He looked at the girl lying white-faced and silent on the bed. "You remember, sweet?"

The girl didn't look at him or answer him.

"She's pooped," Hench said. "I had a gun, a Colt .32, same caliber as that, but a belly gun. A revolver, not an automatic. There's a piece broken off the rubber grip. A Jew named Morris gave it to me three four years ago. We worked together in a bar. I don't have no permit, but I don't carry the gun neither."

Breeze said: "Hitting the hooch like you birds been and having a gun under the pillow sooner or later somebody was going to get shot. You ought to know that."

"Hell, we didn't even know the guy," Hench said. His tie was tied now, very badly. He was cold sober and very shaky. He stood up and picked a coat off the end of the bed and put it on and sat down again. I watched his fingers tremble lighting a cigarette. "We don't know his name. We don't know anything about him. I see him maybe two three times in the hall, but he don't even speak to me. It's the same guy, I guess. I ain't even sure of that."

"It's the fellow that lived there," Breeze said. "Let me see now, this ball game is a studio re-broadcast, huh?"

"Goes on at three," Hench said. "Three to say four-thirty, or sometimes later. We went out about the last half the third. We was gone about an inning and a half, maybe two. Twenty minutes to half an hour. Not more."

"I guess he was shot just before you went out," Breeze said. "The radio would kill the noise of the gun near enough. You must of left your door unlocked. Or even open."

"Could be," Hench said wearily. "You remember, honey?"

Again the girl on the bed refused to answer him or even look at him.

Breeze said: "You left your door open or unlocked. The killer heard you go out. He got into your apartment, wanting to ditch his gun, saw the bed down, walked across and slipped his gun under the pillow, and then imagine his surprise. He found another gun there waiting for him. So he took it along. Now if he meant to ditch his gun, why not do it where he did his killing? Why take the risk of going into another apartment to do it? Why the fancy pants?"

I was sitting in the corner of the davenport by the window. I put in my nickel's worth, saying: "Suppose he had locked himself out of Phillips' apartment before he thought of ditching the gun? Suppose, coming out of the shock of his murder, he found himself in the hall still holding the murder gun. He would want to ditch it fast. Then if Hench's door was open and he had heard them go out along the hall—"

Breeze looked at me briefly and grunted: "I'm not saying it isn't so. I'm just considering." He turned his attention back to Hench. "So now, if this turns out to be the gun that killed Anson, we got to try and trace *your* gun. While we do that we got to have you and the young lady handy. You understand that, of course?"

Hench said: "You don't have any boys that can bounce me hard enough to make me tell it different."

"We can always try," Breeze said mildly. "And we might just as well get started." He stood up, turned and swept the crumpled newspapers off the chair on to the floor. He went over to the door, then turned and stood looking at the girl on the bed. "You all right, sister, or should I call for a matron?"

The girl on the bed didn't answer him.

Hench said: "I need a drink. I need a drink bad."

"Not while I'm watching you," Breeze said and went out of the door.

Hench moved across the room and put the neck of a bottle into his mouth and gurgled liquor. He lowered the bottle, looked at what was left in it and went over to the girl. He pushed her shoulder. "Wake up and have a drink," he growled at her.

The girl stared at the ceiling. She didn't answer him or show that she had heard him.

"Let her alone," I said. "Shock."

Hench finished what was in the bottle, put the empty bottle down carefully and looked at the girl again, then turned his back on her and stood frowning at the floor. "Jeeze, I wish I could remember better," he said under his breath.

Breeze came back into the room with a young fresh-faced plainclothes detective. "This is Lieutenant Spangler," he said. "He'll take you down. Get going, huh?"

Hench went back to the bed and shook the girl's shoulder. "Get on up babe. We gotta take a ride."

The girl turned her eyes without turning her head, and looked at him slowly. She lifted her shoulders off the bed and put a hand under her and swung her legs over the side and stood up, stamping her right foot, as if it was numb.

"Tough, kid—but you know how it is," Hench said.

The girl put a hand to her mouth and bit the knuckle of her little finger, looking at him blankly. Then she swung the hand suddenly and hit him in the face as hard as she could. Then she half ran out of the door.

Hench didn't move a muscle for a long moment. There was a confused noise of men talking outside, a confused noise of cars down below in the street. Hench shrugged and cocked his heavy shoulders back and swept a slow look around the room, as if he didn't expect to see it again very soon, or at all. Then he went out past the young fresh-faced detective.

The detective went out. The door closed. The confused noise outside was dimmed a little and Breeze and I sat looking at each other heavily.

▪ 11 ▪

AFTER A WHILE BREEZE GOT TIRED OF LOOKING AT ME and dug a cigar out of his pocket. He slit the cellophane band with a knife and trimmed the end of the cigar and lit it carefully, turning it around in the flame, and holding the burning match away from it while he stared thoughtfully at nothing and drew on the cigar and made sure it was burning the way he wanted it to burn. Then he shook the match out very slowly and reached over to lay it on the sill of the open window. Then he looked at me some more. "You and me," he said, "are going to get along."

"That's fine," I said.

"You don't think so," he said. "But we are. But not because I took any sudden fancy to you. It's the way I work. Everything is the clear. Everything sensible. Everything quiet. Not like that dame. That's the kind of dame that spends her life looking for trouble and when she finds it, it's the fault of the first guy she can get her fingernails into."

"He gave her a couple of shiners," I said. "That wouldn't make her love him too much."

"I can see," Breeze said, "that you know a lot about dames."

"Not knowing a lot about them has helped me in my business," I said. "I'm open-minded."

He nodded and examined the end of his cigar. He took a piece of paper out of his pocket and read from it. "Delmar B. Hench, 45, bartender, unemployed. Maybelle Masters, 26, dancer. That's all I know about them. I've got a hunch there ain't a lot more to know."

"You don't think he shot Anson?" I asked.

Breeze looked at me without pleasure. "Brother, I just got here." He took a card out of his pocket and read from that. "James B. Pollock, Reliance Indemnity Company, Field Agent. What's the idea?"

"In a neighborhood like this it's bad form to use your own name," I said. "Anson didn't either."

"What's the matter with the neighborhood?"

"Practically everything," I said.

"What I would like to know," Breeze said, "is what you know about the dead guy?"

"I told you already."

"Tell me again. People tell me so much stuff I get it all mixed up."

"I know what it says on his card, that his name is George Anson Phillips, that he claimed to be a private detective. He was outside my office when I went to lunch. He followed me downtown, into the lobby of the Hotel Metropole. I led him there. I spoke to him and he admitted he had been following me and said it was because he wanted to find out if I was smart enough to do business with. That's a lot of baloney, of course. He probably hadn't quite made up his mind what to do and was waiting for something to decide him. He was on a job—he said—he had got leery of and he wanted to join up with somebody, perhaps somebody with a little more experience than he had, if he had any at all. He didn't act as if he had."

Breeze said: "And the only reason he picked on you is that six years ago you worked on a case in Ventura while he was a deputy up there."

I said, "That's my story."

"But you don't have to get stuck with it," Breeze said calmly. "You can always give us a better one."

"It's good enough," I said. "I mean it's good enough in the sense that it's bad enough to be true."

He nodded his big slow head. "What's your idea of all this?" he asked.

"Have you investigated Phillips' office address?"

He shook his head, no.

"My idea is you will find out he was hired because he was simple. He was hired to take this apartment here under a wrong name, and to do something that turned out to be not what he liked. He was scared. He wanted a friend, he wanted help. The fact that he picked me after so long a time and such little knowledge of me showed he didn't know many people in the detective business."

Breeze got his handkerchief out and mopped his head and face again. "But it don't begin to show why he had to follow you around like a lost pup instead of walking right up to your office door and in."

"No," I said, "it doesn't."

"Can you explain that?"

"No. Not really."

"Well, how would you try to explain it?"

"I've already explained it in the only way I know how. He was undecided whether to speak to me or not. He was waiting for something to decide him. I decided by speaking to him."

Breeze said: "That is a very simple explanation. It is so simple it stinks."

"You may be right," I said.

"And as the result of this little hotel lobby conversation this guy, a total stranger to you, asks you to his apartment and hands you his key. Because he wants to talk to you."

I said, "Yes."

"Why couldn't he talk to you then?"

"I had an appointment," I said.

"Business?"

I nodded.

"I see. What you working on?"

I shook my head and didn't answer.

"This is murder," Breeze said. "You're going to have to tell me."

I shook my head again. He flushed a little.

"Look," he said tightly, "you got to."

"I'm sorry, Breeze," I said. "But so far as things have gone, I'm not convinced of that."

"Of course you know I can throw you in the can as a material witness," he said casually.

"On what grounds?"

"On the grounds that you are the one who found the body, that you gave a false name to the manager here, and that you don't give a satisfactory account of your relations with the dead guy."

I said: "Are you going to do it?"

He smiled bleakly. "You got a lawyer?"

"I know several lawyers. I don't have a lawyer on a retainer basis."

"How many of the commissioners do you know personally?"

"None. That is, I've spoken to three of them, but they might not remember me."

"But you have good contacts, in the mayor's office and so on?"

"Tell me about them," I said. "I'd like to know."

"Look, buddy," he said earnestly, "you must got some friends somewhere. Surely."

"I've got a good friend in the Sheriff's office, but I'd rather leave him out of it."

He lifted his eyebrows. "Why? Maybe you're going to need friends. A good word from a cop we know to be right might go a long way."

"He's just a personal friend," I said. "I don't ride around on his back. If I get in trouble, it won't do him any good."

"How about the homicide bureau?"

"There's Randall," I said. "If he's still working out of Central Homicide. I had a little time with him on a case once. But he doesn't like me too well."

Breeze sighed and moved his feet on the floor, rustling the newspapers he had pushed down out of the chair. "Is all this on the level—or are you just being smart? I mean about all the important guys you don't know?"

"It's on the level," I said. "But the way I am using it is smart."

"It ain't smart to say so right out."

"I think it is."

He put a big freckled hand over the whole lower part of his face and squeezed. When he took the hand away there were round red marks on his cheeks from the pressure of thumb and fingers. I watched the marks fade.

"Why don't you go on home and let a man work?" he asked crossly.

I got up and nodded and went towards the door. Breeze said to my back: "Gimme your home address."

I gave it to him. He wrote it down. "So long," he said drearily: "Don't leave town. We'll want a statement—maybe tonight."

I went out. There were two uniformed cops outside on the landing. The door across the way was open and a fingerprint man was still working inside. Downstairs I met two more cops in the hallway, one at each end of it. I didn't see the carroty manager. I went out the front door. There was an ambulance pulling away from the curb. A knot of people hung around on both sides of the street, not as many as would accumulate in some neighborhoods.

I pushed along the sidewalk. A man grabbed me by the arm and said: "What's the damage, Jack?"

I shook his arm off without speaking or looking at his face and went on down the street to where my car was.

■ 12 ■

IT WAS A QUARTER TO SEVEN WHEN I LET MYSELF INTO the office and clicked the light on and picked a piece of paper off the floor. It was a notice from the Green Feather Messenger Service saying that a package was held awaiting my call and would be delivered upon request at any hour of the day or night. I put it on the desk, peeled my coat off and opened the windows. I got a half bottle of Old Taylor out of the deep drawer of the desk and drank a short drink, rolling it around on my tongue. Then I sat there holding the neck of the cool bottle and wondering how it would feel to be a homicide dick and find bodies lying around and not mind at all, not have to sneak out wiping doorknobs, not have to ponder how much I could tell without hurting a client and how little I could tell without too badly hurting myself. I decided I wouldn't like it.

I pulled the phone over and looked at the number on the slip and called it. They said my package could be sent right over. I said I would wait for it.

It was getting dark outside now. The rushing sound of the traffic had died a little and the air from the open window, not yet cool from the night, had that tired end-or-the-day smell of dust, automobile exhaust, sunlight rising from hot walls and sidewalks, the remote smell of food in a thousand restaurants, and perhaps, drifting down from the residential hills above Hollywood—if you had a nose like a hunting dog—a touch of that peculiar tomcat smell that eucalyptus trees give off in warm weather.

73

I sat there smoking. Ten minutes later the door was knocked on and I opened it to a boy in a uniform cap who took my signature and gave me a small square package, not more than two and a half inches wide, if that. I gave the boy a dime and listened to him whistling his way back to the elevators.

The label had my name and address printed on it in ink, in a quite fair imitation of typed letters, larger and thinner than pica. I cut the string that tied the label to the box and unwound the thin brown paper. Inside was a thin cheap cardboard box pasted over with brown paper and stamped *Made in Japan* with a rubber stamp. It would be the kind of box you would get in a Jap store to hold some small carved animal or a small piece of jade. The lid fitted down all the way and tightly. I pulled it off and saw tissue paper and cotton wool. Separating these I was looking at a gold coin about the size of a half dollar, bright and shining as if it had just come from the mint.

The side facing me showed a spread eagle with a shield for a breast and the initials E.B. punched into the left wing. Around these was a circle of beading, between the beading and the smoth unmilled edge of the coin, the legend E PLURIBUS UNUM. At the bottom was the date 1787.

I turned the coin over on my palm. It was heavy and cold and my palm felt moist under it. The other side showed a sun rising or setting behind a sharp peak of mountain, then a double circle of what looked like oak leaves, then more Latin, NOVA EBORACA COLUMBIA EXCELSIOR. At the bottom of this side, in similar capitals, the name BRASHER.

I was looking at the Brasher Doubloon.

There was nothing else in the box or in the paper, nothing on the paper. The handwritten printing meant nothing to me. I didn't know anybody who used it.

I filled an empty tobacco pouch half full, wrapped the coin up in tissue paper, snapped a rubber band around it and tucked it into the tobacco in the pouch and put more in on top. I closed the zipper and put the pouch in my pocket. I locked the paper and string and box and label

up in a filing cabinet, sat down again and dialed Elisha
Morningstar's number on the phone. The bell rang eight
times at the other end of the line. It was not answered. I
hardly expected that. I hung up again, looked Elisha
Morningstar up in the book and saw that he had no
listing for a residence phone in Los Angeles or the
outlying towns that were in the phone book.

I got a shoulder holster out of the desk and strapped it
on and slipped a Colt .38 automatic into it, put on hat
and coat, shut the windows again, put the whiskey away,
clicked the lights off and had the office door unlatched
when the phone rang.

The ringing bell had a sinister sound, for no reason of
itself, but because of the ears to which it rang. I stood
there braced and tense, lips tightly drawn back in a half
grin. Beyond the closed window the neon lights glowed.
The dead air didn't move. Outside the corridor was still.
The bell rang in darkness, steady and strong.

I went back and leaned on the desk and answered.
There was a click and a droning on the wire and beyond
that nothing. I depressed the connection and stood there
in the dark, leaning over, holding the phone with one
hand and holding the flat riser on the pedestal down
with the other. I didn't know what I was waiting for.

The phone rang again. I made a sound in my throat
and put it to my ear again, not saying anything at all.

So we were there silent, both of us, miles apart maybe,
each one holding a telephone and breathing and listening and hearing nothing, not even the breathing. Then
after what seemed a very long time there was the quiet
remote whisper of a voice saying dimly, without any
tone: "Too bad for you, Marlowe."

Then the click again and the droning on the wire and I
hung up and went back across the office and out.

▪ 13 ▪

I DROVE WEST ON SUNSET, FIDDLED AROUND A FEW BLOCKS without making up my mind whether anyone was trying to follow me, then parked near a drugstore and went into its phone booth. I dropped my nickel and asked the O-operator for a Pasadena number. She told me how much money to put in.

The voice which answered the phone was angular and cold. "Mrs. Murdock's residence."

"Philip Marlowe here. Mrs. Murdock, please."

I was told to wait. A soft but very clear voice said: "Mr. Marlowe? Mrs. Murdock is resting now. Can you tell me what it is?"

"You oughtn't to have told him."

"I—who—?"

"That loopy guy whose handkerchief you cry into."

"How dare you?"

"That's fine," I said. "Now let me talk to Mrs. Murdock. I have to."

"Very well. I'll try." The soft clear voice went away and I waited a long wait. They would have to lift her up on the pillows and drag the port bottle out of her hard gray paw and feed her the telephone. A throat was cleared suddenly over the wire. It sounded like a freight train going through a tunnel.

"This is Mrs. Murdock."

"Could you identify the property we were talking about this morning, Mrs. Murdock? I mean could you pick it out from others just like it?"

"Well—are there others just like it?"

"There must be. Dozens, hundreds for all I know. Anyhow dozens. Of course I don't know where they are."

She coughed. "I don't really know much about it. I suppose I couldn't identify it then. But in the circumstances—"

"That's what I'm getting at, Mrs. Murdock. The identification would seem to depend on tracing the history of the article back to you. At least to be convincing."

"Yes. I suppose it would. Why? Do you know where it is?"

"Morningstar claims to have seen it. He says it was offered to him for sale—just as you suspected. He wouldn't buy. The seller was not a woman, he says. That doesn't mean a thing, because he gave me a detailed description of the party which was either made up or was a description of somebody he knew more than casually. So the seller may have been a woman."

"I see. It's not important now."

"Not important?"

"No. Have you anything else to report?"

"Another question to ask. Do you know a youngish blond fellow named George Anson Phillips? Rather heavy set, wearing a brown suit and dark pork pie hat with a gay band. Wearing that today. Claimed to be a private detective."

"I do not. Why should I?"

"I don't know. He enters the picture somewhere. I think he was the one who tried to sell the article. Morningstar tried to call him up after I left. I snuck back into his office and overheard."

"You what?"

"I snuck."

"Please do not be witty, Mr. Marlowe. Anything else?"

"Yes, I agreed to pay Morningstar one thousand dollars for the return of the—the article. He said he could get it for eight hundred . . ."

"And where were you going to get the money, may I ask?"

"Well, I was just talking. This Morningstar is a downy

bird. That's the kind of language he understands. And then again you might have wanted to pay it. I wouldn't want to persuade you. You could always go to the police. But if for any reason you didn't want to go to the police, it might be the only way you could get it back—buying it back."

I would probably have gone on like that for a long time, not knowing just what I was trying to say, if she hadn't stopped me with a noise like a seal barking. "This is all very unnecessary now, Mr. Marlowe. I have decided to drop the matter. The coin has been returned to me."

"Hold the wire a minute," I said. I put the phone down on the shelf and opened the booth door and stuck my head out, filling my chest with what they were using for air in the drugstore. Nobody was paying any attention to me. Up front the druggist, in a pale blue smock, was chatting across the cigar counter. The counter boy was polishing glasses at the fountain. Two girls in slacks were playing the pinball machine. A tall narrow party in a black shirt and a pale yellow scarf was fumbling magazines at the rack. He didn't look like a gunman.

I pulled the booth shut and picked up the phone and said: "A rat was gnawing my foot. It's all right now. You got it back, you said. Just like that. How?"

"I hope you are not too disappointed," she said in her uncompromising baritone. "The circumstances are a little difficult. I may decide to explain and I may not. You may call at the house tomorrow morning. Since I do not wish to proceed with the investigation, you will keep the retainer as payment in full."

"Let me get this straight," I said. "You actually got the coin back—not a promise of it, merely?"

"Certainly not. And I'm getting tired. So, if you—"

"One moment, Mrs. Murdock. It isn't going to be as simple as all that. Things have happened."

"In the morning you may tell me about them," she said sharply, and hung up.

I pushed out of the booth and lit a cigarette with thick awkward fingers. I went back along the store. The druggist was alone now. He was sharpening a pencil with a small knife, very intent, frowning.

"That's a nice sharp pencil you have there," I told him.

He looked up, surprised. The girls at the pinball machine looked at me, surprised. I went over and looked at myself in the mirror behind the counter. I looked surprised. I sat down on one of the stools and said: "A double Scotch, straight."

The counter man looked surprised. "Sorry, this isn't a bar, sir. You can buy a bottle at the liquor counter."

"So it is," I said. "I mean, so it isn't. I've had a shock. I'm a little dazed. Give me a cup of coffee, weak, and a very thin ham sandwish on stale bread. No, I better not eat yet either. Good-by."

I got down off the stool and walked to the door in a silence that was as loud as a ton of coal going down a chute. The man in the black shirt and yellow scarf was sneering at me over the New Republic. "You ought to lay off that fluff and get your teeth into something solid, like a pulp magazine," I told him, just to be friendly.

I went on out. Behind me somebody said: "Hollywood's full of them."

▪ 14 ▪

The wind had risen and had a dry taut feeling, tossing the tops of trees, and making the swung arc light up the side street cast shadows like crawling lava. I turned the car and drove east again.

The hock shop was on Santa Monica, near Wilcox, a quiet old-fashioned little place, washed gently by the lapping waves of time. In the front window there was everything you could think of, from a set of trout flies in a thin wooden box to a portable organ, from a folding baby carriage to a portrait camera with a four-inch lens, from a mother-of-pearl lorgnette in a faded plush case to a Single Action Frontier Colt, .44 caliber, the model they still make for Western peace officers whose grandfathers taught them how to file the trigger and shoot by fanning the hammer back.

I went into the shop and a bell jangled over my head and somebody shuffled and blew his nose far at the back and steps came. An old Jew in a tall black skull cap came along behind the counter, smiling at me over cut out glasses.

I got my tobacco pouch out, got the Brasher Doubloon out of that and laid it on the counter. The window in front was clear glass and I felt naked. No paneled cubicles with hand-carved spittoons and doors that locked themselves as you closed them.

The Jew took the coin and lifted it on his hand. "Gold, is it? A gold hoarder you are maybe," he said, twinkling.

"Twenty-five dollars," I said. "The wife and the kiddies are hungry."

"Oi, that is terrible. Gold, it feels, by the weight. Only gold and maybe platinum it could be." He weighed it casually on a pair of small scales. "Gold it is," he said. "So ten dollars you are wanting?"

"Twenty-five dollars."

"For twenty-five dollars what would I do with it? Sell it, maybe? For fifteen dollars worth of gold is maybe in it. Okay. Fifteen dollars."

"You got a good safe?"

"Mister, in this business are the best safes money can buy. Nothing to worry about here. It is fifteen dollars, is it?"

"Make out the ticket."

He wrote it out partly with his pen and partly with his tongue. I gave my true name and address. Bristol Apartments, 1634 North Bristol Avenue, Hollywood.

"You are living in that district and you are borrowing fifteen dollars," the Jew said sadly, and tore off my half of the ticket and counted out the money.

I walked down to the corner drugstore and bought an

envelope and borrowed a pen and mailed the pawn ticket to myself.

I was hungry and hollow inside. I went over to Vine to eat, and after that I drove downtown again. The wind was still rising and it was drier than ever. The steering wheel had a gritty feeling under my fingers and the inside of my nostrils felt tight and drawn.

The lights were on here and there in the tall buildings. The green and chromium clothier's store on the corner of Ninth and Hill was a blaze of it. In the Belfont Building a few windows glowed here and there, but not many. The same old plowhorse sat in the elevator on his piece of folded burlap, looking straight in front of him, blank-eyed, almost gathered to history. I said: "I don't suppose you know where I can get in touch with the building superintendent?"

He turned his head slowly and looked past my shoulder. "I hear how in Noo York they got elevators that just whiz. Go thirty floors at a time. High speed. That's in Noo York."

"The hell with New York," I said. "I like it here."

"Must take a good man to run them fast babies."

"Don't kid yourself, dad. All those cuties do is push buttons, say 'Good Morning, Mr. Whoosis,' and look at their beauty spots in the car mirror. Now you take a Model T job like this—it takes a man to run it. Satisfied?"

"I work twelve hours a day," he said. "And glad to get it."

"Don't let the union hear you."

"You know what the union can do?" I shook my head. He told me. Then he lowered his eyes until they almost looked at me. "Didn't I see you before somewhere?"

"About the building super," I said gently.

"Year ago he broke his glasses," the old man said. "I could of laughed. Almost did."

"Yes. Where could I get in touch with him this time of the evening?"

He looked at me a little more directly. "Oh, the building super? He's home, ain't he?"

"Sure. Probably. Or gone to the pictures. But where is home? What's his name?"

"You want something?"

"Yes." I squeezed a fist in my pocket and tried to keep from yelling. "I want the address of one of the tenants. The tenant I want the address of isn't in the phone book—at his home. I mean where he lives when he's not in his office. You know, home." I took my hands out and made a shape in the air, writing the leters slowly, h o m e.

The old man said: "Which one?" It was so direct that it jarred me.

"Mr. Morningstar."

"He ain't home. Still in his office."

"Are you sure?"

"Sure I'm sure. I don't notice people much. But he's old like me and I notice him. He ain't been down yet."

I got into the car and said: "Eight."

He wrestled the doors shut and we ground our way up. He didn't look at me any more. When the car stopped and I got out he didn't speak or look at me again. He just sat there blank-eyed, hunched on the burlap and the wooden stool. As I turned the angle of the corridor he was still sitting there. And the vague expression was back on his face.

At the end of the corridor two doors were alight. They were the only two in sight that were. I stopped outside to light a cigarette and listen, but I didn't hear any sound of activity. I opened the door marked *Entrance* and stepped into the narrow office with the small closed typewriter desk. The wooden door was still ajar. I walked along to it and knocked on the wood and said: "Mr. Morningstar."

No answer. Silence. Not even a sound of breathing. The hairs moved on the back of my neck. I stepped around the door. The ceiling light glowed down on the glass cover of the jeweller's scales, on the old polished wood around the leather desk top, down the side of the desk, on a square-toed, elastic-sided black shoe, with a white cotton sock above it. The shoe was at the wrong angle, pointing to the corner of the ceiling. The rest of the leg was behind the corner of the big safe. I seemed to be wading through mud as I went on into the room.

He lay crumpled on his back. Very lonely, very dead.

The safe door was wide open and keys hung in the lock of the inner compartment. A metal drawer was pulled out. It was empty now. There may have been money in it once.

Nothing else in the room seemed to be different.

The old man's pockets had been pulled out, but I didn't touch him except to bend over and put the back of my hand against his livid, violet-colored face. It was like touching a frog's belly. Blood had oozed from the side of his forehead where he had been hit. But there was no powder smell on the air this time, and the violet color of his skin showed that he had died of a heart stoppage, due to shock and fear, probably. That didn't make it any less murder.

I left the lights burning, wiped the doorknobs, and walked down the fire stairs to the sixth floor. I read the names on the doors going along, for no reason at all. *H. R. Teager Dental Laboratories, L. Pridview, Public Accountant, Dalton and Rees Typewriting Service, Dr. E. J. Blaskowitz,* and underneath the name in small letters: *Chiropractic Physician.*

The elevator came growling up and the old man didn't look at me. His face was as empty as my brain.

I called the Receiving Hospital from the corner, giving no name.

■ 15 ■

THE CHESSMEN, RED AND WHITE BONE, WERE LINED UP ready to go and had that sharp, competent and complicated look they always have at the beginning of a game. It was ten o'clock in the evening, I was home at the apartment, I had a pipe in my mouth, a drink at my elbow and nothing on my mind except two murders and the mystery of how Mrs. Elizabeth Bright Murdock had got her Brasher Doubloon back while I still had it in my pocket.

I opened a little paper-bound book of tournament games published in Leipzig, picked out a dashing-looking Queen's Gambit, moved the white pawn to Queen's four, and the bell rang at the door.

I stepped around the table and picked the Colt .38 off the drop leaf of the oak desk and went over to the door holding it down beside my right leg. "Who is it?"

"Breeze."

I went back to the desk to lay the gun down again before I opened the door. Breeze stood there looking just as big and sloppy as ever, but a little more tired. The young, fresh-faced dick named Spangler was with him. They rode me back into the room without seeming to and Spangler shut the door. His bright young eyes flicked this way and that while Breeze let his older and harder ones stay on my face for a long moment, then he walked around me to the davenport. "Look around," he said out of the corner of his mouth.

Spangler left the door and crossed the room to the dinette, looked in there, recrossed and went into the hall. The bathroom door squeaked, his steps went farther along.

Breeze took his hat off and mopped his semi-bald dome. Doors opened and closed distantly. Closets. Spangler came back.

"Nobody here," he said.

Breeze nodded and sat down, placing his panama beside him.

Spangler saw the gun lying on the desk. He said: "Mind if I look?"

I said: "Phooey on both of you."

Spangler walked to the gun and held the muzzle to his nose, sniffing. He broke the magazine out, ejected the shell in the chamber, picked it up and pressed it into the magazine. He laid the magazine on the desk and held the gun so that light went into the open bottom of the breech. Holding it that way he squinted down the barrel.

"A little dust," he said. "Not much."

"What did you expect?" I said. "Rubies?"

He ignored me, looked at Breeze and added: "I'd say this gun has not been fired within twenty-four hours. I'm sure of it."

Breeze nodded and chewed his lip and explored my face with his eyes. Spangler put the gun together neatly and laid it aside and went and sat down. He put a cigarette between his lips and lit it and blew smoke contentedly. "We know damn well it wasn't a long .38 anyway," he said. "One of those things will shoot through a wall. No chance of the slug staying inside a man's head."

"Just what are you guys talking about?" I asked.

Breeze said: "The usual thing in our business. Murder. Have a chair. Relax. I thought I heard voices in here. Maybe it was the next apartment."

"Maybe," I said.

"You always have a gun lying around on your desk?"

"Except when it's under my pillow," I said. "Or under my arm. Or in the drawer of the desk. Or somewhere I can't just remember where I happened to put it. That help you any?"

"We didn't come here to get tough, Marlowe."

"That's fine," I said. "So you prowl my apartment and handle my property without asking my permission. What do you do when you get tough—knock me down and kick me in the face?"

"Aw hell," he said and grinned. I grinned back. We all grinned. Then Breeze said: "Use your phone?"

I pointed to it. He dialed a number and talked to someone named Morrison, saying: "Breeze at—" He looked down at the base of the phone and read the number off— "Anytime now. Marlowe is the name that goes with it. Sure. Five or ten minutes is okay." He hung up and went back to the davenport. "I bet you can't guess why we're here."

"I'm always expecting the brothers to drop in," I said.

"Murder ain't funny, Marlowe."

"Who said it was?"

"Don't you kind of act as if it was?"

"I wasn't aware of it."

He looked at Spangler and shrugged. Then he looked at the floor. Then he lifted his eyes slowly, as if they were heavy, and looked at me again. I was sitting down by the chess table now. "You play a lot of chess?" he asked, looking at the chessmen.

"Not a lot. Once in a while I fool around with a game here, thinking things out."

"Don't it take two guys to play chess?"

"I play over tournament games that have been recorded and published. There's a whole literature about chess. Once in a while I work out problems. They're not chess, properly speaking. What are we talking about chess for? Drink?"

"Not right now," Breeze said. "I talked to Randall about you. He remembers you very well, in connection with a case down at the beach." He moved his feet on the carpet, as if they were very tired. His solid old face was lined and gray with fatigue. "He said you wouldn't murder anybody. He says you are a nice guy, on the level."

"That was friendly of him," I said.

"He says you make good coffee and you get up kind of late in the mornings and are apt to run to a very bright line of chatter and that we should believe anything you say, provided we can check it by five independent witnesses."

"To hell with him," I said.

Breeze nodded exactly as though I had said just what he wanted me to say. He wasn't smiling and he wasn't tough, just a big solid man working at his job. Spangler had his head back on the chair and his eyes half closed and was watching the smoke from his cigarette.

"Randall says we should look out for you. He says you are not as smart as you think you are, but that you are a guy things happen to, and a guy like that could be a lot more trouble than a very smart guy. That's what he says, you understand. You look all right to me. I like everything in the clear. That's why I'm telling you."

I said it was nice of him.

The phone rang. I looked at Breeze, but he didn't move, so I reached for it and answered it. It was a girl's voice. I thought it was vaguely familiar, but I couldn't place it.

"Is this Mr. Philip Marlowe?"

"Yes."

"Mr. Marlowe, I'm in trouble, very great trouble. I want to see you very badly. When can I see you?"

I said: "You mean tonight? Who am I talking to?"

"My name is Gladys Crane. I live at the Hotel Normandy on Rampart. When can you—"

"You mean you want me to come over there tonight?" I asked, thinking about the voice, trying to place it.

"I—" The phone clicked and the line was dead. I sat there holding it, frowning at it, looking across it at Breeze. His face was quietly empty of interest.

"Some girl says she's in trouble," I said. "Connection broken." I held the plunger down on the base of the phone waiting for it to ring again. The two cops were completely silent and motionless. Too silent, too motionless.

The bell rang again and I let the plunger up and said: "You want to talk to Breeze, don't you?"

"Yeah." It was a man's voice and it sounded a little surprised.

"Go on, be tricky," I said, and got up from the chair and went out to the kitchen. I heard Breeze talking very briefly then the sound of the phone being returned to the cradle.

I got a bottle of Four Roses out of the kitchen closet and three glasses. I got ice and ginger ale from the icebox and mixed three highballs and carried them in on a tray and sat the tray down on the cocktail table in front of the davenport where Breeze was sitting. I took two of the glasses, handed one to Spangler, and took the other to my chair.

Spangler held the glass uncertainly, pinching his lower

lip between thumb and finger, looking at Breeze to see whether he would accept the drink.

Breeze looked at me very steadily. Then he sighed. Then he picked the glass up and tasted it and sighed again and shook his head sideways with a half smile; the way a man does when you give him a drink and he needs it very badly and it is just right and the first swallow is like a peek into a cleaner, sunnier, brighter world. "I guess you catch on pretty fast, Mr. Marlowe," he said, and leaned back on the davenport completely relaxed. "I guess now we can do some business together."

"Not that way," I said.

"Huh?" He bent his eyebrows together. Spangler leaned forward in his chair and looked bright and attentive.

"Having stray broads call me up and give me a song and dance so you can say they said they recognized my voice somewhere sometime."

"The girl's name is Gladys Crane," Breeze said.

"So she told me. I never heard of her."

"Okay," Breeze said. "Okay." He showed me the flat of his freckled hand. "We're not trying to pull anything that's not legitimate. We only hope you ain't, either."

"Ain't either what?"

"Ain't either trying to pull anything not legitimate. Such as holding out on us."

"Just why shouldn't I hold out on you, if I feel like it?" I asked. "You're not paying my salary."

"Look, don't get tough, Marlowe."

"I'm not tough. I don't have any idea of being tough. I know enough about cops not to get tough with them. Go ahead and speak your piece and don't try to pull any more phonies like that telephone call."

"We're on a murder case," Breeze said. "We have to try to run it the best we can. You found the body. You had talked to the guy. He had asked you to come to his apartment. He gave you his key. You said you didn't know what he wanted to see you about. We figured that maybe with time to think back you could have remembered."

"In other words I was lying the first time," I said.

Breeze smiled a tired smile. "You been around enough to know that people always lie in murder cases."

"The trouble with that is how are you going to know when I stop lying?"

"When what you say begins to make sense, we'll be satisfied."

I looked at Spangler. He was leaning forward so far he was almost out of his chair. He looked as if he was going to jump. I couldn't think of any reason why he should jump, so I thought he must be excited. I looked back at Breeze. He was about as excited as a hole in the wall. He had one of his cellophane-wrapped cigars between his thick fingers and he was slitting the cellophane with a penknife. I watched him get the wrapping off and trim the cigar end with the blade and put the knife away, first wiping the blade carefully on his pants. I watched him strike a wooden match and light the cigar carefully, turning it around in the flame, then hold the match away from the cigar, still burning, and draw on the cigar until he decided it was properly lighted. Then he shook the match out and laid it down beside the crumpled cellophane on the glass top of the cocktail table. Then he leaned back and pulled up one leg of his pants and smoked peacefully. Every motion had been exactly as it had been when he lit a cigar in Hench's apartment, and exactly as it always would be whenever he lit a cigar. He was that kind of man, and that made him dangerous. Not as dangerous as a brilliant man, but much more dangerous than a quick excitable one like Spangler.

"I never saw Phillips before today," I said. "I don't count that he said he saw me up in Ventura once, because I don't remember him. I met him just the way I told you. He tailed me around and I braced him. He wanted to talk to me, he gave me his key, I went to his apartment, used the key to let myself in when he didn't answer—as he had told me to do. He was dead. The police were called and through a set of events or incidents that had nothing to do with me, a gun was found under Hench's pillow. A gun that had been fired. I told you this and it's true."

Breeze said: "When you found him you went down to the apartment manager, guy named Passmore, and got him to go up with you without telling him anybody was dead. You gave Passmore a phony card and talked about jewelry."

I nodded. "With people like Passmore and apartment houses like that one, it pays to be a little on the cagey side. I was interested in Phillips. I thought Passmore might tell me something about him, if he didn't know he was dead, that he wouldn't be likely to tell me, if he knew the cops were going to bounce in on him in a brief space of time. That's all there was to that."

Breeze drank a little of his drink and smoked a little of his cigar and said: "What I'd like to get in the clear is this. Everything you just told us might be strictly the truth, and yet you might not be telling us the truth. If you get what I mean."

"Like what?" I asked, getting perfectly well what he meant.

He tapped on his knee and watched me with a quiet up from under look. Not hostile, not even suspicious. Just a quiet man doing his job. "Like this. You're on a job. We don't know what it is. Phillips was playing at being a private dick. He was on a job. He tailed you around. How can we know, unless you tell us, that his job and your job don't tie in somewhere? And if they do, that's our business. Right?"

"That's one way to look at it," I said. "But it's not the only way, and it's not my way."

"Don't forget this is a murder case, Marlowe."

"I'm not. But don't you forget I've been around this town a long time, more than fifteen years. I've seen a lot of murder cases come and go. Some have been solved, some couldn't be solved, and some could have been solved that were not solved. And one or two or three of them have been solved wrong. Somebody was paid to take a rap, and the chances are it was known or strongly suspected. And winked at. But skip that. It happens, but not often. Consider a case like the Cassidy case. I guess you remember it, don't you?"

Breeze looked at his watch. "I'm tired," he said. "Let's forget the Cassidy case. Let's stick to the Phillips case."

I shook my head. "I'm going to make a point, and it's an important point. Just look at the Cassidy case. Cassidy was a very rich man, a multimillionaire. He had a grown-up son. One night the cops were called to his home and young Cassidy was on his back on the floor with blood all over his face and a bullet hole in the side of his head. His secretary was lying on *his* back in an adjoining bathroom, with his head against the second bathroom door, leading to a hall, and a cigarette burned out between the fingers of his left hand, just a short burned out stub that had scorched the skin between his fingers. A gun was lying by his right hand. He was shot in the head, not a contact wound. A lot of drinking had been done. Four hours had elapsed since the deaths and the family doctor had been there for three of them. Now, what did you do with the Cassidy case?"

Breeze sighed. "Murder and suicide during a drinking spree. The secretary went haywire and shot young Cassidy. I read it in the papers or something. Is that what you want me to say?"

"You read it in the papers," I said, "but it wasn't so. What's more you knew it wasn't so and the D.A. knew it wasn't so and the D.A.'s investigators were pulled off the case within a matter of hours. There was no inquest. But every crime reporter in town and every cop on every homicide detail knew it was Cassidy that did the shooting, that it was Cassidy that was crazy drunk, that it was the secretary who tried to handle him and couldn't and at last tried to get away from him, but wasn't quick enough. Cassidy's was a contact wound and the secretary's was not. The secretary was left-handed and he had a cigarette in his left hand when he was shot. Even if you are right-handed, you don't change a cigarette over to your other hand and shoot a man while casually holding the cigarette. They might do that on *Gang Busters*, but rich men's secretaries don't do it. And what were the family and the family doctor doing during the four hours they didn't call the cops? Fixing it so there would only be a superficial investigation. And why were no tests of the hands made for nitrates? Because you didn't want the truth. Cassidy was too big. But this was a murder case too, wasn't it?"

"The guys were both dead," Breeze said. "What the hell difference did it make who shot who?"

"Did you ever stop to think," I asked, "that Cassidy's secretary might have had a mother or a sister or a sweetheart—or all three? That they had their pride and their faith and their love for a kid who was made out to be a drunken paranoiac because his boss's father had a hundred million dollars?"

Breeze lifted his glass slowly and finished his drink slowly and put it down slowly and turned the glass slowly on the glass top of the cocktail table. Spangler sat rigid, all shining eyes and lips parted in a sort of rigid half smile.

Breeze said: "Make your point."

I said: "Until you guys own your own souls you don't own mine. Until you guys can be trusted every time and always, in all times and conditions, to seek the truth out and find it and let the chips fall where they may—until that time comes, I have a right to listen to my conscience, and protect my client the best way I can. Until I'm sure you won't do him more harm than you'll do the truth good. Or until I'm hauled before somebody that can make me talk."

Breeze said: "You sound to me just a little like a guy who is trying to hold his conscience down."

"Hell," I said. "Let's have another drink. And then you can tell me about that girl you had me talk to on the phone."

He grinned: "That was a dame that lives next door to Phillips. She heard a guy talking to him at the door one evening. She works days as an usherette. So we thought maybe she ought to hear your voice. Think nothing of it."

"What kind of voice was it?"

"Kind of a mean voice. She said she didn't like it."

"I guess that's what made you think of me," I said.

I picked up the three glasses and went out to the kitchen with them.

■ 16 ■

WHEN I GOT OUT THERE I HAD FORGOTTEN WHICH GLASS was which, so I rinsed them all out and dried them and was starting to make more drinks when Spangler strolled out and stood just behind my shoulder.

"It's all right," I said. "I'm not using any cyanide this evening."

"Don't get too foxy with the old guy," he said quietly to the back of my neck. "He knows more angles than you think."

"Nice of you," I said.

"Say, I'd like to read up on that Cassidy case," he said. "Sounds interesting. Must have been before my time."

"It was a long time ago," I said. "And it never happened. I was just kidding." I put the glasses on the tray and carried them back into the living room and set them around. I took mine over to my chair behind the chess table.

"Another phony," I said. "Your sidekick sneaks out to the kitchen and gives me advice behind your back about how careful I ought to keep on account of the angles you know that I don't think you know. He has just the right face for it. Friendly and open and an easy blusher."

Spangler sat down on the edge of his chair and blushed. Breeze looked at him casually, without meaning.

"What did you find out about Phillips?" I asked.

"Yes," Breeze said. "Phillips. Well, George Anson Phillips is a kind of pathetic case. He thought he was a detective, but it looks as if he couldn't get anybody to agree with him. I talked to the sheriff at Ventura. He said George was a nice kind, maybe a little too nice to make a good cop, even if he had any brains. George did what they said and he would do it pretty well, provided they told him which foot to start on and how many steps to take which way and little things like that. But he didn't develop much, if you get what I mean. He was the sort of cop who would be likely to hang a pinch on a chicken thief, if he saw the guy steal the chicken and the guy fell down running away and hit his head on a post or something and knocked himself out. Otherwise it might get a little tough and George would have to go back to the office for instructions. Well, it wore the sheriff down after a while and he let George go."

Breeze drank some more of his drink and scratched his chin with a thumbnail like the blade of a shovel.

"After that George worked in a general store at Simi for a man named Sutcliff. It was a credit business with little books for each customer and George would have trouble with the books. He would forget to write the stuff down or write it in the wrong book and some of the customers would straighten him out and some would let George forget. So Sutcliff thought maybe George would do better at something else, and George came to L.A. He had come into a little money, not much, but enough for him to get a license and put up a bond and get himself a piece of an office. I was over there. What he had was desk room with another guy who claims he is selling Christmas cards. Name of Marsh. If George had a customer, the arrangement was Marsh would go for a walk. Marsh says he didn't know where George lived and George didn't have any customers. That is, no business came into the office that Marsh knows about. But George put an ad in the paper and he might have got a customer out of that. I guess he did, because about a week ago Marsh found a note on his desk that George would be out of town for a few days. That's the last he heard of him. So George went over to Court Street and took an apartment under the name of Anson and got bumped off. And that's all we know about George so far. Kind of a pathetic case." He looked at me with a level uncurious gaze and raised his glass to his lips.

"What about this ad?"

Breeze put the glass down and dug a thin piece of paper out of his wallet and put it down on the cocktail table. I went over and picked it up and read it. It said: *Why worry? Why be doubtful or confused? Why be gnawed by suspicion? Consult cool, careful, confidential, discreet investigator. George Anson Phillips. Glenview 9521.*

I put it down on the table again.

"It ain't any worse than lots of business personals," Breeze said. "It don't seem to be aimed at the carriage trade."

Spangler said: "The girl in the office wrote it for him. She said she could hardly keep from laughing, but George thought it was swell. The Hollywood Boulevard office of the *Chronicle*."

"You checked that fast," I said.

"We don't have any trouble getting information," Breeze said. "Except maybe from you."

"What about Hench?"

"Nothing about Hench. Him and the girl were having a liquor party. They would drink a little and sing a little and scrap a little and listen to the radio and go out to eat once in a while, when they thought of it. I guess it had been going on for days. Just as well we stopped it. The girl has two bad eyes. The next round Hench might have broken her neck. The world is full of bums like Hench—and his girl."

"What about the gun Hench said wasn't his?"

"It's the right gun. We don't have the slug yet, but we have the shell. It was under George's body and it checks. We had a couple more fired and comparisoned the ejector marks and the firing pin dents."

"You believe somebody planted it under Hench's pillow?"

"Sure. Why would Hench shoot Phillips? He didn't know him."

"How do you know that?"

"I know it," Breeze said, spreading his hands. "Look, there are things you know because you have them down in black and white. And there are things you know because they are reasonable and have to be so. You don't shoot somebody and then make a lot of racket calling attention to yourself, and all the time you have the gun under your pillow. The girl was with Hench all day. If Hench shot anybody, she would have some idea. She doesn't have any such idea. She would spill, if she had. What is Hench to her? A guy to play around with, no more. Look, forget Hench. The guy who did the shooting hears the loud radio and knows it will cover a shot. But all the same he saps Phillips and drags him into the bathroom and shuts the door before he shoots him. He's not drunk. He's minding his own business, and careful. He goes out, shuts the bathroom door, the radio stops, Hench and the girl go out to eat. Just happens that way."

"How do you know the radio stopped?"

"I was told," Breeze said calmly. "Other people live in that dump. Take it the radio stopped and they went out. Not quiet. The killer steps out of the apartment and Hench's door is open. That must be because otherwise he wouldn't think anything about Hench's door."

"People don't leave their doors open in apartment houses. Especially in districts like that."

"Drunks do. Drunks are careless. Their minds don't focus well. And they only think of one thing at a time. The door was open—just a little maybe, but open. The killer went in and ditched his gun on the bed and found another gun there. He took that away, just to make it worse for Hench."

"You can check the gun," I said.

"Hench's gun? We'll try to, but Hench says he doesn't know the number. If we find it, we might do something there. I doubt it. The gun we have we will try to check, but you know how those things are. You get just so far along and you think it is going to open up for you, and then the trail dies out cold. A dead end. Anything else you can think of that we might know that might be a help to you in your business?"

"I'm getting tired," I said. "My imagination isn't working very well."

"You were doing fine a while back," Breeze said. "On the Cassidy case."

I didn't say anything. I filled my pipe up again but it was too hot to light. I laid it on the edge of the table to cool off.

"It's God's truth," Breeze said slowly, "that I don't know what to make of you. I can't see you deliberately covering up on any murder. And neither can I see you knowing as little about all this as you pretend to know."

I didn't say anything, again.

Breeze leaned over to revolve his cigar butt in the tray until he had killed the fire. He finished his drink, put on his hat and stood up. "How long you expect to stay dummied up?" he asked.

"I don't know."

"Let me help you out. I give you till tomorrow noon, a little better than twelve hours. I won't get my post mortem report before that anyway. I give you till then to talk things over with your party and decide to come clean."

"And after that?"

"After that I see the Captain of Detectives and tell him a private eye named Philip Marlowe is withholding information which I need in a murder investigation, or I'm pretty sure he is. And what about it? I figure he'll pull you in fast enough to singe your breeches."

I said: "Uh-huh. Did you go through Phillips' desk?"

"Sure. A very neat young feller. Nothing in it at all, except a little kind of diary. Nothing in that either, except about how he went to the beach or took some girl to the pictures and she didn't warm up much. Or how he sat in the office and no business come in. One time he got a little sore about his laundry and wrote a whole page. Mostly it was just three or four lines. There was only one thing about it. It was all done in a kind of printing."

I said: "Printing?"

"Yeah, printing in pen and ink. Not big block caps like people trying to disguise things. Just neat fast little printing as if the guy could write that way as fast and easy as any way."

"He didn't write like that on the card he gave me," I said.

Breeze thought about that for a moment. Then he nodded. "True. Maybe it was this way. There wasn't any name in the diary either, in the front. Maybe the printing was just a little game he played with himself."

"Like Pepys' shorthand," I said.

"What was that?"

"A diary a man wrote in a private shorthand, a long time ago."

Breeze looked at Spangler, who was standing up in front of his chair, tipping the last few drops of his glass. "We better beat it," Breeze said. "This guy is warming up for another Cassidy case."

Spangler put his glass down and they both went over to the door. Breeze shuffled a foot and looked at me sideways, with his hand on the doorknob. "You know any tall blonds?"

"I'd have to think," I said. "I hope so. How tall?"

"Just tall. I don't know how tall that is. Except that it would be tall to a guy who is tall himself. A wop named Palermo owns that apartment house on Court Street. We went across to see him in his funeral parlors. He owns them too. He says he saw a tall blond come out of the apartment house about three-thirty. The manager, Passmore, don't place anybody in the joint that he would call a tall blond. The wop says she was a looker. I give some weight to what he says because he give us a good description of you. He didn't see this tall blond go in, just saw her come out. She was wearing slacks and a sports jacket and a wrap-around. But she had light blond hair and plenty of it under the wrap-around."

"Nothing comes to me," I said. "But I just remembered

something else. I wrote the license number of Phillips' car down on the back of an envelope. That will give you his former address, probably. I'll get it." They stood there while I went to get it out of my coat in the bedroom. I handed the piece of envelope to Breeze and he read what was on it and tucked it into his billfold.

"So you just thought of this, huh?"

"That's right."

"Well, well," he said. "Well, well." The two of them went along the hallway towards the elevator, shaking their heads.

I shut the door and went back to my almost untasted second drink. It was flat. I carried it to the kitchen and hardened it up from the bottle and stood there holding it and looking out of the window at the eucalyptus trees tossing their limber tops against the bluish dark sky. The wind seemed to have risen again. It thumped at the north window and there was a heavy slow pounding noise on the wall of the building, like a thick wire banging the stucco between insulators.

I tasted my drink and wished I hadn't wasted the fresh whiskey on it. I poured it down the sink and got a fresh glass and drank some ice water.

Twelve hours to tie up a situation which I didn't even begin to understand. Either that or turn up a client and let the cops go to work on her and her whole family. Hire Marlowe and get your house full of law. Why worry? Why be doubtful and confused? Why be gnawed by suspicion? Consult cockeyed, careless, clubfooted, dissipated investigator Philip Marlowe, Glenview 7537. See me and you meet the best cops in town. Why despair? Why be lonely? Call Marlowe and watch the wagon come.

This didn't get me anywhere either. I went back to the living room and put a match to the pipe that had cooled off now on the edge of the chess table. I drew the smoke in slowly, but it still tasted like the smell of hot rubber. I put it away and stood in the middle of the floor pulling my lower lip out and letting it snap back against my teeth.

The telephone rang. I picked it up and growled into it.

"Marlowe?" The voice was a harsh low whisper. It was a harsh low whisper I had heard before.

"All right," I said. "Talk it up whoever you are. Whose pocket have I got my hand in now?"

"Maybe you're a smart guy," the harsh whisper said. "Maybe you would like to do yourself some good."

"How much good?"

"Say about five C's worth of good."

"That's grand," I said. "Doing what?"

"Keeping your nose clean," the voice said. "Want to talk about it?"

"Where, when and who to?"

"Idle Valley Club. Morny. Any time you get here."

"Who are you?"

A dim chuckle came over the wire. "Just ask at the gate for Eddie Prue." The phone clicked dead. I hung it up.

It was near eleven-thirty when I backed my car out of the garage and drove towards Cahuenga Pass.

■ 17 ■

ABOUT TWENTY MILES NORTH OF THE PASS A WIDE BOULE-vard with flowering moss in the parkways turned towards the foothills. It ran for five blocks and died—without a house in its entire length. From its end a curving asphalt road dove into the hills. This was Idle Valley.

Around the shoulder of the first hill there was a low white building with a tiled roof beside the road. It had a roofed porch and a floodlighted sign on it read: *Idle Valley Patrol*. Open gates were folded back on the shoulders of the road, in the middle of which a square white sign standing on its point said STOP in letters sprinkled with reflector buttons. Another floodlight blistered the space of road in front of the sign.

I stopped. A uniformed man with a star and a strapped-on gun in a woven leather holster looked at my car, then at a board on a post. He came over to the car. "Good evening. I don't have your car. This is a private road. Visiting?"

"Going to the club."

"Which one?"

"Idle Valley Club."

"Eighty-seven Seventy-seven. That's what we call it here. You mean Mr. Morny's place?"

"Right."

"You're not a member, I guess."

"No."

"I have to check you in. To somebody who is a member or to somebody who lives in the valley. All private property here, you know."

"No gate crashers, huh?"

He smiled. "No gate crashers."

"The name is Philip Marlowe," I said. "Calling on Eddie Prue."

"Prue?"

"He's Mr. Morny's secretary. Or something."

"Just a minute, please."

He went to the door of the building, and spoke. Another uniformed man inside, plugged in on a PBX. A car came up behind me and honked. The clack of a typewriter came from the open door of the patrol office. The man who had spoken to me looked at the honking car and waved it in. It slid around me and scooted off into the dark, a green long open convertible sedan with three dizzy-looking dames in the front seat, all cigarettes and arched eyebrows and go-to-hell expressions. The car flashed around a curve and was gone.

The uniformed man came back to me and put a hand on the car door. "Okay, Mr. Marlowe. Check with the officer at the club, please. A mile ahead on your right. There's a lighted parking lot and the number on the wall. Just the number. Eight-seven Seventy-seven. Check with the officer there, please."

I said: "Why would I do that?"

He was very calm, very polite, and very firm. "We have to know exactly where you go. There's a great deal to protect in Idle Valley."

"Suppose I don't check with him?"

"You kidding me?" His voice hardened.

"No. I just wanted to know."

"A couple of cruisers would start looking for you."

"How many are you in the patrol?"

"Sorry," he said. "About a mile ahead on the right, Mr. Marlowe."

I looked at the gun strapped to his hip, the special badge pinned to his shirt. "And they call this a democracy," I said.

He looked behind him and then spat on the ground and put a hand on the sill of the car door. "Maybe you got company," he said. "I knew a fellow belonged to the John Reed Club. Over in Boyle Heights, it was."

"Tovarich," I said.

"The trouble with revolutions," he said, "is that they get in the hands of the wrong people."

"Check," I said.

"On the other hand," he said, "could they be any wronger than the bunch of rich phonies that live around here?"

"Maybe you'll be living in here yourself someday," I said.

He spat again. "I wouldn't live in here if they paid me fifty thousand a year and let me sleep in chiffon pajamas with a string of matched pearls around my neck."

"I'd hate to make you the offer," I said.

"You make me the offer any time," he said. "Day or night. Just make me the offer and see what it gets you."

"Well, I'll run along now and check with the officer of the club," I said.

"Tell him to go spit up his left pants leg," he said. "Tell him I said so."

"I'll do that," I said.

A car came up behind and honked. I drove off. Half a block of dark limousine blew me off the road with its horn and went past me making a noise like dead leaves falling.

The wind was quiet out here and the valley moonlight was so sharp that the black shadows looked as if they had been cut with an engraving tool.

Around the curve the whole valley spread out before me. A thousand white houses built up and down the hills, ten thousand lighted windows and the stars hanging down over them politely, not getting too close, on account of the patrol.

The wall of the club building that faced the road was white and blank, with no entrance door, no windows on the lower floor. The number was small but bright in violet-colored neon. 8777. Nothing else. To the side, under rows of hooded, downward-shining lights, were even rows of cars, set out in the white lined slots on the smooth black asphalt. Attendants in crisp clean uniforms moved in the lights.

The road went around to the back. A deep concrete porch there, with an overhanging canopy of glass and chromium, but very dim lights. I got out of the car and received a check with the license number on it, carried it over to a small desk where a uniformed man sat and dumped it in front of him.

"Philip Marlowe," I said. "Visitor."

"Thank you, Mr. Marlowe." He wrote the name and number down, handed me back my check and picked up a telephone.

A Negro in a white linen doublebreasted guards uniform, gold epaulettes, a cap with a broad gold band, opened the door for me.

The lobby looked like a high-budget musical. A lot of light and glitter, a lot of scenery, a lot of clothes, a lot of sound, an all-star cast, and a plot with all the originality and drive of a split fingernail. Under the beautiful soft indirect lighting the walls seemed to go up forever and to be lost in soft lascivious stars that really twinkled. You could just manage to walk on the carpet without waders.

At the back was a free-arched stairway with a chromium and white enamel gangway going up in wide shallow carpeted steps. At the entrance to the dining room a chubby captain of waiters stood negligently with a two-inch satin stripe on his pants and a bunch of goldplated menus under his arm. He had the sort of face that can turn from a polite simper to cold-blooded fury almost without moving a muscle.

The bar entrance was to the left. It was dusky and quiet and a bartender moved mothlike against the faint glitter of piled glassware. A tall handsome blond in a dress that looked like seawater sifted over with gold dust came out of the Ladies' Room touching up her lips and turned toward the arch, humming. The sound of rhumba music came through the archway and she nodded her gold head in time to it, smiling. A short fat man with a red face and glittering eyes waited for her with a white wrap over his arm. He dug his thick fingers into her bare arm and leered up at her.

A check girl in peach-bloom Chinese pajamas came over to take my hat and disapprove of my clothes. She had eyes like strange sins. A cigarette girl came down the gangway. She wore an egret plume in her hair, enough clothes to hide behind a toothpick, one of her long beautiful naked legs was silver, and one was gold. She had the utterly disdainful expression of a dame who makes her dates by long distance.

I went into the bar and sank into a leather bar seat packed with down. Glasses tinkled gently, lights glowed softly, there were quiet voices whispering of love, or ten per cent, or whatever they whisper about in a place like that.

A tall fine-looking man in a gray suit cut by an angel suddenly stood up from a small table by the wall and walked over to the bar and started to curse one of the barmen. He cursed him in a loud clear voice for a long minute, calling him about nine names that are not usually mentioned by tall fine-looking men in well cut gray suits. Everybody stopped talking and looked at him quietly. His voice cut through the muted rhumba music like a shovel through snow.

The barman stood perfectly still, looking at the man. The barman had curly hair and a clear warm skin and wide-set careful eyes. He didn't move or speak. The tall man stopped talking and stalked out of the bar. Everybody watched him out except the barman. The barman moved slowly along the bar to the end where I sat and stood looking away from me, with nothing in his face but pallor. Then he turned to me and said: "Yes, sir?"

"I want to talk to a fellow named Eddie Prue."

"So?"

"He works here," I said.

"Works here doing what?" His voice was perfectly level and as dry as dry sand.

"I understand he's the guy that walks behind the boss. If you know what I mean."

"Oh. Eddie Prue." He moved one lip slowly over the other and made small tight circles on the bar with his bar cloth.

"Your name?"

"Marlowe."

"Marlowe. Drink while waiting?"

"A dry martini will do."

"A martini. Dry. Veddy, veddy dry."

"Okay."

"Will you eat it with a spoon or a knife and fork?"

"Cut it in strips," I said. "I'll just nibble it."

"On your way to school," he said. "Should I put the olive in a bag for you?"

"Sock me on the nose with it," I said. "If it will make you feel any better."

"Thank you, sir," he said. "A dry martini."

He took three steps away from me, and then came back and leaned across the bar and said: "I made a mistake in a drink. The gentleman was telling me about it."

"I heard him."

"He was telling me about it as gentlemen tell you

about things like that. As big shot directors like to point out to you your little errors. And you heard him."

"Yeah," I said, wondering how long this was going to go on.

"He made himself heard—the gentleman did. So I come over here and practically insult you."

"I got the idea," I said.

He held up one of his fingers and looked at it thoughtfully. "Just like that," he said. "A perfect stranger."

"It's my big brown eyes," I said. "They have that gentle look."

"Thanks, chum," he said, and quietly went away.

I saw him talking into a phone at the end of the bar. Then I saw him working with a shaker. When he came back with the drink he was all right again.

■ 18 ■

I CARRIED THE DRINK OVER TO A SMALL TABLE AGAINST the wall and sat down there and lit a cigarette. Five minutes went by. The music that was coming through the fret had changed in tempo without my noticing it. A girl was singing. She had a rich deep down around the ankles contralto that was pleasant to listen to. She was singing Dark Eyes and the band behind her seemed to be falling asleep. There was a heavy round of applause and some whistling when she ended.

A man at the next table said to his girl: "They got Linda Conquest back with the band. I heard she got married to some rich guy in Pasadena, but it didn't take."

The girl said: "Nice voice. If you like female crooners."

I started to get up but a shadow fell across my table and a man was standing there. A great long gallows of a man with a ravaged face and a haggard frozen right eye that had a clotted iris and the steady look of blindness. He was so tall that he had to stoop to put his hand on the back of the chair across the table from me. He stood there sizing me up without saying anything and I sat there sipping the last of my drink and listening to the contralto voice singing another song. The customers seemed to like corny music in there. Perhaps they were all tired out trying to be ahead of the minute in the place where they worked.

"I'm Prue," the man said in his harsh whisper.

"So I gathered. You want to talk to me, I want to talk to you, and I want to talk to the girl that just sang."

"Let's go."

There was a locked door at the back end of the bar. Prue unlocked it and held it for me and we went through that and up a flight of carpeted steps to the left. A long straight hallway with several closed doors. At the end of it a bright star cross-wired by the mesh of a screen. Prue knocked on a door near the screen and opened it and stood aside for me to pass him. It was a cozy sort of office, not too large. There was a built-in upholstered corner seat by the French windows and a man in a white dinner jacket was standing with his back to the room, looking out. He had gray hair. There was a large black and chromium safe, some filing cases, a large globe in a stand, a small built-in bar, and the usual broad heavy executive desk with the usual high-backed padded leather chair behind it.

I looked at the ornaments on the desk. Everything standard and all copper. A copper lamp, pen set and pencil tray, a glass and copper ashtray with a copper elephant on the rim, a copper letter opener, a copper thermos bottle on a copper tray, copper corners on the blotter holder. There was a spray of almost copper-colored sweet peas in a copper vase.

It seemed like a lot of copper.

The man at the window turned around and showed me that he was going on fifty and had soft ash gray hair and plenty of it, and a heavy handsome face with nothing unusual about it except a short puckered scar in his left cheek that had almost the effect of a deep dimple. I remembered the dimple. I would have forgotten the man. I remembered that I had seen him in pictures a long time ago, at least ten years ago. I didn't remember the pictures or what they were about or what he did in them, but I remembered the dark heavy handsome face and the puckered scar. His hair had been dark then.

He walked over to his desk and sat down and picked up his letter opener and poked at the ball of his thumb with the point. He looked at me with no expression and said: "You're Marlowe?"

I nodded.

"Sit down." I sat down. Eddie Prue sat in a chair against the wall and tilted the front legs off the floor.

"I don't like peepers," Morny said.

I shrugged.

"I don't like them for a lot of reasons," he said. "I don't like them in any way or at any time. I don't like them when they bother my friends. I don't like them when they bust in on my wife."

I didn't say anything.

"I don't like them when they question my driver or when they get tough with my guests," he said.

I didn't say anything.

"In short," he said. "I just don't like them."

"I'm beginning to get what you mean," I said.

He flushed and his eyes glittered. "On the other hand," he said, "just at the moment I might have a use for you. It might pay you to play ball with me. It might be a good idea. It might pay you to keep your nose clean."

"How much might it pay me?" I asked.

"It might pay you in time and health."

"I seem to have heard this record somewhere," I said. "I just can't put a name to it."

He laid the letter opener down and swung open a door in the desk and got a cut glass decanter out. He poured liquid out of it in a glass and drank it and put the stopper back in the decanter and put the decanter back in the desk. "In my business," he said, "tough boys come a dime a dozen. And would-be tough boys come a nickel a gross. Just mind your business and I'll mind my business and we won't have any trouble." He lit a cigarette. His hand shook a little.

I looked across the room at the tall man sitting tilted against the wall, like a loafer in a country store. He just sat there without motion, his long arms hanging, his lined gray face full of nothing.

"Somebody said something about some money," I said to Morny. "What's that for? I know what the bawling out is for. That's you trying to make yourself think you can scare me."

"Talk like that to me," Morny said, "and you are liable to be wearing lead buttons on your vest."

"Just think," I said. "Poor old Marlowe with lead buttons on his vest."

Eddie Prue made a dry sound in his throat that might have been a chuckle.

"And as for me minding my own business and not minding yours," I said, "it might be that my business and your business would get a little mixed up together. Through no fault of mine."

"It better not," Morny said. "In what way?" He lifted his eyes quickly and dropped them again.

"Well, for instance, your hard boy here calling me up on the phone and trying to scare me to death. And later in the evening calling me up and talking about five C's and how it would do me some good to drive out here and talk to you. And for instance that same hard boy or somebody who looks just like him—which is a little un-likely—following around after a fellow in my business who happened to get shot this afternoon, on Court Street on Bunker Hill."

Morny lifted his cigarette away from his lips and narrowed his eyes to look at the tip. Every motion, every gesture, right out of the catalogue. "Who got shot?"

"A fellow named Phillips, a youngish blond kid. You wouldn't like him. He was a peeper." I described Phillips to him.

"I never heard of him," Morny said.

"And also for instance, a tall blond who didn't live

there was seen coming out of the apartment house just after he was killed," I said.

"What tall blond?" His voice had changed a little. There was urgency in it.

"I don't know that. She was seen and the man who saw her could identify her, if he saw her again. Of course she need not have anything to do with Phillips."

"This man Phillips was a shamus?"

I nodded. "I told you that twice."

"Why was he killed and how?"

"He was sapped and shot in his apartment. We don't know why he was killed. If we knew that, we would likely know who killed him. It seems to be that kind of a situation."

"Who is 'we'?"

"The police and myself. I found him dead. So I had to stick around."

Prue let the front legs of his chair down on the carpet very quietly and looked at me. His good eye had a sleepy expression I didn't like.

Morny said: "You told the cops what?"

I said: "Very little. I gather from your opening remarks to me here that you know I am looking for Linda Conquest. Mrs. Leslie Murdock. I've found her. She's singing here. I don't know why there should have been any secret about it. It seems to me that your wife or Mr. Vannier might have told me. But they didn't."

"What my wife would tell a peeper," Morny said, "you could put in a gnat's eye."

"No doubt she has her reasons," I said. "However that's not very important now. In fact it's not very important that I see Miss Conquest. Just the same I'd like to talk to her a little. If you don't mind."

"Suppose I mind," Morny said.

"I guess I would like to talk to her anyway," I said. I got a cigarette out of my pocket and rolled it around in my fingers and admired his thick and still-dark eyebrows. They had a fine shape, an elegant curve.

Prue chuckled. Morny looked at him and frowned and

looked back at me, keeping the frown on his face. "I asked you what you told the cops," he said.

"I told them as little as I could. This man Phillips asked me to come and see him. He implied he was too deep in a job he didn't like and needed help. When I got there he was dead. I told the police that. They didn't think it was quite the whole story. It probably isn't. I have until tomorrow noon to fill it out. So I'm trying to fill it out."

"You wasted your time coming here," Morny said.

"I got the idea that I was asked to come here."

"You can go to hell back any time you want to," Morny said. "Or you can do a little job for me—for five hundred dollars. Either way you leave Eddie and me out of any conversations you might have with the police."

"What's the nature of the job?"

"You were at my house this morning. You ought to have an idea."

"I don't do divorce business," I said.

His face turned white. "I love my wife," he said. "We've only been married eight months. I don't want any divorce. She's a swell girl and she knows what time it is, as a rule. But I think she's playing with a wrong number at the moment."

"Wrong in what way?"

"I don't know. That's what I want found out."

"Let me get this straight," I said. "Are you hiring me on a job—or off a job I already have."

Prue chuckled again against the wall. Morny poured himself some more brandy and tossed it quickly down his throat. Color came back into his face. He didn't answer me.

"And let me get another thing straight," I said. "You don't mind your wife playing around, but you don't want her playing with somebody named Vannier. Is that it?"

"I trust her heart," he said slowly. "But I don't trust her judgment. Put it that way."

"And you want me to get something on this man Vannier?"

"I want to find out what he is up to."

"Oh. Is he up to something?"

"I think he is. I don't know what."

"You think he is—or you want to think he is?"

He stared at me levelly for a moment, then he pulled the middle drawer of his desk out, reached in and tossed a folded paper across to me. I picked it up and unfolded it. It was a carbon copy of a gray billhead. *Cal-Western Dental Supply Company*, and an address. The bill was for *30 lbs. Kerr's Crystobolite, $15.75*, and *25 lbs. White's Albastone, $7.75*, plus tax. It was made out to *H. R. Teager, Will Call*, and stamped *Paid* with a rubber stamp. It was signed for in the corner: *L. G. Vannier.* I put it down on the desk.

"That fell out of his pocket one night when he was here," Morny said. "About ten days ago. Eddie put one of his big feet on it and Vannier didn't notice he had dropped it."

I looked at Prue, then at Morny, then at my thumb. "Is this supposed to mean something to me?"

"I thought you were a smart detective. I figured you could find out."

I looked at the paper again, folded it and put it in my pocket. "I'm assuming you wouldn't give it to me unless it meant something," I said.

Morny went to the black and chromium safe against the wall and opened it. He came back with five new bills spread out in his fingers like a poker hand. He smoothed them edge to edge, riffled them lightly, and tossed them on the desk in front of me. "There's your five C's," he said. "Take Vannier out of my wife's life and there will be the same again for you. I don't care how you do it and I don't want to know anything about how you do it. Just do it."

I poked at the crisp new bills with a hungry finger. Then I pushed them away. "You can pay me when—and if—I deliver," I said. "I'll take my payment tonight in a short interview with Miss Conquest."

Morny didn't touch the money. He lifted the square bottle and poured himself another drink. This time he poured one for me and pushed it across the desk.

"And as for this Phillips murder," I said, "Eddie here was following Phillips a little. You want to tell me why?"

"No."

"The trouble with a case like this is that the information might come from somebody else. When a murder gets into the papers you never know what will come out. If it does, you'll blame me."

He looked at me steadily and said: "I don't think so. I was a bit rough when you came in, but you shape up pretty good. I'll take a chance."

"Thanks," I said. "Would you mind telling me why you had Eddie call me up and give me the shakes?"

He looked down and tapped on the desk. "Linda's an old friend of mine. Young Murdock was out here this afternoon to see her. He told her you were working for old lady Murdock. She told me. I didn't know what the job was. You say you don't take divorce business, so it couldn't be that the old lady hired you to fix anything like that up." He raised his eyes on the last words and stared at me.

I stared back at him and waited.

"I guess I'm just a fellow who likes his friends," he said. "And doesn't want them bothered by dicks."

"Murdock owes you some money, doesn't he?"

He frowned. "I don't discuss things like that." He finished his drink, nodded and stood up. "I'll send Linda up to talk to you. Pick your money up."

He went to the door and out. Eddie Prue unwound his long body and stood up and gave me a dim gray smile that meant nothing and wandered off after Morny.

I lit another cigarette and looked at the dental supply company's bill again. Something squirmed at the back of my mind, dimly. I walked to the window and stood looking out across the valley. A car was winding up a hill towards a big house with a tower that was half glass brick with light behind it. The headlights of the car moved across it and turned in toward a garage. The lights went out and the valley seemed darker. It was very quiet and quite cool now. The dance band seemed to be somewhere under my feet. It was muffled, and the tune was indistinguishable.

Linda Conquest came in through the open door behind me and shut it and stood looking at me with a cold light in her eyes.

■ 19 ■

SHE LOOKED LIKE HER PHOTO AND NOT LIKE IT. SHE HAD the wide cool mouth, the short nose, the wide cool eyes, the dark hair parted in the middle and the broad white line between the parting. She was wearing a white coat over her dress, with the collar turned up. She had her hands in the pockets of the coat and a cigarette in her mouth. She looked older, her eyes were harder, and her lips seemed to have forgotten to smile. They would smile when she was singing, in that staged artificial smile. But in repose they were thin and tight and angry.

She moved over to the desk and stood looking down, as if counting the copper ornaments. She saw the cut glass decanter, took the stopper out, poured herself a drink and tossed it down with a quick flip of the wrist. "You're a man named Marlowe?" she asked, looking at me. She put her hips against the end of the desk and crossed her ankles.

I said I was a man named Marlowe.

"By and large," she said, "I am quite sure I am not going to like you one damned little bit. So speak your piece and drift away."

"What I like about this place is everything runs so true to type," I said. "The cop on the gate, the shine on the door, the cigarette and check girls, the fat greasy sensual man with the tall stately bored showgirl, the well-dressed, drunk and horribly rude director cursing the barman, the silent guy with the gun, the night club owner with the soft gray hair and the B-picture mannerisms, and now you—the tall dark torcher with the negligent sneer, the husky voice, the hard-boiled vocabulary."

She said: "Is that so?" and fitted her cigarette between her lips and drew slowly on it. "And what about the wise-cracking snooper with the last year's gags and the come-hither smile?"

"And what gives me the right to talk to you at all?" I said.

"I'll bite. What does?"

"She wants it back. Quickly. It has to be fast or there will be trouble."

"I thought—" she started to say and stopped cold. I watched her remove the sudden trace of interest from her face by monkeying with her cigarette and bending her face over it. "She wants what back, Mr. Marlowe?"

"The Brasher Doubloon."

She looked up at me and nodded, remembering—letting me see her remembering. "Oh, the Brasher Doubloon."

"I bet you completely forgot it," I said.

"Well, no. I've seen it a number of times," she said. "She wants it back, you said. Do you mean she thinks I took it?"

"Yeah. Just that."

"She's a dirty old liar," Linda Conquest said.

"What you think doesn't make you a liar," I said. "It only sometimes makes you mistaken. Is she wrong?"

"Why would I take her silly old coin?"

"Well—it's worth a lot of money. She thinks you might need money. I gather she was not too generous."

She laughed, a tight sneering little laugh. "No," she said. "Mrs. Elizabeth Bright Murdock would not rate as very generous."

"Maybe you just took it for spite, kind of," I said hopefully.

"Maybe I ought to slap your face." She killed her cigarette in Morny's copper goldfish bowl, speared the crushed stub absently with the letter opener and dropped it into the wastebasket.

"Passing on from that to perhaps more important matters," I said, "will you give him a divorce?"

"For twenty-five grand," she said, not looking at me, "I should be glad to."

"You're not in love with the guy, huh?"

"You're breaking my heart, Marlowe."

"He's in love with you," I said. "After all you did marry him."

She looked at me lazily. "Mister, don't think I didn't pay for that mistake." She lit another cigarette. "But a girl has to live. And it isn't always as easy as it looks. And so a girl can make a mistake, marry the wrong guy and the wrong family, looking for something that isn't there. Security, or whatever."

"But not needing any love to do it," I said.

"I don't want to be too cynical, Marlowe. But you'd be surprised how many girls marry to find a home, especially girls whose arm muscles are all tired out fighting off the kind of optimists that come into these gin and glitter joints."

"You had a home and you gave it up."

"It got to be too dear. That port-sodden old fake made the bargain too rough. How do you like her for a client?"

"I've had worse."

She picked a shred of tobacco off her lip. "You notice what she's doing to that girl?"

"Merle? I noticed she bullied her."

"It isn't just that. She has her cutting out dolls. The girl had a shock of some kind and the old brute has used the effect of it to dominate the girl completely. In company she yells at her but in private she's apt to be stroking her hair and whispering in her ear. And the kid sort of shivers."

"I didn't quite get all that," I said.

"The kid's in love with Leslie, but she doesn't know it. Emotionally, she's about ten years old. Something funny is going to happen in that family one of these days. I'm glad I won't be there."

I said: "You're a smart girl, Linda. And you're tough and you're wise. I suppose when you married him you thought you could get your hands on plenty."

She curled her lip. "I thought it would at least be a vacation. It wasn't even that. That's a smart ruthless woman, Marlowe. Whatever she's got you doing, it's not what she says. She's up to something. Watch your step."

"Would she kill a couple of men?"

She laughed.

"No kidding," I said. "A couple of men have been killed and one of them at least is connected with rare coins."

"I don't get it," she looked at me levelly. "Murdered, you mean?"

I nodded.

"You tell Morny all that?"

"About one of them."

"You tell the cops?"

"About one of them. The same one."

She moved her eyes over my face. We stared at each other. She looked a little pale, or just tired. I thought she had grown a little paler than before. "You're making that up," she said between her teeth.

I grinned and nodded. She seemed to relax then.

"About the Brasher Doubloon?" I said. "You didn't take it. Okay. About the divorce, what?"

"That's none of your affair."

"I agree. Well, thanks for talking to me. Do you know a fellow named Vannier?"

"Yes." Her face froze hard now. "Not well. He's a friend of Lois."

"A very good friend."

"One of these days he's apt to turn out to be a small quiet funeral too."

"Hints," I said, "have sort of been thrown in that direction. There's something about the guy. Every time his name comes up the party freezes."

She stared at me and said nothing. I thought that an idea was stirring at the back of her eyes, but if so it didn't come out. She said quietly: "Morny will sure as hell kill him, if he doesn't lay off Lois."

"Go on with you. Lois flops at the drop of a hat. Anybody can see that."

"Perhaps Alex is the one person who can't see it."

"Vannier hasn't anything to do with my job anyway. He has no connection with the Murdocks."

She lifted a corner of her lip at me and said: "No? Let me tell you something. No reason why I should. I'm just a great big open-hearted kid. Vannier knows Elizabeth Bright Murdock and well. He never came to the house but once while I was there, but he called on the phone plenty of times. I caught some of the calls. He always asked for Merle."

"Well—that's funny," I said. "Merle, huh?"

She bent to crush out her cigarette and again she speared the stub and dropped it into the wastebasket. "I'm very tired," she said suddenly. "Please go away."

I stood there for a moment, looking at her and wondering. Then I said: "Good night and thanks. Good luck." I went out and left her standing there with her hands in the pockets of the white coat, her head bent and her eyes looking at the floor.

It was two o'clock when I got back to Hollywood and put the car away and went upstairs to my apartment. The wind was all gone but the air still had that dryness and lightness of the desert. The air in the apartment was dead and Breeze's cigar butt had made it a little worse than dead. I opened windows and flushed the place through while I undressed and stripped the pockets of my suit. Out of them with other things came the dental supply company's bill. It still looked like a bill to one H. R. Teager for 30 lbs. of crystobolite and 25 lbs. of albastone.

I dragged the phone book up on the desk in the living room and looked up Teager. Then the confused memory clicked into place. His address was 422 West Ninth Street. The address of the Belfont Building was 422 West Ninth Street. H. R. Teager Dental Laboratories had been one of the names on doors on the sixth floor of the Belfont Building when I did my backstairs crawl away from the office of Elisha Morningstar.

But even the Pinkertons have to sleep, and Marlowe needed far, far more sleep than the Pinkertons. I went to bed.

■ **20** ■

IT WAS JUST AS HOT IN PASADENA AS THE DAY BEFORE AND the big dark red brick house on Dresden Avenue looked just as cool and the little painted Negro waiting by the hitching block looked just as sad. The same butterfly landed on the same hydrangea bush—or it looked like the same one—the same heavy scent of summer lay on the morning, and the same middle-aged sourpuss with the frontier voice opened to my ring.

She led me along the same hallways to the same sunless sunroom. In it Mrs. Elizabeth Bright Murdock sat in the same reed chaise longue and as I came into the room she was pouring herself a slug from what looked like the same port bottle but was more probably a grandchild.

The maid shut the door, I sat down and put my hat on the floor, just like yesterday, and Mrs. Murdock gave me the same hard level stare and said: "Well?"

"Things are bad," I said. "The cops are after me."

She looked as flustered as a side of beef. "Indeed. I thought you were more competent than that."

I brushed it off. "When I left here yesterday morning a man followed me in a coupé. I don't know what he was doing here or how he got here. I suppose he followed me here, but I feel doubtful about that. I shook him off, but he turned up again in the hall outside my office. He followed me again, so I invited him to explain why and he said he knew who I was and he needed help and asked me to come to his apartment on Bunker Hill and talk to him. I went, after I had seen Mr. Morningstar, and found the man shot to death on the floor of his bathroom."

Mrs. Murdock sipped a little port. Her hand might have shaken a little, but the light in the room was too dim for me to be sure. She cleared her throat. "Go on."

"His name is George Anson Phillips. A young, blond fellow, rather dumb. He claimed to be a private detective."

"I never heard of him," Mrs. Murdock said coldly. "I never saw him to my knowledge and don't know anything about him. Did you think I employed him to follow you?"

"I didn't know what to think. He talked about pooling our resources and he gave me the impression that he was working for some member of your family. He didn't say so in so many words."

"He wasn't. You can be quite definite on that." The baritone voice was as steady as a rock.

"I don't think you know quite as much about your family as you think you do, Mrs. Murdock."

"I know you have been questioning my son—contrary to my orders," she said coldly.

"I didn't question him. He questioned me. Or tried to."

"We'll go into that later," she said harshly. "What about this man you found shot? You are involved with the police on account of him?"

"Naturally. They want to know why he followed me, what I was working on, why he spoke to me, why he asked me to come to his apartment and why I went. But that is only the half of it."

She finished her port and poured herself another glass. "How's your asthma?" I asked.

"Bad," she said. "Get on with your story."

"I saw Morningstar. I told you about that over the phone. He pretended not to have the Brasher Doubloon, but admitted it had been offered to him and said he could get it. As I told you. Then you told me it had been returned to you, so that was that." I waited, thinking she would tell me some story about how the coin had been returned, but she just stared at me bleakly over the wine glass. "So, as I had made a sort of arrangement with Mr. Morningstar to pay him a thousand dollars for the coin—"

"You had no authority to do anything like that," she barked.

I nodded, agreeing with her. "Maybe I was kidding him a little," I said. "And I know I was kidding myself. Anyway after what you told me over the phone I tried to get in touch with him to tell him the deal was off. He's not in the phone book except at his office. I went to his office. This was quite late. The elevator man said he was still in his office. He was lying on his back on the floor, dead. Killed by a blow on the head and shock, apparently. Old men die easily. The blow might not have been intended to kill him. I called the Receiving Hospital, but didn't give my name."

"That was wise of you," she said.

"Was it? It was considerate of me, but I don't think I'd call it wise. I want to be nice, Mrs. Murdock. You understand that in your rough way, I hope. But two murders happened in a matter of hours and both the bodies were found by me. And both the victims were connected—in some manner—with your Brasher Doubloon."

"I don't understand. This other, younger man also?"

"Yes. Didn't I tell you over the phone? I thought I did." I wrinkled my brow, thinking back. I knew I had.

She said calmly: "It's possible. I wasn't paying a great deal of attention to what you said. You see, the doubloon had already been returned. And you sounded a little drunk."

"I wasn't drunk. I might have felt a little shock, but I wasn't drunk. You take all this very calmly."

"What do you want me to do?"

I took a deep breath. "I'm connected with one murder already, by having found the body and reported it. I may presently be connected with another, by having found the body and not reported it. Which is much more serious for me. Even as far as it goes, I have until noon today to disclose the name of my client."

"That," she said, still much too calm for my taste, "would be a breach of confidence. You are not going to do that, I'm sure."

"I wish you'd leave that damn port alone and make some effort to understand the position," I snapped at her.

She looked vaguely surprised and pushed her glass away—about four inches away.

"This fellow Phillips," I said, "had a license as a private detective. How did I happen to find him dead? Because he followed me and I spoke to him and he asked me to come to his apartment. And when I got there he was dead. The police know all this. They may even believe it. But they don't believe the connection between Phillips and me is quite that much of a coincidence. They think there is a deeper connection between Phillips and me and they insist on knowing what I am doing, who I am working for. Is that clear?"

"You'll find a way out of all that," she said. "I expect it to cost me a little more money, of course."

I felt myself getting pinched around the nose. My mouth felt dry. I needed air. I took another deep breath and another dive into the tub of blubber that was sitting across the room from me on the reed chaise longue, looking as unperturbed as a bank president refusing a loan.

"I'm working for you," I said, "now, this week, today. Next week I'll be working for somebody else, I hope. And the week after that for still somebody else. In order to do that I have to be on reasonably good terms with the police. They don't have to love me, but they have to be fairly sure I am not cheating on them. Assume Phillips knew nothing about the Brasher Doubloon. Assume, even, that he knew about it, but that his death had nothing to do with it. I still have to tell the cops what I know about him. And they have to question anybody they want to question. Can't you understand that?"

"Doesn't the law give you the right to protect a

client?" she snapped. "If it doesn't, what is the use of anyone's hiring a detective?"

I got up and walked around my chair and sat down again. I leaned forward and took hold of my kneecaps and squeezed them until my knuckles glistened.

"The law, whatever it is, is a matter of give and take, Mrs. Murdock. Like most other things. Even if I had the legal right to stay clammed up—refuse to talk—and got away with it once, that would be the end of my business. I'd be a guy marked for trouble. One way or another they would get me. I value your business, Mrs. Murdock, but not enough to cut my throat for you and bleed in your lap."

She reached for her glass and emptied it. "You seem to have made a nice mess of the whole thing," she said. "You didn't find my daughter-in-law and you didn't find my Brasher Doubloon. But you found a couple of dead men that I have nothing to do with and you have neatly arranged matters so that I must tell the police all my private and personal business in order to protect you from your own incompetence. That's what I see. If I am wrong, pray correct me."

She poured some more wine and gulped it too fast and went into a paroxysm of coughing. Her shaking hand slid the glass on to the table, slopping the wine. She threw herself forward in her seat and got purple in the face. I jumped up and went over and landed one on her beefy back that would have shaken the City Hall. She let out a long strangled wail and drew her breath in rackingly and stopped coughing. I pressed one of the keys on her dictaphone box and when somebody answered, metallic and loud, through the metal disk I said: "Bring Mrs. Murdock a glass of water, quick!" and then let the key up again.

I sat down again and watched her pull herself together. When her breath was coming evenly and without effort, I said: "You're not tough. You just think you're tough. You've been living too long with people that are scared of you. Wait'll you meet up with some law. Those boys are professionals. You're just a spoiled amateur."

The door opened and the maid came in with a pitcher of ice water and a glass. She put them down on the table and went out.

I poured Mrs. Murdock a glass of water and put it in her hand. "Sip it, don't drink it. You won't like the taste of it, but it won't hurt you."

She sipped, then drank half of the glass, then put the glass down and wiped her lips. "To think," she said raspingly, "that out of all the snoopers for hire I could have employed, I had to pick out a man who would bully me in my own home."

"That's not getting you anywhere either," I said. "We don't have a lot of time. What's our story to the police going to be?"

"The police mean nothing to me. Absolutely nothing. And if you give them my name, I shall regard it as a thoroughly disgusting breach of faith."

That put me back where we started. "Murder changes everything, Mrs. Murdock. You can't dummy up on a murder case. We'll have to tell them why you employed me and what to do. They won't publish it in the papers, you know. That is, they won't if they believe it. They certainly won't believe you hired me to investigate Elisha Morningstar just because he called up and wanted to buy the doubloon. They may not find out that you couldn't have sold the coin, if you wanted to, because they might not think of that angle. But they won't believe you hired a private detective just to investigate a possible purchaser. Why should you?"

"That's my business, isn't it?"

"No. You can't fob the cops off that way. You have to satisfy them that you are being frank and open and have nothing to hide. As long as they think you are hiding something they never let up. Give them a reasonable and plausible story and they go away cheerful. And the most reasonable and plausible story is always the truth. Any objection to telling it?"

"Every possible objection," she said. "But it doesn't seem to make much difference. Do we have to tell them that I suspected my daughter-in-law of stealing the coin and that I was wrong?"

"It would be better."

"And that it has been returned and how?"

"It would be better."

"That is going to humiliate me very much."

I shrugged.

"You're a callous brute," she said. "You're a cold-blooded fish. I don't like you. I deeply regret ever having met you."

"Mutual," I said.

She reached a thick finger to a key and barked into the talking box. "Merle. Ask my son to come in here at once. And I think you may as well come in with him." She released the key, pressed her broad fingers together and let her hands drop heavily to her thighs. Her bleak eyes went up to the ceiling. Her voice was quiet and sad, saying: "My son took the coin, Mr. Marlowe. My son. My own son."

I didn't say anything. We sat there glaring at each other. In a couple of minutes they both came in and she barked at them to sit down.

▪ 21 ▪

LESLIE MURDOCK WAS WEARING A GREENISH SLACK SUIT and his hair looked damp, as if he had just been taking a shower. He sat hunched forward, looking at the white buck shoes on his feet, and turning a ring on his finger. He didn't have his long black cigarette holder and he looked a little lonely without it. Even his mustache seemed to droop a little more than it had in my office.

Merle Davis looked just the same as the day before. Probably she always looked the same. Her copper blond hair was dragged down just as tight, her shell-rimmed glasses looked just as large and empty, her eyes behind them just as vague. She was even wearing the same one-piece linen dress with short sleeves and no ornament of any kind, not even earrings.

I had the curious feeling of reliving something that had already happened.

Mrs. Murdock sipped her port and said quietly: "All right, son. Tell Mr. Marlowe about the doubloon. I'm afraid he has to be told."

Murdock looked up at me quickly and then dropped his eyes again. His mouth twitched. When he spoke his voice had the toneless quality, a flat tired sound, like a man making a confession after an exhausting battle with his conscience. "As I told you yesterday in your office I owe Morny a lot of money. Twelve thousand dollars. I denied it afterwards, but it's true. I do owe it. I didn't want Mother to know. He was pressing me pretty hard for payment. I suppose I knew I would have to tell her in the end, but I was weak enough to want to put it off. I took the doubloon, using her keys one afternoon when she was asleep and Merle was out. I gave it to Morny and he agreed to hold it as security because I explained to him that he couldn't get anything like twelve thousand dollars for it unless he could give its history and show that it was legitimately in his possession."

He stopped talking and looked up at me to see how I was taking it. Mrs. Murdock had her eyes on my face, practically puttied there. The little girl was looking at Murdock with her lips parted and an expression of suffering on her face.

Murdock went on. "Morny gave me a receipt, in which he agreed to hold the coin as collateral and not to convert it without notice and demand. Something like that. I don't profess to know how legal it was. When this man Morningstar called up and asked about the coin I immediately became suspicious that Morny either was trying to sell it or that he was at least thinking of selling it and was trying to get a valuation on it from somebody who knew about rare coins. I was badly scared."

He looked up and made a sort of face at me. Maybe it was the face of somebody being badly scared. Then he took his handkerchief out and wiped his forehead and sat holding it between his hands.

"When Merle told me Mother had employed a detective—Merle ought not to have told me, but Mother has promised not to scold her for it—" He looked at his mother. The old warhorse clamped her jaws and looked grim. The little girl had her eyes still on his face and didn't seem to be very worried about the scolding. He went on: "—then I was sure she had missed the doubloon and had hired you on that account. I didn't really believe she had hired you to find Linda. I knew where Linda was all the time. I went to your office to see what I could find out. I didn't find out very much. I went to see Morny yesterday afternoon and told him about it. At first he laughed in my face, but when I told him that even my mother couldn't sell the coin without violating the terms of Jasper Murdock's will and that she would certainly set the police on him when I told her where the coin was, then he loosened up. He got up and went to the safe and got the coin out and handed it to me without a word. I gave him back his receipt and he tore it up. So I brought the coin home and told Mother about it."

He stopped talking and wiped his face again. The little girl's eyes moved up and down with the motions of his hand.

In the silence that followed I said: "Did Morny threaten you?"

He shook his head. "He said he wanted his money and he needed it and I had better get busy and dig it up. But he wasn't threatening. He was very decent, really. In the circumstances."

"Where was this?"

"At the Idle Valley Club, in his private office."

"Was Eddie Prue there?"

The little girl tore her eyes away from his face and looked at me. Mrs. Murdock said thickly: "Who is Eddie Prue?"

"Morny's bodyguard," I said. "I didn't waste *all* my

time yesterday, Mrs. Murdock." I looked at her son, waiting.

He said: "No, I didn't see him. I know him by sight, of course. You would only have to see him once to remember him. But he wasn't around yesterday."

I said: "Is that all?"

He looked at his mother. She said harshly: "Isn't it enough?"

"Maybe," I said. "Where is the coin now?"

"Where would you expect it to be?" she snapped.

I almost told her, just to see her jump. But I managed to hold it in. I said: "That seems to take care of that, then."

Mrs. Murdock said heavily: "Kiss your mother, son, and run along."

He got up dutifully and went over and kissed her on the forehead. She patted his hand. He went out of the room with his head down and quietly shut the door. I said to Merle: "I think you had better have him dictate that to you just the way he told it and make a copy of it and get him to sign it."

She looked startled. The old woman snarled: "She certainly won't do anything of the sort. Go back to your work, Merle. I wanted you to hear this. But if I ever again catch you violating my confidence, you know what will happen."

The little girl stood up and smiled at her with shining eyes. "Oh yes, Mrs. Murdock. I never will. Never. You can trust me."

"I hope so," the old dragon growled. "Get out."

Merle went out softly.

Two big tears formed themselves in Mrs. Murdock's eyes and slowly made their way down the elephant hide of her cheeks, reached the corners of her fleshy nose and slid down her lip. She scrabbled around for a handkerchief, wiped them off and then wiped her eyes. She put the handkerchief away, reached for her wine and said placidly: "I'm very fond of my son, Mr. Marlowe. Very fond. This grieves me deeply. Do you think he will have to tell this story to the police?"

"I hope not," I said. "He'd have a hell of a time getting them to believe it."

Her mouth snapped open and her teeth glinted at me in the dim light. She closed her lips and pressed them tight, scowling at me with her head lowered. "Just what do you mean by that?" she snapped.

"Just what I said. The story doesn't ring true. It has a fabricated, over-simple sound. Did he make it up himself or did you think it up and teach it to him?"

"Mr. Marlowe," she said in a deadly voice, "you are treading on very thin ice."

I waved a hand. "Aren't we all? All right, suppose it's true. Morny will deny it, and we'll be right back where we started. Morny will have to deny it, because otherwise it would tie him to a couple of murders."

"Is there anything so unlikely about that being the exact situation?" she blared.

"Why would Morny, a man with backing, protection and some influence, tie himself to a couple of small murders in order to avoid tying himself to something trifling, like selling a pledge? It doesn't make sense to me."

She stared, saying nothing. I grinned at her, because for the first time she was going to like something I said.

"I found your daughter-in-law, Mrs. Murdock. It's a little strange to me that your son, who seems so well under your control, didn't tell you where she was."

"I didn't ask him," she said in a curiously quiet voice, for her.

"She's back where she started, singing with the band at the Idle Valley Club. I talked to her. She's a pretty hard sort of girl in a way. She doesn't like you very well. I don't find it impossible to think that she took the coin all right, partly from spite. And I find it slightly less impossible to believe that Leslie knew it or found it out and cooked up that yarn to protect her. He says he's very much in love with her."

She smiled. It wasn't a beautiful smile, being on slightly the wrong kind of face. But it was a smile. "Yes," she said gently. "Yes. Poor Leslie. He would do just that. And in that case—" she stopped and her smile widened until it was almost ecstatic—"in that case my dear daughter-in-law may be involved in murder."

I watched her enjoying the idea for a quarter of a minute. "And you'd just love that," I said.

She nodded, still smiling, getting the idea she liked before she got the rudeness in my voice. Then her face stiffened and her lips came together hard. Between them and her teeth she said: "I don't like your tone. I don't like your tone at all."

"I don't blame you," I said. "I don't like it myself. I don't like anything. I don't like this house or you or the air of repression in the joint, or the squeezed down face of the little girl or that twerp of a son you have, or this case or the truth I'm not told about it and the lies I am told about it and—"

She started yelling then, noise out of a splotched furious face, eyes tossing with fury, sharp with hate: "Get out! Get out of this house at once! Don't delay one instant! Get out!"

I stood up and reached my hat off the carpet and said: "I'll be glad to."

I gave her a sort of a tired leer and picked my way to the door and opened it and went out. I shut it quietly, holding the knob with a stiff hand and clicking the lock gently into place. For no reason at all.

■ 22 ■

STEPS GIBBERED ALONG AFTER ME AND MY NAME WAS called and I kept on going until I was in the middle of the living room. Then I stopped and turned and let her catch up with me, out of breath, her eyes trying to pop through her glasses and her shining copper-blond hair catching funny little lights from the high windows. "Mr. Marlowe? Please! Please don't go away. She wants you. She really does!"

"I'll be darned. You've got Sub-deb Bright on your mouth this morning. Looks all right too."

She grabbed my sleeve. "Please!"

"The hell with her," I said. "Tell her to jump in the lake. Marlowe can get sore too. Tell her to jump in two lakes, if one won't hold her. Not clever, but quick."

I looked down at the hand on my sleeve and patted it. She drew it away swiftly and her eyes looked shocked. "Please, Mr. Marlowe. She's in trouble. She needs you."

"I'm in trouble too," I growled. "I'm up to my ear flaps in trouble. What are you crying about?"

"Oh, I'm really very fond of her. I know she's rough and blustery, but her heart is pure gold."

"To hell with her heart too," I said. "I don't expect to get intimate enough with her for that to make any difference. She's a fat-faced old liar. I've had enough of her. I think she's in trouble all right, but I'm not in the excavating business. I have to get told things."

"Oh, I'm sure if you would only be patient—"

I put my arm around her shoulders, without thinking. She jumped about three feet and her eyes blazed with panic. We stood there staring at each other, making breath noises, me with my mouth open as it too frequently is, she with her lips pressed tight and her little pale nostrils quivering. Her face was as pale as the unhandy makeup would let it be.

"Look," I said slowly, "did something happen to you when you were a little girl?"

She nodded, very quickly.

"A man scared you or something like that?"

She nodded again. She took her lower lip between her little white teeth.

"And you've been like this ever since?"

She just stood there, looking white.

"Look," I said, "I won't do anything to you that will scare you. Not ever." Her eyes melted with tears. "If I touched you," I said, "it was just like touching a chair or a door. It didn't mean anything. Is that clear?"

"Yes." She got a word out at last. Panic still twitched in the depths of her eyes, behind the tears. "Yes."

"That takes care of me," I said. "I'm all adjusted. Nothing to worry about in me any more. Now take Leslie. He has his mind on other things. You know he's all right—in the way we mean. Right?"

"Oh, yes," she said. "Yes, indeed." Leslie was aces. With her. With me he was a handful of bird gravel.

"Now take the old wine barrel," I said. "She's rough and she's tough and she thinks she can eat walls and spit bricks, and she bawls you out, but she's fundamentally decent to you, isn't she?"

"Oh, she is, Mr. Marlowe. I was trying to tell you—"

"Sure. Now why don't you get over it? Is he still around—this other one that hurt you?"

She put her hand to her mouth and gnawed the fleshy part at the base of the thumb, looking at me over it, as if it were a balcony. "He's dead," she said. "He fell out of a—out of a—a window."

I stopped her with my big right hand. "Oh, that guy. I heard about him. Forget it, can't you?"

"No," she said, shaking her head seriously behind the hand. "I can't. I can't seem to forget it at all. Mrs. Murdock is always telling me to forget it. She talks to me for the longest times telling me to forget it. But I just can't."

"It would be a darn sight better," I snarled, "if she would keep her fat mouth shut about it for the longest times. She just keeps it alive."

She looked surprised and rather hurt at that. "Oh, that isn't all," she said. "I was his secretary. She was his wife. He was her first husband. Naturally she doesn't forget it either. How could she?"

I scratched my ear. That seemed sort of non-committal. There was nothing much in her expression now except that I didn't really think she realized that I was there. I was a voice coming out of somewhere, but rather impersonal. Almost a voice in her own head. Then

I had one of my funny and often unreliable hunches. "Look," I said, "is there someone you meet that has that effect on you? Some one person more than another?"

She looked all around the room. I looked with her. Nobody was under a chair or peeking at us through a door or a window. "Why do I have to tell you?" she breathed.

"You don't. It's just how you feel about it."

"Will you promise not to tell anybody—anybody in the whole world, not even Mrs. Murdock?"

"Her last of all," I said. "I promise."

She opened her mouth and put a funny little confiding smile on her face, and then it went wrong. Her throat froze up. She made a croaking noise. Her teeth actually rattled.

I wanted to give her a good hard squeeze but I was afraid to touch her. We stood. Nothing happened. We stood. I was about as much use as a hummingbird's spare egg would have been.

Then she turned and ran. I heard her steps going along the hall. I heard a door close.

I went after her along the hall and reached the door. She was sobbing behind it. I stood there and listened to the sobbing. There was nothing I could do about it. I wondered if there was anything anybody could do about it.

I went back to the glass porch and knocked on the door and opened it and put my head in. Mrs. Murdock sat just as I had left her. She didn't seem to have moved at all. "Who's scaring the life out of that little girl?" I asked her.

"Get out of my house," she said between her fat lips.

I didn't move. Then she laughed at me hoarsely. "Do you regard yourself as a clever man, Mr. Marlowe?"

"Well, I'm not dripping with it," I said.

"Suppose you find out for yourself."

"At your expense?"

She shrugged her heavy shoulders. "Possibly. It depends. Who knows?"

"You haven't bought a thing," I said. "I'm still going to have to talk to the police."

"I haven't bought anything," she said, "and I haven't paid for anything. Except the return of the coin. I'm satisfied to accept that for the money I have already given you. Now go away. You bore me. Unspeakably."

I shut the door and went back. No sobbing behind the door. Very still. I went on.

I let myself out of the house. I stood there, listening to the sunshine burn the grass. A car started up in back and a gray Mercury came drifting along the drive at the side of the house. Mr. Leslie Murdock was driving it. When he saw me he stopped. He got out of the car and walked quickly over to me. He was nicely dressed; cream colored gabardine now, all fresh clothes, slacks, black and white shoes, with polished black toes, a sport coat of very small black and white check, black and white handkerchief, cream shirt, no tie. He had a pair of green sun glasses on his nose. He stood close to me and said in a low timid sort of voice: "I guess you think I'm an awful heel."

"On account of that story you told about the doubloon?"

"Yes."

"That didn't affect my way of thinking about you in the least," I said.

"Well—"

"Just what do you want me to say?"

He moved his smoothly tailored shoulders in a deprecatory shrug. His silly little reddish brown mustache glittered in the sun. "I suppose I like to be liked," he said.

"I'm sorry, Murdock. I like your being that devoted to your wife. If that's what it is."

"Oh. Didn't you think I was telling the truth? I mean, did you think I was saying all that just to protect her?"

"There was that possibility."

"I see." He put a cigarette into the long black holder, which he took from behind his display handkerchief. "Well—I guess I can take it that you don't like me." The dim movement of his eyes was visible behind the green lenses, fish moving in a deep pool.

"It's a silly subject," I said. "And damned unimportant. To both of us."

He put a match to the cigarette and inhaled. "I see," he said quietly. "Pardon me for being crude enough to bring it up."

He turned on his heel and walked back to his car and got in. I watched him drive away before I moved. Then I went over and patted the little painted Negro boy on the head a couple of times before I left. "Son," I said to him, "you're the only person around this house that's not nuts."

■ **23** ■

THE POLICE LOUDSPEAKER BOX ON THE WALL GRUNTED and a voice said: "KGPL. Testing." A click and it went dead. Detective-Lieutenant Jesse Breeze stretched his arms high in the air and yawned and said: "Couple of hours late, ain't you?"

I said: "Yes. But I left a message for you that I would be. I had to go to the dentist."

"Sit down."

He had a small littered desk across one corner of the room. He sat in the angle behind it, with a tall bare window to his left and a wall with a large calendar about eye height to his right. The days that had gone down to dust were crossed off carefully in soft black pencil, so that Breeze glancing at the calendar always knew exactly what day it was.

Spangler was sitting sideways at a smaller and much neater desk. It had a green blotter and an onyx pen set and a small brass calendar and an abalone shell full of ashes and matches and cigarette stubs. Spangler was flipping a handful of bank pens at the felt back of a seat cushion on end against the wall, like a Mexican knife thrower flipping knives at a target. He wasn't getting anywhere with it. The pens refused to stick.

The room had that remote, heartless, not quite dirty, not quite clean, not quite human smell that such rooms always have. Give a police department a brand new building and in three months all its rooms will smell like that. There must be something symbolic in it. A New York police reporter wrote once that when you pass in beyond the green lights of a precinct station you pass clear out of this world, into a place beyond the law.

I sat down. Breeze got a cellophane-wrapped cigar out of his pocket and the routine with it started. I watched it detail by detail, unvarying, precise. He drew in smoke, shook his match out, laid it gently in the black glass ashtray, and said: "Hi, Spangler."

Spangler turned his head and Breeze turned his head. They grinned at each other. Breeze poked the cigar at me. "Watch him sweat," he said.

Spangler had to move his feet to turn far enough around to watch me sweat. If I was sweating, I didn't know it.

"You boys are as cute as a couple of lost golf balls," I said. "How in the world do you do it?"

"Skip the wisecracks," Breeze said. "Had a busy little morning?"

"Fair," I said.

He was still grinning. Spangler was still grinning. Whatever it was Breeze was tasting he hated to swallow it. Finally he cleared his throat, straightened his big freckled face out, turned his head enough so that he was not looking at me but could still see me and said in a vague empty sort of voice: "Hench confessed."

Spangler swung clear around to look at me. He leaned forward on the edge of his chair and his lips were parted in an ecstatic half smile that was almost indecent.

I said: "What did you use on him—a pickax?"

"Nope."

They were both silent, staring at me.

"A wop," Breeze said.

"A what?"

"Boy, are you glad?" Breeze said.

"Are you going to tell me or are you just going to sit there looking fat and complacent and watch me being glad?"

"We like to watch a guy being glad," Breeze said. "We don't often get a chance."

I put a cigarette in my mouth and jiggled it up and down.

"We used a wop on him," Breeze said. "A wop named Palermo."

"Oh. You know something?"

"What?" Breeze asked.

"I just thought of what is the matter with policemen's dialogue."

"What?"

"They think every line is a punch line."

"And every pinch is a good pinch," Breeze said calmly. "You want to know—or you want to just crack wise?"

"I want to know."

"Was like this, then. Hench was drunk. I mean he was drunk deep inside, not just on the surface. Screwy drunk. He'd been living on it for weeks. He'd practically quit eating and sleeping. Just liquor. He'd got to the point where liquor wasn't making him drunk, it was keeping him sober. It was the last hold he had on the real world. When a guy gets like that and you take his liquor away and don't give him anything to hold him down, he's a lost cuckoo."

I didn't say anything. Spangler still had the same erotic leer on his young face. Breeze tapped the side of his cigar and no ash fell off and he put it back in his mouth and went on. "He's a psycho case, but we don't want any psycho case made out of our pinch. We make that clear. We want a guy that don't have any psycho record."

"I thought you were sure Hench was innocent."

Breeze nodded vaguely. "That was last night. Or

maybe I was kidding a little. Anyway in the night, bang, Hench is bugs. So they drag him over to the hospital ward and shoot him full of hop. The jail doc does. That's between you and me. No hop in the record. Get the idea?"

"All too clearly," I said.

"Yeah." He looked vaguely suspicious of the remark, but he was too full of his subject to waste time on it. "Well, this a.m. he is fine. Hop still working, the guy is pale but peaceful. We go see him. How you doing, kid? Anything you need? Any little thing at all? Be glad to get it for you. They treating you nice in here? You know the line."

"I do," I said. "I know the line."

Spangler licked his lips in a nasty way.

"So after a while he opens his trap just enough to say 'Palermo.' Palermo is the name of the wop across the street that owns the funeral home and the apartment house and stuff. You remember? Yeah, you remember. On account of he said something about a tall blond. All hooey. Them wops got tall blonds on the brain. In sets of twelve. But this Palermo is important. I asked around. He gets the vote out up there. He's a guy that can't be pushed around. Well, I don't aim to push him around. I say to Hench, 'You mean Palermo's a friend of yours?' He says, 'Get Palermo.' So we come back here to the hutch and phone Palermo and Palermo says he will be right down. Okay. He is here very soon. We talk like this: Hench wants to see you, Mr. Palermo. I wouldn't know why. He's a poor guy. Palermo says. A nice guy. I think he's okay. He wanta see me, that'sa fine. I see him. I see him alone. Without any coppers. I say, Okay, Mr. Palermo, and we go over to the hospital ward and Palermo talks to Hench and nobody listens. After a while Palermo comes out and he says, Okay, copper. He make the confess. I pay the lawyer, maybe. I like the poor guy. Just like that. He goes away."

I didn't say anything. There was a pause. The loudspeaker on the wall put out a bulletin and Breeze cocked his head and listened to ten or twelve words and then ignored it.

"So we go in with a steno and Hench gives us the dope Phillips made a pass at Hench's girl. That was day before yesterday, out in the hall. Hench was in the room and he saw it, but Phillips got into his apartment and shut the door before Hench could get out. But Hench was sore. He socked the girl in the eye. But that didn't satisfy him. He got to brooding, the way a drunk will brood. He says to himself, that guy can't make a pass at my girl. I'm the boy that will give him something to remember me by. So he keeps an eye open for Phillips. Yesterday afternoon he sees Phillips go into his apartment. He tells the girl to go for a walk. She don't want to go for a walk, so Hench socks her in the other eye. She goes for a walk. Hench knocks on Phillips' door and Phillips opens it. Hench is a little surprised at that, but I told him Phillips was expecting you. Anyway the door opens and Hench goes in and tells Phillips how he feels and what he is going to do and Phillips is scared and pulls a gun. Hench hits him with a sap. Phillips falls down and Hench ain't satisfied. You hit a guy with a sap and he falls down and what have you? No satisfaction, no revenge. Hench picks the gun off the floor and he is very drunk there being dissatisfied and Phillips grabs for his ankle. Hench doesn't know why he did what he did then. He's all fuzzy in the head. He drags Phillips into the bathroom and gives him the business with his own gun. You like it?"

"I love it," I said. "But what is the satisfaction in it for Hench?"

"Well, you know how a drunk is. Anyway he gives him the business. Well it ain't Hench's gun, you see, but he can't make a suicide out of it. There wouldn't be any satisfaction for him in that. So Hench takes the gun away and puts it under his pillow and takes his own gun out and ditches it. He won't tell us where. Probably passes it to some tough guy in the neighborhood. Then he finds the girl and they eat."

"That was a lovely touch," I said. "Putting the gun

under his pillow. I'd never in the world have thought of that."

Breeze leaned back in his chair and looked at the ceiling. Spangler, the big part of the entertainment over, swung around in his chair and picked up a couple of bank pens and threw one at the cushion.

"Look at it this way," Breeze said. "What was the effect of that stunt? Look how Hench did it. He was drunk, but he was smart. He found that gun and showed it before Phillips was found dead. First we get the idea that a gun is under Hench's pillow that killed a guy—been fired anyway—and then we get the stiff. We believed Hench's story. It seemed reasonable. Why would we think any man would be such a sap as to do what Hench did? It doesn't make any sense. So we believed somebody put the gun under Hench's pillow and took Hench's gun away and ditched it. And suppose Hench ditched the death gun instead of his own, would he have been any better off? Things being what they were we would be bound to suspect him. And that way he wouldn't have started our minds thinking any particular way about him. The way he did he got us thinking he was a harmless drunk that went out and left his door open and somebody ditched a gun on him."

He waited, with his mouth a little open and the cigar in front of it, held up by a hard freckled hand and his pale blue eyes full of dim satisfaction.

"Well," I said, "if he was going to confess anyway, it wouldn't have made very much difference. Will he cop a plea?"

"Sure. I think so. I figured Palermo could get him off with manslaughter. Naturally I'm not sure."

"Why would Palermo want to get him off with anything?"

"He kind of likes Hench. And Palermo is a guy we can't push around."

I said: "I see." I stood up. Spangler looked at me sideways along glistening eyes. "What about the girl?"

"Won't say a word. She's smart. We can't do anything to her. Nice neat little job all around. You wouldn't kick, would you? Whatever your business is, it's still your business. Get me?"

"And the girl is a tall blond," I said. "Not of the freshest, but still a tall blond. Although only one. Maybe Palermo doesn't mind."

"Hell, I never thought of that," Breeze said. He thought about it and shook it off. "Nothing in that, Marlowe. Not enough class."

"Cleaned up and sober, you never can tell," I said. "Class is a thing that has a way of dissolving rapidly in alcohol. That all you want with me?"

"Guess so." He slanted the cigar up and aimed it at my eye. "Not that I wouldn't like to hear your story. But I don't figure I have an absolute right to insist on it the way things are."

"That's white of you, Breeze," I said. "And you too, Spangler. A lot of the good things in life to both of you."

They watched me go out, both with their mouths a little open. I rode down to the big marble lobby and went and got my car out of the official parking lot.

▪ 24 ▪

MR. PIETRO PALERMO WAS SITTING IN A ROOM WHICH, EX-cept for a mahogany roll-top desk, a sacred triptych in gilt frames and a large ebony and ivory crucifixion, looked exactly like a Victorian parlor. It contained a horseshoe sofa and chairs with carved mahogany frames and antimacassars of fine lace. There was an ormolu clock on the gray green marble mantel, a grandfather clock ticking lazily in the corner, and some wax flowers under a glass dome on an oval table with a marble top and curved elegant legs. The carpet was thick and full of gentle sprays of flowers. There was even a cabinet for bric-a-brac and there was plenty of bric-a-brac in it, little cups of fine china, little figurines in glass and porcelain, odds and ends of ivory and dark rosewood, painted saucers, an early American set of swan salt cellars, stuff like that.

Long lace curtains hung across the windows, but the room faced south and there was plenty of light. Across the street I could see the windows of the apartment where George Anson Phillips had been killed. The street between was sunny and silent. The tall Italian with the dark skin and the handsome head of iron gray hair read my card and said: "I got business in twelve minutes. What you want, Meester Marlowe?"

"I'm the man that found the dead man across the street yesterday. He was a friend of mine."

His cold black eyes looked me over silently. "That'sa not what you tell Luke."

"Luke?"

"He manage the joint for me."

"I don't talk much to strangers, Mr. Palermo."

"That'sa good. You talk to me, huh?"

"You're a man of standing, an important man. I can talk to you. You saw me yesterday. You described me to the police. Very accurately, they said."

"Si. I see much," he said without emotion.

"You saw a tall blond woman come out of there yesterday."

He studied me. "Not yesterday. Wasa two three days ago. I tell the coppers yesterday." He snapped his long dark fingers. "The coppers, bah!"

"Did you see any strangers yesterday, Mr. Palermo?"

"Is back way in and out," he said. "Is stair from second floor also." He looked at his wrist watch.

"Nothing there then," I said. "This morning you saw Hench."

He lifted his eyes and ran them lazily over my face. "The coppers tell you that, huh?"

"They told me you got Hench to confess. They said he was a friend of yours. How good a friend they didn't know, of course."

"Hench make the confess, huh?" He smiled, a sudden brilliant smile.

"Only Hench didn't do the killing," I said.

"No?"

"No."

"That'sa interesting. Go on, Meester Marlowe."

"The confession is a lot of baloney. You got him to make it for some reason of your own."

He stood up and went to the door and called out: "Tony." He sat down again. A short tough-looking Italian came into the room, looked at me and sat down against the wall in a straight chair. "Tony, thees man a Meester Marlowe. Look, take the card." Tony came to get the card and sat down with it. "You look at thees man very good, Tony. Not forget him, huh?"

Tony said : "Leave it to me, Mr. Palermo."

Palermo said: "Was a friend to you, huh? A good friend, huh?"

"Yes."

"That'sa bad. Yeah. That'sa bad. I tell you something. A man's friend is a man's friend. So I tell you. But you don' tell anybody else. Not the damn coppers, huh?"

"No."

"That'sa promise, Meester Marlowe. That'sa something not to forget. You not forget?"

"I won't forget."

"Tony, he not forget you. Get the idea?"

"I gave you my word. What you tell me is between us here."

"That'sa fine. Okay. I come of large family. Many sisters and brothers. One brother very bad. Almost so bad as Tony."

Tony grinned.

"Okay, thees brother live very quiet. Across the street. Gotta move. Okay, the coppers fill the joint up. Not so good. Ask too many questions. Not good for business, not good for thees bad brother. You get the idea?"

"Yes," I said. "I get the idea."

"Okay, thees Hench no good, but poor guy, drunk, no job. Pay no rent, but I got lotsa money. So I say, look,

Hench, you make the confess. You sick man. Two three weeks sick. You go into court. I have a lawyer for you. You say to hell with the confess. I was drunk. The damn coppers are stuck. The judge he turn you loose and you come back to me and I take care of you. Okay? So Hench say okay, make the confess. That'sa all."

I said: "And after two or three weeks the bad brother is a long way from here and the trail is cold and the cops will likely just write the Phillips killing off as unsolved. Is that it?"

"Si." He smiled again. A brilliant warm smile, like the kiss of death.

"That takes care of Hench, Mr. Palermo," I said. "But it doesn't help me much about my friend."

He shook his head and looked at his watch again. I stood up. Tony stood up. He wasn't going to do anything, but it's better to be standing up. You move faster.

"The trouble with you birds," I said, "is you make mystery of nothing. You have to give the password before you bite a piece of bread. If I went down to headquarters and told the boys everything you have told me, they would laugh in my face. And I would be laughing with them."

"Tony don't laugh much," Palermo said.

"The earth is full of people who don't laugh much, Mr. Palermo," I said. "You ought to know. You put a lot of them where they are."

"Is my business," he said, shrugging enormously.

"I'll keep my promise," I said. "But in case you should get to doubting that, don't try to make any business for yourself out of me. Because in my part of town I'm a pretty good man and if the business got made out of Tony instead, it would be strictly on the house. No profit."

Palermo laughed. "That'sa good," he said. "Tony. One funeral—on the house. Okay."

He stood up and held his hand out, a fine strong warm hand.

■ 25 ■

IN THE LOBBY OF THE BELFONT BUILDING, IN THE SINGLE elevator that had light in it, on the piece of folded burlap, the same watery-eyed relic sat motionless, giving his imitation of the forgotten man. I got in with him and said: "Six."

The elevator lurched into motion and pounded its way upstairs. It stopped at six, I got out, and the old man leaned out of the car to spit and said in a dull voice: "What's cookin'?"

I turned around all in one piece, like a dummy on a revolving platform. I stared at him.

He said: "You got a gray suit on today."

"So I have," I said. "Yes."

"Looks nice," he said. "I like the blue you was wearing yesterday too."

"Go on," I said. "Give out."

"You rode up to eight," he said. "Twice. Second time was late. You got back on at six. Shortly after that the boys in blue came bustlin' in."

"Any of them up there now?"

He shook his head. His face was like a vacant lot. "I ain't told them anything," he said. "Too late to mention it now. They'd eat my ass off."

I said: "Why?"

"Why I ain't told them? The hell with them. You talked to me civil. Damn few people do that. Hell, I know you didn't have nothing to do with that killing."

"I played you wrong," I said. "Very wrong." I got a card out and gave it to him. He fished a pair of metal-

145

framed glasses out of his pocket, perched them on his nose and held the card a foot away from them. He read it slowly, moving his lips, looked at me over the glasses, handed me back the card.

"Better keep it," he said. "Case I get careless and drop it. Mighty interestin' life yours, I guess."

"Yes and no. What was the name?"

"Grandy. Just call me Pop. Who killed him?"

"I don't know. Did you notice anybody going up there or coming down—anybody that seemed out of place in this building, or strange to you?"

"I don't notice much," he said. "I just happened to notice you."

"A tall blond, for instance, or a tall slender man with sideburns about thirty-five years old."

"Nope."

"Everybody going up or down about then would ride in your car."

He nodded his worn head. "'Less they used the fire stairs. They come out in the alley, bar-lock door. Party would have to come in this way, but there's stairs back of the elevator to the second floor. From there they can get to the fire stairs. Nothing to it."

I nodded. "Mr. Grandy, could you use a five dollar bill—not as a bribe in any sense, but as a token of esteem from a sincere friend?"

"Son, I could use a five dollar bill so rough Abe Lincoln's whiskers would be all lathered up with sweat."

I gave him one. I looked at it before I passed it over. It was Lincoln on the five, all right.

He tucked it small and put it away deep in his pocket. "That's right nice of you," he said. "I hope to hell you didn't think I was fishin'."

I shook my head and went along the corridor, reading the names again, *Dr. E. J. Blaskowitz, Chiropractic Physician. Dalton and Rees, Typewriting Service. L. Pridview, Public Accountant.* Four blank doors. *Moss Mailing Company.* Two more blank doors. *H. R. Teager, Dental Laboratories.* In the same relative position as the Morningstar office two floors above, but the rooms were cut up differently. Teager had only one door and there was more wall space in between his door and the next one.

The knob didn't turn. I knocked. There was no answer. I knocked harder, with the same result. I went back to the elevator. It was still at the sixth floor. Pop Grandy watched me come as if he had never seen me before.

"Know anything about H. R. Teager?" I asked him.

He thought. "Heavy-set, oldish, sloppy clothes, dirty fingernails, like mine. Come to think I didn't see him in today."

"Do you think the super would let me into his office to look around?"

"Pretty nosey, the super is. I wouldn't recommend it." He turned his head very slowly and looked up the side of the car. Over his head on a big metal ring a key was hanging. A pass-key. Pop Grandy turned his head back to normal position, stood up off his stool and said: "Right now I gotta go to the can."

He went. When the door had closed behind him I took the key off the cage wall and went back along to the office of H. R. Teager, unlocked it and went in.

Inside was a small windowless anteroom on the furnishings of which a great deal of expense had been spared. Two chairs, a smoking stand from a cut rate drugstore, a standing lamp from the basement of some borax emporium, a flat stained wood table with some old picture magazines on it. The door closed behind me on the door closer and the place went dark except for what little light came through the pebbled glass panel. I pulled the chain switch of the lamp and went over to the inner door in a wall that cut across the room. It was marked: *H. R. Teager. Private.* It was not locked.

Inside it there was a square office with two uncurtained east windows and very dusty sills. There was a swivel chair and two straight chairs, both plain hard stained wood, and there was a squarish flat-topped desk. There was nothing on the top of it except an old blotter and a cheap pen set and a round glass ashtray with cigar ash in it. The drawers of the desk contained some dusty paper linings, a few wire clips, rubber bands, worn down pencils, pens, rusty pen points, used blotters, four uncancelled two-cent stamps, and some printed letter-heads, envelopes and bill forms.

The wire paper basket was full of junk. I almost wasted ten minutes going through it rather carefully. At the end of that time I knew what I was pretty sure of already: that H. R. Teager carried on a small business as a dental technician doing laboratory work for a number of dentists in unprosperous sections of the city, the kind of dentists who have shabby offices on second floor walk-ups over stores, who lack both the skill and the equipment to do their own laboratory work, and who like to send it out to men like themselves, rather than to the big efficient hard-boiled laboratories who wouldn't give them any credit.

I did find one thing. Teager's home address at 1354B Toberman Street on the receipted part of a gas bill.

I straightened up, dumped the stuff back into the basket and went over to the wooden door marked *Laboratory*. It had a new Yale lock on it and the pass-key didn't fit it. That was that. I switched off the lamp in the outer office and left.

The elevator was downstairs again. I rang for it and when it came up I sidled in around Pop Grandy, hiding the key, and hung it up over his head. The ring tinkled against the cage. He grinned.

"He's gone," I said. "Must have left last night. Must have been carrying a lot of stuff. His desk is cleaned out."

Pop Grandy nodded. "Carried two suitcases. I wouldn't notice that, though. Most always does carry a suitcase. I figure he picks up and delivers his work."

"Work such as what?" I asked as the car growled down. Just to be saying something.

"Such as makin' teeth that don't fit," Pop Grandy said. "For poor old bastards like me."

"You wouldn't notice," I said, as the doors struggled open on the lobby, "you wouldn't notice the color of a hummingbird's eye at fifty feet. Not much you wouldn't."

He grinned. "What's he done?"

"I'm going over to his house and find out," I said. "I think most likely he's taken a cruise to nowhere."

"I'd shift places with him," Pop Grandy said. "Even if he only got to Frisco and got pinched there, I'd shift places with him."

■ 26 ■

TOBERMAN STREET, A WIDE DUSTY STREET, OFF PICO. NO. 1354B was an upstairs flat, south, in a yellow and white frame building. The entrance door was on the porch, beside another marked 1352B. The entrances to the downstairs flats were at right angles, facing each other across the width of the porch. I kept on ringing the bell, even after I was sure that nobody would answer it. In a neighborhood like that there is always an expert window-peeker.

Sure enough the door of 1354A was pulled open and a small bright-eyed woman looked out at me. Her dark hair had been washed and waved and was an intricate mass of bobby pins. "You want Mrs. Teager?" she shrilled.

"Mr. or Mrs."

"They gone away last night on their vacation. They loaded up and gone away late. They had me stop the milk and the paper. They didn't have much time. Kind of sudden, it was."

"Thanks. What kind of car do they drive?"

The heartrending dialogue of some love serial came out of the room behind her and hit me in the face like a wet dish-towel.

The bright-eyed woman said: "You a friend of theirs?"

In her voice, suspicion was as thick as the ham in her radio.

"Never mind," I said in a tough voice. "All we want is our money. Lots of ways to find out what car they were driving."

The woman cocked her head, listening. "That's Beula May," she told me with a sad smile. "She won't go to the dance with Doctor Myers. I was scared she wouldn't."

"Aw hell," I said, and went back to my car and drove on home to Hollywood.

The office was empty. I unlocked my inner room and threw the windows up and sat down.

Another day drawing to its end, the air dull and tired, the heavy growl of homing traffic on the boulevard, and Marlowe in his office nibbling a drink and sorting the day's mail. Four ads; two bills; a handsome colored postcard from a hotel in Santa Rosa where I had stayed for four days last year, working on a case; a long, badly typed letter from a man named Peabody in Sausalito, the general and slightly cloudy drift of which was that a sample of the handwriting of a suspected person would, when exposed to the searching Peabody examination, reveal the inner emotional characteristics of the individual, classified according to both the Freudian and Jung systems.

There was a stamped addressed envelope inside. As I tore the stamp off and threw the letter and envelope away I had a vision of a pathetic old rooster in long hair, black felt hat and black bow tie, rocking on a rickety porch in front of a lettered window, with the smell of ham hocks and cabbage coming out of the door at his elbow.

I sighed, retrieved the envelope, wrote its name and address on a fresh one, folded a dollar bill into a sheet of paper and wrote on it: "This is positively the last contribution." I signed my name, sealed the envelope, stuck a stamp on it and poured another drink.

I filled and lit my pipe and sat there smoking. Nobody came in, nobody called, nothing happened, nobody cared whether I died or went to El Paso.

Little by little the roar of the traffic quieted down. The sky lost its glare. Over in the west it would be red. An early neon light showed a block away, diagonally over roofs. The ventilator churned dully in the wall of the coffee shop down in the alley. A truck filled and backed and growled its way out on to the boulevard. Finally the telephone rang. I answered it and the voice said: "Mr. Marlowe? This is Mr. Shaw. At the Bristol."

"Yes, Mr. Shaw. How are you?"

"I'm very well thanks, Mr. Marlowe. I hope you are the same. There's a young lady here asking to be let into your apartment. I don't know why."

"Me neither, Mr. Shaw. I didn't order anything like that. Does she give a name?"

"Oh yes. Quite. Her name is Davis. Miss Merle Davis. She is—what shall I say?—quite verging on the hysterical."

"Let her in," I said, rapidly. "I'll be there in ten minutes. She's the secretary of a client. It's a business matter entirely."

"Quite. Oh yes. Shall I—er—remain with her?"

"Whatever you think," I said and hung up.

Passing the open door of the wash cabinet I saw a stiff excited face in the glass.

■ 27 ■

AS I TURNED THE KEY IN MY DOOR AND OPENED IT SHAW was already standing up from the davenport. He was a tall man with glasses and a high domed bald head that made his ears look as if they had slipped down on his head. He had the fixed smile of polite idiocy on his face. The girl sat in my easy chair behind the chess table. She wasn't doing anything, just sitting there.

"Ah, there you are, Mr. Marlowe," Shaw chirped. "Yes.

Quite. Miss Davis and I have been having such an interesting little conversation. I was telling her I originally came from England. She hasn't—er—told me where she came from." He was halfway to the door saying this.

"Very kind of you, Mr. Shaw," I said.

"Not at all," he chirped. "Not at all. I'll just run along now. My dinner, possibly—"

"It's very nice of you," I said, "I appreciate it."

He nodded and was gone. The unnatural brightness of his smile seemed to linger in the air after the door closed, like the smile of the Cheshire Cat.

I said: "Hello, there."

She said: "Hello." Her voice was quite calm, quite serious. She was wearing a brownish linen coat and skirt, a broad-brimmed low-crowned straw hat with a brown velvet band that exactly matched the color of her shoes and the leather trimming on the edges of her linen envelope bag. The hat was tilted rather daringly, for her. She was not wearing her glasses.

Except for her face she would have looked all right. In the first place her eyes were quite mad. There was white showing all around the iris and they had a sort of fixed look. When they moved the movement was so stiff that you could almost hear something creak. Her mouth was in a tight line at the corners, but the middle part of her upper lip kept lifting off her teeth, upwards and outwards as if fine threads attached to the edge of the lip were pulling it. It would go up so far that it didn't seem possible, and then the entire lower part of her face would go into a spasm and when the spasm was over her mouth would be tight shut, and then the process would slowly start all over again. In addition to this there was something wrong with her neck, so that very slowly her head was drawn around to the left about forty-five degrees. It would stop there, her neck would twitch, and her head would slide back the way it had come. The combination of these two movements, taken with the immobility of her body, the tight-clasped hands in her lap, and the fixed stare of her eyes, was enough to start anybody's nerves backfiring.

There was a can of tobacco on the desk, between which and her chair was the chess table with the chessmen in their box. I got the pipe out of my pocket and went over to fill it at the can of tobacco. That put me just on the other side of the chess table from her. Her bag was lying on the edge of the table, in front of her and a little to one side. She jumped a little when I went over there, but after that she was just like before. She even made an effort to smile.

I filled the pipe and struck a paper match and lit it and stood there holding the match after I had blown it out. "You're not wearing your glasses," I said.

She spoke. Her voice was quiet, composed. "Oh, I only wear them around the house and for reading. They're in my bag."

"You're in the house now," I said. "You ought to be wearing them."

I reached casually for the bag. She didn't move. She didn't watch my hands. Her eyes were on my face. I turned my body a little as I opened the bag. I fished the glass case out and slid it across the table. "Put them on," I said.

"Oh, yes, I'll put them on," she said. "But I'll have to take my hat off, I think . . ."

"Yes, take your hat off," I said.

She took her hat off and held it on her knees. Then she remembered about the glasses and forgot about the hat. The hat fell on the floor while she reached for the glasses. She put them on. That helped her appearance a lot, I thought.

While she was doing this I got the gun out of her bag and slid it into my hip pocket. I didn't think she saw me. It looked like the same Colt .25 automatic with the walnut grip that I had seen in the top right hand drawer of her desk the day before.

I went back to the davenport and sat down and said: "Well, here we are. What do we do now? Are you hungry?"

"I've been over to Mr. Vannier's house," she said.

"Oh."

"He lives in Sherman Oaks. At the end of Escamillo Drive. At the very end."

"Quite, probably," I said without meaning, and tried to blow a smoke ring, but didn't make it. A nerve in my cheek was trying to twang like a wire. I didn't like it.

"Yes," she said in her composed voice, with her upper lip still doing the hoist and flop movement and her chin still swinging around at anchor and back again. "It's very quiet there. Mr. Vannier has been living there three years now. Before that he lived up in the Hollywood hills, on Diamond Street. Another man lived with him there, but they didn't get along very well, Mr. Vannier said."

"I feel as if I could understand that too," I said, "How long have you known Mr. Vannier?"

"I've known him eight years. I haven't known him very well. I have had to take him a—a parcel now and then. He liked to have me bring it myself."

I tried again with a smoke ring. Nope.

"Of course," she said, "I never liked him very well. I was afraid he would—I was afraid he—"

"But he didn't," I said.

For the first time her face got a human natural expression—surprise. "No," she said, "He didn't. That is, he didn't really. But he had his pajamas on."

"Taking it easy," I said. "Lying around all afternoon with his pajamas on. Well, some guys have all the luck, don't they?"

"Well you have to know something," she said seriously. "Something that makes people pay you money. Mrs. Murdock has been wonderful to me, hasn't she?"

"She certainly has," I said. "How much were you taking him today?"

"Only five hundred dollars. Mrs. Murdock said that was all she could spare, and she couldn't really spare that. She said it would have to stop. It couldn't go on. Mr. Vannier would always promise to stop, but he never did."

"It's a way they have," I said.

"So there was only one thing to do. I've known that for

years, really. It was all my fault and Mrs. Murdock has been so wonderful to me. It couldn't make me any worse than I was already, could it?"

I put my hand up and rubbed my cheek hard, to quiet the nerve. She forgot that I hadn't answered her and went on again. "So I did it," she said. "He was there in his pajamas, with a glass beside him. He was leering at me. He didn't even get up to let me in. But there was a key in the front door. Somebody had left a key there. It was—it was—" her voice jammed in her throat.

"It was a key in the front door," I said. "So you were able to get in."

"Yes." She nodded and almost smiled again. "There wasn't anything to it, really. I don't even remember hearing the noise. But there must have been a noise, of course. Quite a loud noise."

"I suppose so," I said.

"I went over quite close to him, so I couldn't miss," she said.

"And what did Mr. Vannier do?"

"He didn't do anything at all. He just leered, sort of. Well, that's all there is to it. I didn't like to go back to Mrs. Murdock and make any trouble for her. And for Leslie." Her voice hushed on the name, and hung suspended, and a little shiver rippled over her body. "So I came here," she said. "And when you didn't answer the bell, I found the office and asked the manager to let me in and wait for you. I knew you would know what to do."

"And what did you touch in the house while you were there?" I asked. "Can you remember at all? I mean, besides the front door. Did you just go in at the door and come out without touching anything in the house?"

She thought and her face stopped moving. "Oh, I remember one thing," she said. "I put the light out. Before I left. It was a lamp. One of these lamps that shine upwards, with big bulbs. I put that out."

I nodded and smiled at her. Marlowe, one smile, cheerful. "What time was this—how long ago?"

"Oh just before I came over here. I drove. I had Mrs.

Murdock's car. The one you asked about yesterday. I forgot to tell you that she didn't take it when she went away. Or did I? No, I remember now I did tell you."

"Let's see," I said. "Half an hour to drive here anyway. You've been here close to an hour. That would be about five-thirty when you left Mr. Vannier's house. And you put the light off."

"That's right." She nodded again, quite brightly. Pleased at remembering. "I put the light out."

"Would you care for a drink?" I asked her.

"Oh, no." She shook her head quite vigorously. "I never drink anything at all."

"Would you mind if I had one?"

"Certainly not. Why should I?"

I stood up, gave her a studying look. Her lip was still going up and her head was still going around, but I thought not so far. It was like a rhythm which is dying down. It was difficult to know how far to go with this. It might be that the more she talked, the better. Nobody knows very much about the time of absorption of a shock. I said: "Where is your home?"

"Why—I live with Mrs. Murdock. In Pasadena."

"I mean, your real home. Where your folks are."

"My parents live in Wichita," she said. "But I don't go there—ever. I write once in a while, but I haven't seen them for years."

"What does your father do?"

"He has a dog and cat hospital. He's a veterinarian. I hope they won't have to know. They didn't about the other time. Mrs. Murdock kept it from everybody."

"Maybe they won't have to know," I said. "I'll get my drink."

I went out around the back of her chair to the kitchen and poured it and made it a drink that was a drink. I put it down in a lump and took the little gun off my hip and saw that the safety was on. I smelled the muzzle, broke out the magazine. There was a shell in the chamber, but it was one of those guns that won't fire when the magazine is out. I held it so that I could look into the breech. The shell in there was the wrong size and was crooked against the breech block. It looked like a .32. The shells in the magazine were the right size, .25's. I fitted the gun together again and went back to the living room.

I hadn't heard a sound. She had just slid forward in a pile in front of the chair, on top of her nice hat. She was as cold as a mackerel.

I spread her out a little and took her glasses off and made sure she hadn't swallowed her tongue. I wedged my folded handkerchief into the corner of her mouth so that she wouldn't bite her tongue when she came out of it. I went to the phone and called Carl Moss.

"Phil Marlowe, Doc. Any more patients or are you through?"

"All through," he said. "Leaving. Trouble?"

"I'm home," I said. "Four-o-eight Bristol Apartments, if you don't remember. I've got a girl here who has pulled a faint. I'm not afraid of the faint, I'm afraid she may be nuts when she comes out of it."

"Don't give her any liquor," he said. "I'm on my way."

I hung up and knelt down beside her. I began to rub her temples. She opened her eyes. The lip started to lift. I pulled the handkerchief out of her mouth. She looked up at me and said: "I've been over to Mr. Vannier's house. He lives in Sherman Oaks. I—"

"Do you mind if I lift you up and put you on the davenport? You know me—Marlowe, the big boob that goes around asking all the wrong questions."

"Hello," she said.

I lifted her. She went stiff on me, but she didn't say anything. I put her on the davenport and tucked her skirt down over her legs and put a pillow under her head and picked her hat up. It was as flat as a flounder. I did what I could to straighten it out and laid it aside on the desk.

She watched me sideways, doing this. "Did you call the police?" she asked softly.

"Not yet," I said. "I've been too busy."

She looked surprised. I wasn't quite sure, but I thought she looked a little hurt, too.

I opened up her bag and turned my back to her to slip

the gun back into it. While I was doing that I took a look at what else was in the bag. The usual oddments, a couple of handkerchiefs, lipstick, a silver and red enamel compact with powder in it, a couple of tissues, a purse with some hard money and a few dollar bills, no ciga-rettes, no matches, no tickets to the theater.

I pulled open the zipper pocket at the back. That held her driver's license and a flat packet of bills, ten fifties. I riffled them. None of them brand new. Tucked into the rubber band that held them was a folded paper. I took it out and opened it and read it. It was neatly typewritten, dated that day. It was a common receipt form and it would, when signed, acknowledge the receipt of $500. "Payment on Account."

It didn't seem as if it would ever be signed now. I slipped money and receipt into my pocket. I closed the bag and looked over at the davenport. She was looking at the ceiling and doing that with her face again. I went into my bedroom and got a blanket to throw over her. Then I went to the kitchen for another drink.

■ 28 ■

DR. CARL MOSS WAS A BIG BURLY MAN WITH A HITLER mustache, pop eyes and the calmness of a glacier. He put his hat and bag in a chair and went over and stood looking down at the girl on the davenport inscrutably. "I'm Dr. Moss," he said. "How are you?"

She said: "Aren't you the police?"

He bent down and felt her pulse and then stood there watching her breathing. "Where does it hurt, Miss—"

"Davis," I said. "Miss Merle Davis."

"Miss Davis."

"Nothing hurts me," she said, staring up at him. "I—I

don't even know why I'm lying here like this. I thought you were the police. You see, I killed a man."

"Well, that's a normal human impulse," he said. "I've killed dozens." He didn't smile.

She lifted her lip and moved her head around for him.

"You know you don't have to do that," he said, quite gently. "You feel a twitch of the nerves here and there and you proceed to build it up and dramatize it. You can control it, if you want to."

"Can I?" she whispered.

"If you want to," he said. "You don't have to. It doesn't make any difference to me either way. Nothing pains at all, eh?"

"No." She shook her head.

He patted her shoulder and walked out to the kitchen. I went after him. He leaned his hips against the sink and gave me a cool stare. "What's the story?"

"She's the secretary of a client. A Mrs. Murdock in Pasadena. The client is rather a brute. About eight years ago a man made a hard pass at Merle. How hard I don't know. Then—I don't mean immediately—but around that time he fell out of a window or jumped. Since then she can't have a man touch her—not in the most casual way, I mean."

"Uh-huh." His pop eyes continued to read my face. "Does she think he jumped out of the window on her account?"

"I don't know. Mrs. Murdock is the man's widow. She married again and her second husband is dead too. Merle has stayed with her. The old woman treats her like a rough parent treats a naughty child."

"I see. Regressive."

"What's that?"

"Emotional shock, and the subconscious attempt to escape back to childhood. If Mrs. Murdock scolds her a good deal, but not too much, that would increase the tendency. Identification of childhood subordination with childhood protection."

"Do we have to go into that stuff?" I growled.

He grinned at me calmly. "Look, pal. The girl's obvi-

ously a neurotic. It's partly induced and partly deliberate. I mean to say that she really enjoys a lot of it. Even
if she doesn't realize that she enjoys it. However, that's
not of immediate importance. What's this about killing a
man?"

"A man named Vannier who lives in Sherman Oaks.
There seems to be some blackmail angle. Merle had to
take him his money, from time to time. She was afraid of
him. I've seen the guy. A nasty type. She went over there
this afternoon and she says she shot him."

"Why?"

"She says she didn't like the way he leered at her."

"Shot him with what?"

"She had a gun in her bag. Don't ask me why. I don't
know. But if she shot him, it wasn't with that. The gun's
got a wrong cartridge in the breech. It can't be fired as it
is. Also it hasn't been fired."

"This is too deep for me," he said. "I'm just a doctor.
What did you want me to do with her?"

"Also," I said, ignoring the question, "she said the lamp
was turned on and it was about five-thirty of a nice
summery afternoon. And the guy was wearing his sleeping suit and there was a key in the lock of the front door.
And he didn't get up to let her in. He just sort of sat
there sort of leering."

He nodded and said: "Oh." He pushed a cigarette
between his heavy lips and lit it. "If you expect me to
tell you whether she really thinks she shot him, I can't do
it. From your description I gather that the man is shot.
That so?"

"Brother, I haven't been there. But that much seems
pretty clear."

"If she thinks she shot him and isn't just acting—and
God, how these types do act!—that indicates it was not a
new idea to her. You say she carried a gun. So perhaps it
wasn't. She may have a guilt complex. Wants to be
punished, wants to expiate some real or imaginary crime.
Again I ask what do you want me to do with her? She's
not sick, she's not loony."

"She's not going back to Pasadena."

"Oh." He looked at me curiously. "Any family?"

"In Wichita. Father's a vet. I'll call him, but she'll have to stay here tonight."

"I don't know about that. Does she trust you enough to spend the night in your apartment?"

"She came here of her own free will, and not socially. So I guess she does."

He shrugged and fingered the sidewall of his coarse black mustache. "Well, I'll give her some nembutal and we'll put her to bed. And you can walk the floor wrestling with your conscience."

"I have to go out," I said. "I have to go over there and see what has happened. And she can't stay here alone. And no man, not even a doctor is going to put her to bed. Get a nurse. I'll sleep somewhere else."

"Phil Marlowe," he said, "the shop-soiled Galahad. Okay. I'll stick around until the nurse comes."

He went back into the living room and telephoned the Nurses' Registry. Then he telephoned his wife. While he was telephoning, Merle sat up on the davenport and clasped her hands primly in her lap.

"I don't see why the lamp was on," she said. "It wasn't dark in the house at all. Not that dark."

I said: "What's your dad's first name?"

"Dr. Wilbur Davis. Why?"

"Wouldn't you like something to eat?"

At the telephone Carl Moss said to me: "Tomorrow will do for that. This is probably just a lull." He finished his call, hung up, went to his bag and came back with a couple of yellow capsules in his hand on a fragment of cotton. He got a glass of water, handed her the capsules and said: "Swallow."

"I'm not sick, am I?" she said, looking up at him.

"Swallow, my child, swallow."

She took them and put them in her mouth and took the glass of water and drank.

I put my hat on and left.

On the way down in the elevator I remembered that there hadn't been any keys in her bag, so I stopped at the lobby floor and went out through the lobby to the

Bristol Avenue side. The car was not hard to find. It was parked crookedly about two feet from the curb. It was a gray Mercury convertible and its license number was 2X1111. I remembered that this was the number of Linda Murdock's car.

A leather keyholder hung in the lock. I got into the car, started the engine, saw that there was plenty of gas, and drove it away. It was a nice eager little car. Over Cahuenga Pass it had the wings of a bird.

■ **29** ■

ESCAMILLO DRIVE MADE THREE JOGS IN FOUR BLOCKS, FOR no reason that I could see. It was very narrow, averaged about five houses to a block and was overhung by a section of shaggy brown foothill on which nothing lived at this season except sage and manzanita. In its fifth and last block, Escamillo Drive did a neat little curve to the left, hit the base of the hill hard, and died without a whimper. In this last block were three houses, two on the opposite entering corners, one at the dead end. This was Vannier's. My spotlight showed the key still in the door.

It was a narrow English type bungalow with a high roof, leaded front windows, a garage to the side, and a trailer parked beside the garage. The early moon lay quietly on its small lawn. A large oak tree grew almost on the front porch. There was no light in the house now, none visible from the front at least.

From the lay of the land a light in the living room in the daytime did not seem utterly improbable. It would be a dark house except in the morning. As a love nest the place had its points, but as a residence for a blackmailer I didn't give it very high marks. Sudden death can come to you anywhere, but Vannier had made it too easy.

I turned into his driveway, backed to get myself pointed out of the dead end, and then drove down to the
corner and parked there. I walked back in the street
because there was no sidewalk. The front door was made
of iron-bound oak planks, bevelled where they joined.
There was a thumb latch instead of a knob. The head
of the flat key projected from the lock. I rang the bell,
and it rang with that remote sound of a bell ringing at
night in an empty house. I walked around the oak tree
and poked the light of my pencil flash between the
leaves of the garage door. There was a car in there. I
went back around the house and looked at a small
flowerless yard, walled in by a low wall of fieldstone.
Three more oak trees, a table and a couple of all metal
chairs under one of them. A rubbish burner at the back. I
shone my light into the trailer before I went back to the
front. There didn't seem to be anybody in the trailer. Its
door was locked.

I opened the front door, leaving the key in the lock. I
wasn't going to work any dipsy-doodle in this place.
Whatever was, was. I just wanted to make sure. I felt
around on the wall inside the door for a light switch,
found one and tilted it up. Pale flame bulbs in pairs in
wall brackets went on all around the room, showing me
the big lamp Merle had spoken of, as well as other things.
I went over to switch the lamp on, then back to switch
the wall light off. The lamp had a big bulb inverted in
porcelain glass bowl. You could get three different inten-
sities of light. I clicked the button switch around until I
had all there was.

The room ran from front to back, with a door at the
back and an arch up front to the right. Inside that was a
small dining room. Curtains were half drawn across the
arch, heavy pale green brocade curtains, far from new.
The fireplace was in the middle of the left wall, book-
shelves opposite and on both sides of it, not built in. Two
davenports angled across the corners of the room and
there was one gold chair, one pink chair, one brown
chair, one brown and gold jacquard chair with footstool.
Yellow pajama legs were on the footstool, bare ankles,

feet in dark green morocco leather slippers. My eyes ran up from the feet, slowly, carefully. A dark green figured silk robe, tied with a tasseled belt. Open above the belt showing a monogram on the pocket of the pajamas. A handkerchief neat in the pocket, two stiff points of white linen. A yellow neck, the face turned sideways, pointed at a mirror on the wall. I walked around and looked in the mirror. The face leered all right.

The left arm and hand lay between a knee and the side of the chair, the right arm hung outside the chair, the ends of the fingers touching the rug. Touching also the butt of a small revolver, about .32 caliber, a belly gun, with practically no barrel. The right side of the face was against the back of the chair, but the right shoulder was dark brown with blood and there was some on the right sleeve. Also on the chair. A lot of it on the chair.

I didn't think his head had taken that position natural-ly. Some sensitive soul had not liked the right side of it.

I lifted my foot and gently pushed the footstool side-ways a few inches. The heels of the slippers moved reluctantly over the jacquard surface, not with it. The man was as stiff as a board. So I reached down and touched his ankle. Ice was never as cold.

On a table at his right elbow was half of a dead drink, an ashtray full of butts and ash. Three of the butts had lipstick on them. Bright Chinese red lipstick. What a blond would use. There was another ashtray beside an-other chair. Matches in it and a lot of ash, but no stubs.

On the air of the room a rather heavy perfume strug-gled with the smell of death, and lost. Although de-feated, it was still there.

I poked through the rest of the house, putting lights on and off. Two bedrooms, one furnished in light wood, one in red maple. The light one seemed to be a spare. A nice bathroom with tan and mulberry tiling and a stall shower with a glass door. The kitchen was small. There were a lot of bottles in the sink. Lots of bottles, lots of glass, lots of fingerprints, lots of evidence. Or not, as the case may be.

I went back to the living room and stood in the middle

of the floor breathing with my mouth as far as possible and wondering what the score would be when I turned this one in. Turn this one in and report that I was the fellow who had found Morningstar and run away. The score would be low, very low. Marlowe, three murders. Marlowe practically knee-deep in dead men. And no reasonable, logical, friendly account of himself whatsoever. But that wasn't the worst of it. The minute I opened up I would cease to be a free agent. I would be through with doing whatever it was I was doing and with finding out whatever it was I was finding out.

Carl Moss might be willing to protect Merle with the mantle of Aesculapius, up to a point. Or he might think it would do her more good in the long run to get it all off her chest, whatever it was.

I wandered back to the jacquard chair and set my teeth and grabbed enough of his hair to pull the head away from the chair back. The bullet had gone in at the temple. The set-up could be for suicide. But people like Louis Vannier do not commit suicide. A blackmailer, even a scared blackmailer, has a sense of power, and loves it.

I let the head go back where it wanted to go and leaned down to scrub my hand on the nap of the rug. Leaning down I saw the corner of a picture frame under the lower shelf of the table at Vannier's elbow. I went around and reached for it with a handkerchief.

The glass was cracked across. It had fallen off the wall. I could see the small nail. I could make a guess how it had happened. Somebody standing at Vannier's right, even leaning over him, somebody he knew and had no fear of, had suddenly pulled a gun and shot him in the right temple. And then, startled by the blood or the recoil of the shot, the killer had jumped back against the wall and knocked the picture down. It had landed on a corner and jumped under the table. And the killer had been too careful to touch it, or too scared.

I looked at it. It was a small picture, not interesting at all. A guy in doublet and hose, with lace at his sleeve ends, and one of those round puffy velvet hats with a feather, leaning far out of a window and apparently calling out to somebody downstairs. Downstairs not being in the picture. It was a color reproduction of something that had never been needed in the first place.

I looked around the room. There were other pictures, a couple of rather nice water colors, some engravings—very old-fashioned this year, engravings, or are they? Half a dozen in all. Well, perhaps the guy liked the picture, so what? A man leaning out of a high window. A long time ago.

I looked at Vannier. He wouldn't help me at all. A man leaning out of a high window, a long time ago.

The touch of the idea at first was so light that I almost missed it and passed on. A touch of a feather, hardly that. The touch of a snowflake. A high window, a man leaning out—a long time ago.

It snapped in place. It was so hot it sizzled. Out of a high window a long time ago—eight years ago—a man leaning—too far—a man falling—to his death. A man named Horace Bright.

"Mr. Vannier," I said with a little touch of admiration, "you played that rather neatly."

I turned the picture over. On the back dates and amounts of money were written. Dates over almost eight years, amounts mostly of $500, a few $750's, two for $1000. There was a running total in small figures. It was $11,100. Mr. Vannier had not received the latest payment. He had been dead when it arrived. It was not a lot of money, spread over eight years. Mr. Vannier's customer had bargained hard.

The cardboard back was fastened into the frame with steel victrola needles. Two of them had fallen out. I worked the cardboard loose and tore it a little getting it loose. There was a white envelope between the back and the picture. Sealed, blank. I tore it open. It contained two square photographs and a negative. The photos were just the same. They showed a man leaning far out of a window with his mouth open, yelling. His hands were on the brick edges of the window frame. There was a woman's face behind his shoulder. He was a thinnish dark-haired man. His face was not very clear, nor the face of the woman behind him. He was leaning out of a window and yelling or calling out.

There I was holding the photograph and looking at it. And so far as I could see it didn't mean a thing. I knew it had to. I just didn't know why. But I kept on looking at it. And in a little while something was wrong. It was a very small thing, but it was vital. The position of the man's hands, lined against the corner of the wall where it was cut out to make the window frame. The hands were not holding anything, they were not touching anything. It was the inside of his wrists that lined against the angle of the bricks. The hands were in air.

The man was not leaning. He was falling.

I put the stuff back in the envelope and folded the cardboard back and stuffed that into my pocket also. I hid frame, glass and picture in the linen closet under towels.

All this had taken too long. A car stopped outside the house. Feet came up the walk. I dodged behind the curtains in the archway.

■ 30 ■

THE FRONT DOOR OPENED AND THEN QUIETLY CLOSED. There was a silence, hanging in the air like a man's breath in frosty air, and then a thick scream, ending in a wail of despair. Then a man's voice, tight with fury, saying: "Not bad, not good. Try again."

The woman's voice said: "My God, it's Louis! He's dead!"

The man's voice said: "I may be wrong, but I still think it stinks."

"My God! He's dead, Alex. Do something—for God's sake—*do* something!"

"Yeah," the hard tight voice of Alex Morny said. "I ought to. I ought to make you look just like him. With blood and everything. I ought to make you just as dead, just as cold, just as rotten. No, I don't have to do that. You're that already. Just as rotten. Eight months married and cheating on me with a piece of merchandise like that. My God! What did I ever think of to put in with a chippy like you?" He was almost yelling at the end of it.

The woman made another wailing noise.

"Quit stalling," Morny said bitterly. "What do you think I brought you over here for? You're not kidding anybody. You've been watched for weeks. You were here last night. I've been here already today. I've seen what there is to see. Your lipstick on cigarettes, your glass that you drank out of. I can see you now, sitting on the arm of his chair, rubbing his greasy hair, and then feeding him a slug while he was still purring. Why?"

"Oh, Alex—darling—don't say such awful things."

"Early Lillian Gish," Morny said. "Very early Lillian Gish. Skip the agony, toots. I have to know how to handle this. What the hell do you think I'm here for? I don't give one little flash in hell about you any more. Not any more, toots, not any more, my precious darling angel blond man-killer. But I do care about myself and my reputation and my business. For instance, did you wipe the gun off?"

Silence. Then the sound of a blow. The woman wailed. She was hurt, terribly hurt. Hurt in the depths of her soul. She made it rather good.

"Look, angel," Morny snarled. "Don't feed me the ham. I've been in pictures. I'm a connoisseur of ham. Skip it. You're going to tell me how this was done if I have to drag you around the room by your hair. Now—did you wipe off the gun?"

Suddenly she laughed. An unnatural laugh, but clear and with a nice tinkle to it. Then she stopped laughing, just as suddenly. Her voice said: "Yes."

"And the glass you were using?"

"Yes." Very quiet now, very cool.

"And you put his prints on the gun?"

"Yes."

He thought in the silence. "Probably won't fool them," he said. "It's almost impossible to get a dead man's prints on a gun in a convincing way. However. What else did you wipe off?"

"N-nothing. Oh Alex. Please don't be so brutal."

"Stop it. *Stop it!* Show me how you did it, how you were standing, how you held the gun."

She didn't move.

"Never mind about the prints," Morny said. "I'll put better ones on. Much better ones."

She moved slowly across the opening of the curtains and I saw her. She was wearing pale green gabardine slacks, a fawn-colored leisure jacket with stitching on it, a scarlet turban with a gold snake in it. Her face was smeared with tears.

"Pick it up," Morny yelled at her. "Show me!"

She bent beside the chair and came up with the gun in her hand and her teeth bared. She pointed the gun across the opening in the curtains, towards the space of room where the door was. Morny didn't move, didn't make a sound. The blond's hand began to shake and the gun did a queer up and down dance in the air. Her mouth trembled and her arm fell. "I can't do it," she breathed. "I ought to shoot you, but I can't." The hand opened and the gun thudded to the floor.

Morny went swiftly past the break in the curtains, pushed her out of the way and with his foot pushed the gun back to about where it had been.

"You couldn't do it," he said thickly. "You couldn't do it. Now watch." He whipped a handkerchief out and bent to pick the gun up again. He pressed something and the gate fell open. He reached his right hand into his pocket and rolled a cartridge in his fingers, moving his fingertips on the metal, pushed the cartridge into a cylinder. He repeated the performance four times more, snapped the gate shut, then opened it and spun it a little to set it in a certain spot. He placed the gun down on the floor, withdrew his hand and handkerchief and straightened up.

"You couldn't shoot me," he sneered, "because there was nothing in the gun but one empty shell. Now it's loaded again. The cylinders are in the right place. One shot has been fired. And your fingerprints are on the gun."

The blond was very still, looking at him with haggard eyes.

"I forgot to tell you," he said softly, "I wiped the gun off. I thought it would be so much nicer to be *sure* your prints were on it. I was pretty sure they were—but I felt as if I would like to be *quite* sure. Get it?"

The girl said quietly: "You're going to turn me in?"

His back was towards me. Dark clothes. Felt hat pulled low. So I couldn't see his face. But I could just about see the leer with which he said: "Yes, angel, I am going to turn you in."

"I see," she said, and looked at him levelly. There was a sudden grave dignity in her over-emphasized chorus girl's face.

"I'm going to turn you in, angel," he said slowly, spacing his words as if he enjoyed his act. "Some people are going to be sorry for me and some people are going to laugh at me. But it's not going to do my business any harm. Not a bit of harm. That's one nice thing about a business like mine. A little notoriety won't hurt it at all."

"So I'm just publicity value to you, now," she said. "Apart, of course, from the danger that you might have been suspected yourself."

"Just so," he said. "Just so."

"How about my motive?" she asked, still calm, still level-eyed and so gravely contemptuous that he didn't get the expression at all.

"I don't know," he said. "I don't care. You were up to something with him. Eddie tailed you downtown to a street on Bunker Hill where you met a blond guy in a brown suit. You gave him something. Eddie dropped you and tailed the guy to an apartment house near there. He tried to tail him some more, but he had a hunch the guy spotted him, and he had to drop it. I don't know what it was all about. I know one thing, though. In that apartment house a young guy named Phillips was shot yesterday. Would you know anything about that, my sweet?"

The blond said: "I wouldn't know anything about it. I don't know anybody named Phillips and strangely enough I didn't just run up and shoot anybody out of sheer girlish fun."

"But you shot Vannier, my dear," Morny said almost gently.

"Oh yes," she drawled. "Of course. We were wondering what my motive was. You get it figured out yet?"

"You can work that out with the johns," he snapped. "Call it a lovers' quarrel. Call it anything you like."

"Perhaps," she said, "when he was drunk he looked just a little like you. Perhaps that was the motive."

He said: "Ah," and sucked his breath in.

"Better looking," she said. "Younger, with less belly. But with the same goddamned self-satisfied smirk."

"Ah," Morny said, and he was suffering.

"Would that do?" she asked him softly.

He stepped forward and swung a fist. It caught her on the side of the face and she went down and sat on the floor, a long leg straight out in front of her, one hand to her jaw, her very blue eyes looking up at him.

"Maybe you oughtn't to have done that," she said. "Maybe I won't go through with it, now."

"You'll go through with it, all right. You won't have any choice. You'll get off easy enough. Christ, I know that. With your looks. But you'll go through with it, angel. Your fingerprints are on that gun."

She got to her feet slowly, still with the hand to her jaw. Then she smiled. "I knew he was dead," she said. "That is my key in the door. I'm quite willing to go downtown and say I shot him. But don't lay your smooth white paw on me again—if you want my story. Yes. I'm quite willing to go to the cops. I'll feel a lot safer with them than I feel with you."

Morny turned and I saw the hard white leer of his face and the scar dimple in his cheek twitching. He walked past the opening in the curtains. The front door opened again. The blond stood still a moment, looked back over her shoulder at the corpse, shuddered slightly, and passed out of my line of vision.

The door closed. Steps on the walk. Then car doors opening and closing. The motor throbbed, and the car went away.

■ 31 ■

AFTER A LONG TIME I MOVED OUT FROM MY HIDING PLACE and stood looking around the living room again. I went over and picked the gun up and wiped it off very carefully and put it down again. I picked the three rouge-stained cigarette stubs out of the tray on the table and carried them into the bathroom and flushed them down the toilet. Then I looked around for the second glass with her fingerprints on it. There wasn't any second glass. The one that was half full of a dead drink I took to the kitchen and rinsed out and wiped on a dish towel.

Then the nasty part. I kneeled on the rug by his chair and picked up the gun and reached for the trailing bone-stiff hand. The prints would not be good, but they would be prints and they would not be Lois Morny's. The gun had a checked rubber grip, with a piece broken off on the left side below the screw. No prints on that. An index print on the right side of the barrel, two fingers on the trigger guard, a thumb print on the flat piece on the left side, behind the chambers. Good enough.

I took one more look around the living room.

I put the lamp down to a lower light. It still glared too much on the dead yellow face. I opened the front door, pulled the key out and wiped it off and pushed it back into the lock. I shut the door and wiped the thumblatch off and went my way down the block to the Mercury.

I drove back to Hollywood and locked the car up and

started along the sidewalk past the other parked cars to the entrance of the Bristol. A harsh whisper spoke to me out of darkness, out of a car. It spoke my name. Eddie Prue's long blank face hung somewhere up near the roof of a small Packard, behind its wheel. He was alone in it. I leaned on the door of the car and looked in at him.

"How you making out, shamus?"

I tossed a match down and blew smoke at his face. I said: "Who dropped that dental supply company's bill you gave me last night? Vannier, or somebody else?"

"Vannier."

"What was I supposed to do with it—guess the life history of a man named Teager?"

"I don't go for dumb guys," Eddie Prue said.

I said: "Why would he have it in his pocket to drop? And if he did drop it, why wouldn't you just hand it back to him? In other words, seeing that I'm a dumb guy, explain to me why a bill for dental supplies should get anybody all excited and start trying to hire private detectives. Especially gents like Alex Morny, who don't like private detectives."

"Morny's a good head," Eddie Prue said coldly.

"He's the fellow for whom they coined the phrase, 'as ignorant as an actor.'"

"Skip that. Don't you know what they use that dental stuff for?"

"Yeah. I found out. They use albastone for making molds of teeth and cavities. It's very hard, very fine grain and retains any amount of fine detail. The other stuff, crystobolite, is used to cook out the wax in an invested wax model. It's used because it stands a great deal of heat without distortion. Tell me you don't know what I'm talking about."

"I guess you know how they make gold inlays," Eddie Prue said. "I guess you do, huh?"

"I spent two of my hours learning today. I'm an expert. What does it get me?"

He was silent for a little while, and then he said: "You ever read the paper?"

"Once in a while."

"It couldn't be you read where an old guy named Morningstar was bumped off in the Belfont Building on Ninth Street, just two floors above where this H. R. Teager had his office. It couldn't be you read that, could it?"

I didn't answer him. He looked at me for a moment longer, then he put his hand forward to the dash and pushed the starter button. The motor of his car caught and he started to ease in the clutch. "Nobody could be as dumb as you act," he said softly. "Nobody ain't. Good night to you." The car moved away from the curb and drifted down the hill towards Franklin. I was grinning into the distance as it disappeared.

I went up to the apartment and unlocked the door and pushed it open a few inches and then knocked gently. There was movement in the room. The door was pulled open by a strong-looking girl with a black stripe on the cap of her white nurse's uniform.

"I'm Marlowe. I live here."

"Come in, Mr. Marlowe. Dr. Moss told me."

I shut the door quietly and we spoke in low voices. "How is she?" I asked.

"She's asleep. She was already drowsy when I got here. I'm Miss Lymington. I don't know very much about her except that her temperature is normal and her pulse still rather fast, but going down. A mental disturbance, I gather."

"She found a man murdered," I said. "It shot her full of holes. Is she hard enough asleep so that I could go in and get a few things to take to the hotel?"

"Oh, yes. If you're quiet. She probably won't wake. If she does, it won't matter."

I went over and put some money on the desk. "There's coffee and bacon and eggs and bread and tomato juice and oranges and liquor here," I said. "Anything else you'll have to phone for."

"I've already investigated your supplies," she said, smiling. "We have all we need until after breakfast tomorrow. Is she going to stay here?"

"That's up to Dr. Moss. I think she'll be going home as

soon as she is fit for it. Home being quite a long way off, in Wichita."

"I'm only a nurse," she said. "But I don't think there is anything the matter with her that a good night's sleep won't cure."

"A good night's sleep and a change of company," I said, but that didn't mean anything to Miss Lymington.

I went along the hallway and peeked into the bedroom. They had put a pair of my pajamas on her. She lay almost on her back with one arm outside the bedclothes. The sleeve of the pajama coat was turned up six inches or more. The small hand below the end of the sleeve was in a tight fist. Her face looked drawn and white and quite peaceful. I poked about in the closet and got a suitcase and put some junk in it. As I started back out I looked at Merle again. Her eyes opened and looked straight up at the ceiling. Then they moved just enough to see me and a faint little smile tugged at the corners of her lips. "Hello." It was a weak spent little voice, a voice that knew its owner was in bed and had a nurse and everything.

"Hello."

I went around near her and stood looking down, with my polished smile on my clean-cut features.

"I'm all right," she whispered. "I'm fine. Amn't I?"

"Sure."

"Is this your bed I'm in?"

"That's all right. It won't bite you."

"I'm not afraid," she said. A hand came sliding towards me and lay palm up, waiting to be held. I held it. "I'm not afraid of you. No woman would ever be afraid of you, would she?"

"Coming from you," I said, "I guess that's meant to be a compliment."

Her eyes smiled, then got grave again. "I lied to you," she said softly. "I—didn't shoot anybody."

"I know. I was over there. Forget it. Don't think about it."

"People are always telling you to forget unpleasant

things. But you never do. It's so kind of silly to tell you to, I mean."

"Okay," I said, pretending to be hurt. "I'm silly. How about making some more sleep?"

She turned her head until she was looking into my eyes. I sat on the edge of the bed, holding her hand.

"Will the police come here?" she asked.

"No. And try not to be disappointed."

She frowned. "You must think I'm an awful fool."

"Well—maybe."

A couple of tears formed in her eyes and slid out at the corners and rolled gently down her cheeks. "Does Mrs. Murdock know where I am?"

"Not yet. I'm going over and tell her."

"Will you have to tell her—everything?"

"Yeah, why not?"

She turned the head away from me. "She'll understand," her voice said softly. "She knows the awful thing I did eight years ago. The frightful terrible thing."

"Sure," I said. "That's why she's been paying Vannier money all this time."

"Oh dear," she said, and brought her other hand out from under the bedclothes and pulled away the one I was holding so that she could squeeze them tightly together. "I wish you hadn't had to know that. I wish you hadn't. Nobody ever knew but Mrs. Murdock. My parents never knew. I wish you hadn't."

The nurse came in at the door and looked at me severely. "I don't think she ought to be talking like this, Mr. Marlowe. I think you should leave now."

"Look, Miss Lymington, I've known this little girl two days. You've only known her two hours. This is doing her a lot of good."

"It might bring on another—er—spasm," she said severely, avoiding my eyes.

"Well, if she has to have it, isn't it better for her to have it now, while you're here, and get it over with? Go on out to the kitchen and buy yourself a drink."

"I never drink on duty," she said coldly. "Besides somebody might smell my breath."

"You're working for me now. All my employees are required to get liquored up from time to time. Besides, if you had a good dinner and were to eat a couple of the Chasers in the kitchen cabinet, nobody would smell your breath."

She gave me a quick grin and went back out of the room. Merle had been listening to this as if it was a frivolous interruption to a very serious play. Rather annoyed.

"I want to tell you all about it," she said breathlessly. "I—"

I reached over and put a paw over her two locked hands. "Skip it. I know. Marlowe knows everything—except how to make a decent living. It doesn't amount to beans. Now you're going back to sleep and tomorrow I'm going to take you on the way back to Wichita—to visit your parents. At Mrs. Murdock's expense."

"Why, that's wonderful of her," she cried, her eyes opening wide and shining. "But she's always been wonderful to me."

I got up off the bed. "She's a wonderful woman," I said, grinning down at her. "Wonderful. I'm going over there now and we're going to have a perfectly lovely little talk over the teacups. And if you don't go to sleep right now, I won't let you confess to any more murders."

"You're horrid," she said. "I don't like you." She turned her head away and put her arms back under the bedclothes and shut her eyes.

I went towards the door. At the door I swung around and looked back quickly. She had one eye open, watching me. I gave her a leer and it snapped shut in a hurry.

I went back to the living room, gave Miss Lymington what was left of my leer, and went out with my suitcase.

I drove over to Santa Monica Boulevard. The hockshop was still open. The old Jew in the tall black skullcap seemed surprised that I was able to redeem my pledge so soon. I told him that was the way it was in Hollywood.

He got the envelope out of the safe and tore it open and took my money and pawnticket and slipped the shining gold coin out on his palm. "So valuable this is I am hating to give it back to you," he said. "The workmanship, you understand, the workmanship, is beautiful."

"And the gold in it must be worth all of twenty dollars," I said.

He shrugged and smiled and I put the coin in my pocket and said goodnight to him.

■ **32** ■

THE MOONLIGHT LAY LIKE A WHITE SHEET ON THE FRONT lawn except under the deodar where there was the thick darkness of black velvet. Lights in two lower windows were lit and in one upstairs room visible from the front. I walked across the stumble stones and rang the bell. I didn't look at the little painted Negro by the hitching block. I didn't pat his head tonight. The joke seemed to have worn thin.

A white-haired, red-faced woman I hadn't seen before opened the door and I said: "I'm Philip Marlowe. I'd like to see Mrs. Murdock. Mrs. Elizabeth Murdock."

She looked doubtful. "I think she's gone to bed," she said. "I don't think you can see her."

"It's only nine o'clock."

"Mrs. Murdock goes to bed early." She started to close the door.

She was a nice old thing and I hated to give the door the heavy shoulder. I just leaned against it. "It's about Miss Davis," I said. "It's important. Could you tell her that?"

"I'll see."

I stepped back and let her shut the door.

A mockingbird sang in a dark tree nearby. A car tore down the street much too fast and skidded around the next corner. The thin shreds of a girl's laughter came back along the dark street as if the car had spilled them out in its rush.

The door opened after a while and the woman said: "You can come in."

I followed her across the big empty entrance room. A single dim light burned in one lamp, hardly reaching to the opposite wall. The place was too still, and the air needed freshening. We went along the hall to the end and up a flight of stairs with a carved handrail and newel post. Another hall at the top, a door open towards the back.

I was shown in at the open door and the door was closed behind me. It was a big sitting room with a lot of chintz, blue and silver wallpaper, a couch, a blue carpet and French windows open on a balcony. There was an awning over the balcony. Mrs. Murdock was sitting in a padded wing chair with a card table in front of her. She was wearing a quilted robe and her hair looked a little fluffed out. She was playing solitaire. She had the pack in her left hand and she put a card down and moved another one before she looked up at me. Then she said: "Well?"

I went over by the card table and looked down at the game. It was Canfield. "Merle's at my apartment," I said. "She threw an ing-bing."

Without looking up she said: "And just what is an ing-bing, Mr. Marlowe?"

She moved another card, then two more quickly.

"A case of the vapors, they used to call it," I said. "Ever catch yourself cheating at that game?"

"It's no fun if you cheat," she said gruffly. "And very little if you don't. What's this about Merle? She has never stayed out like this before. I was getting worried about her."

I pulled a slipper chair over and sat down across the table from her. It put me too low down. I got up and got a better chair and sat in that.

"No need to worry about her," I said. "I got a doctor and a nurse. She's asleep. She was over to see Vannier."

She laid the pack of cards down and folded her big gray hands on the edge of the table and looked at me solidly. "Mr. Marlowe," she said, "you and I had better have something out. I made a mistake calling you in the first place. That was my dislike of being played for a sucker, as you would say, by a hardboiled little animal like Linda. But it would have been much better, if I had not raised the point at all. The loss of the doubloon would have been much easier to bear than you are. Even if I had never got it back."

"But you did get it back," I said.

She nodded. Her eyes stayed on my face. "Yes. I got it back. You heard how."

"I didn't believe it."

"Neither did I," she said calmly. "My fool of a son was simply taking the blame for Linda. An attitude I find childish."

"You have a sort of knack," I said, "of getting yourselves surrounded with people who take such attitudes."

She picked her cards up again and reached down to put a black ten on a red jack, both cards that were already in the layout. Then she reached sideways to a small heavy table on which was her port. She drank some, put the glass down and gave me a hard level stare. "I have a feeling that you are going to be insolent, Mr. Marlowe."

I shook my head. "Not insolent. Just frank. I haven't done so badly for you, Mrs. Murdock. You did get the doubloon back. I kept the police away from you—so far. I didn't do anything on the divorce, but I found Linda—your son knew where she was all the time—and I don't think you'll have any trouble with her. She knows she made a mistake marrying Leslie. However, if you don't think you got value—"

She made a humph noise and played another card. She got the ace of diamonds up to the top line. "The ace of clubs is buried, darn it. I'm not going to get it out in time."

"Kind of slide it out," I said, "when you're not looking."

"Hadn't you better," she said very quietly, "get on with

telling me about Merle? And don't gloat too much, if you have found out a few family secrets, Mr. Marlowe."

"I'm not gloating about anything. You sent Merle to Vannier's place this afternoon, with five hundred dollars."

"And if I did?" She poured some of her port and sipped, eyeing me steadily over the glass.

"When did he ask for it?"

"Yesterday. I couldn't get it out of the bank until today. What happened?"

"Vannier's been blackmailing you for about eight years, hasn't he? On account of something that happened on April 26th, 1933?"

A sort of panic twitched in the depths of her eyes, but very far back, very dim, and somehow as though it had been there for a long time and had just peeped out at me for a second.

"Merle told me a few things," I said. "Your son told me how his father died. I looked up the records and the papers today. Accidental death. There had been an accident in the street under his office and a lot of people were craning out of windows. He just craned out too far. There was some talk of suicide because he was broke and had fifty thousand life insurance for his family. But the coroner was nice and slid past that."

"Well?" she said. It was a cold hard voice, neither a croak nor a gasp. A cold hard utterly composed voice.

"Merle was Horace Bright's secretary. A queer little girl in a way, overtimid, not sophisticated, a little girl mentality, likes to dramatize herself, very old-fashioned ideas about men, all that sort of thing. I figure he got high one time and made a pass at her and scared her out of her socks."

"Yes?" Another cold hard monosyllable prodding me like a gun barrel.

"She brooded and got a little murderous inside. She got a chance and passed right back at him. While he was leaning out of a window. Anything in it?"

"Speak plainly, Mr. Marlowe. I can stand plain talk."

"Good grief, how plain do you want it? She pushed her

employer out of a window. Murdered him, in two words. And got away with it. With your help."

She looked down at the left hand clenched over her cards. She nodded. Her chin moved a short inch, down, up.

"Did Vannier have any evidence?" I asked. "Or did he just happen to see what happened and put the bite on you and you paid him a little now and then to avoid scandal—and because you were really very fond of Merle?"

She played another card before she answered me. Steady as a rock. "He talked about a photograph," she said. "But I never believed it. He couldn't have taken one. And if he had taken one, he would have shown it to me—sooner or later."

I said: "No, I don't think so. It would have been a very fluky shot, even if he happened to have the camera in his hand, on account of the doings down below in the street. But I can see he might not have dared to show it. You're a pretty hard woman, in some ways. He might have been afraid you would have him taken care of. I mean that's how it might look to him, a crook. How much have you paid him?"

"That's none—" she started to say, then stopped and shrugged her big shoulders. A powerful woman, strong, rugged, ruthless and able to take it. She thought. "Eleven thousand one hundred dollars, not counting the five hundred I sent him this afternoon."

"Ah. It was pretty darn nice of you, Mrs. Murdock. Considering everything."

She moved a hand vaguely, made another shrug. "It was my husband's fault," she said. "He was drunk, vile. I don't think he really hurt her, but, as you say, he frightened her out of her wits. I—I can't blame her too much. She has blamed herself enough all these years."

"She had to take the money to Vannier in person?"

"That was her idea of penance. A strange penance."

I nodded. "I guess that would be in character. Later you married Jasper Murdock and you kept Merle with you and took care of her. Anybody else know?"

"Nobody. Only Vannier. Surely he wouldn't tell anybody."

"No. I hardly think so. Well, it's all over now. Vannier is through."

She lifted her eyes slowly and gave me a long level gaze. Her gray head was a rock on top of a hill. She put the cards down at last and clasped her hands tightly on the edge of the table. The knuckles glistened.

I said: "Merle came to my apartment when I was out. She asked the manager to let her in. He phoned me and I said yes. I got over there quickly. She told me she had shot Vannier."

Her breath was a faint swift whisper in the stillness of the room.

"She had a gun in her bag, God knows why. Some idea of protecting herself against men, I suppose. But somebody—Leslie, I should guess—had fixed it to be harmless by jamming a wrong size cartridge into the breech. She told me she had killed Vannier and fainted. I got a doctor friend of mine. I went over to Vannier's house. There was a key in the door. He was dead in a chair, long dead, cold, stiff. Dead long before Merle went there. She didn't shoot him. Her telling me that was just drama. The doctor explained it after a fashion, but I won't bore you with it. I guess you understand all right."

She said: "Yes. I think I understand. And now?"

"She's in bed, in my apartment. There's a nurse there. I phoned Merle's father long distance. He wants her to come home. That all right with you?"

She just stared.

"He doesn't know anything," I said quickly. "Not this or the other time. I'm sure of that. He just wants her to come home. I thought I'd take her. It seems to be my responsibility now. I'll need that last five hundred that Vannier didn't get—for expenses."

"And how much more?" she asked brutally.

"Don't say that. You know better."

"Who killed Vannier?"

"Looks like he committed suicide. A gun at his right hand. Temple contact wound. Morny and his wife were there while I was. I hid. Morny's trying to pin it on his wife. She was playing games with Vannier. So she probably thinks he did it, or had it done. But it shapes up like suicide. The cops will be there by now. I don't know what they will make of it. We just have to sit tight and wait it out."

"Men like Vannier," she said grimly, "don't commit suicide."

"That's like saying girls like Merle don't push people out of windows. It doesn't mean anything."

We stared at each other, with that inner hostility that had been there from the first. After a moment I pushed my chair back and went over to the French windows. I opened the screen and stepped out on to the porch. The night was all around, soft and quiet. The white moonlight was cold and clear, like the justice we dream of but don't find.

The trees down below cast heavy shadows under the moon. In the middle of the garden there was a sort of garden within a garden. I caught the glint of an ornamental pool. A lawn swing beside it. Somebody was lying in the lawn swing and a cigarette tip glowed as I looked down.

I went back into the room. Mrs. Murdock was playing solitaire again. I went over to the table and looked down. "You got the ace of clubs out," I said.

"I cheated," she said without looking up.

"There was one thing I wanted to ask you," I said. "This doubloon business is still cloudy, on account of a couple of murders which don't seem to make sense now that you have the coin back. What I wondered was if there was anything about the Murdock Brasher that might identify it to an expert—to a man like old Morningstar."

She thought, sitting still, not looking up. "Yes. There might be. The coinmaker's initials, E. B., are on the left wing of the eagle. Usually, I'm told, they are on the right wing. That's the only thing I can think of."

I said: "I think that might be enough. You did actually

get the coin back, didn't you? I mean that wasn't just something said to stop my ferreting around?"

She looked up swiftly and then down. "It's in the strong room at this moment. If you can find my son, he will show it to you."

"Well, I'll say good night. Please have Merle's clothes packed and sent to my apartment in the morning."

Her head snapped up again and her eyes glared. "You're pretty highhanded about all this, young man."

"Have them packed," I said. "And send them. You don't need Merle any more—now that Vannier is dead."

Our eyes locked hard and held locked for a long moment. A queer stiff smile moved the corners of her lips. Then her head went down and her right hand took the top card off the pack held in her left hand and turned it and her eyes looked at it and she added it to the pile of unplayed cards below the layout, and then turned the next card, quietly, calmly, in a hand as steady as a stone pier in a light breeze.

I went across the room and out, closed the door softly, went along the hall, down the stairs, along the lower hall past the sun room and Merle's little office, and out into the cheerless stuffy unused living room that made me feel like an embalmed corpse just to be in it.

The French doors at the back opened and Leslie Murdock stepped in and stopped, staring at me.

■ 33 ■

HIS SLACK SUIT WAS RUMPLED AND ALSO HIS HAIR. HIS little reddish mustache looked just as ineffectual as ever. The shadows under his eyes were almost pits. He was carrying his long black cigarette holder, empty, and tapping it against the heel of his left hand as he stood not liking me, not wanting to meet me, not wanting to talk to me. "Good evening," he said stiffly. "Leaving?"

"Not quite yet. I want to talk to you."

"I don't think we have anything to talk about. And I'm tired of talking."

"Oh yes we have. A man named Vannier."

"Vannier? I hardly know the man. I've seen him around. What I know I don't like."

"You know him a little better than that," I said.

He came forward into the room and sat down in one of the I-dare-you-to-sit-in-me chairs and leaned forward to cup his chin in his left hand and look at the floor.

"All right," he said wearily. "Get on with it. I have a feeling you are going to be very brilliant. Remorseless flow of logic and intuition and all that rot. Just like a detective in a book."

"Sure. Taking the evidence piece by piece, putting it all together in a neat pattern, sneaking in an odd bit I had on my hip here and there, analyzing the motives and characters and making them out to be quite different from what anybody—or I myself for that matter—thought them to be up to this golden moment—and finally making a sort of world-weary pounce on the least promising suspect."

He lifted his eyes and almost smiled. "Who thereupon turns as pale as paper, froths at the mouth, and pulls a gun out of his right ear."

I sat down near him and got a cigarette out. "That's right. We ought to play it together sometime. You got a gun?"

"Not with me. I have one. You know that."

"Have it with you last night when you called on Vannier?"

He shrugged and bared his teeth. "Oh. Did I call on Vannier last night?"

"I think so. Deduction. You smoke Benson and Hedges Virginia cigarettes. They leave a firm ash that keeps its shape. An ashtray at his house had enough of those little gray rolls to account for at least two cigarettes. But no stubs in the tray. Because you smoke them in a holder and a stub from a holder looks different. So you removed the stubs. Like it?"

"No." His voice was quiet. He looked down at the floor again.

"That's an example of deduction. A bad one. For there might not have been any stubs, but if there had been and they had been removed, it might have been because they had lipstick on them. Of a certain shade that would at least indicate the coloring of the smoker. And your wife has a quaint habit of throwing her stubs into the waste-basket."

"Leave Linda out of this," he said coldly.

"Your mother still thinks Linda took the doubloon and that your story about taking it to give to Alex Morny was just a cover-up to protect her."

"I said leave Linda out of it." The tapping of the black holder against his teeth had a sharp quick sound, like a telegraph key.

"I'm willing to," I said. "But I didn't believe your story for a different reason. This." I took the doubloon out and held it on my hand under his eyes.

He stared at it tightly. His mouth set.

"This morning when you were telling your story this was hocked on Santa Monica Boulevard for safekeeping. It was sent to me by a would-be detective named George Phillips. A simple sort of fellow who allowed himself to get into a bad spot through poor judgment and over-eagerness for a job. A thickset blond fellow in a brown suit, wearing dark glasses and a rather gay hat. Driving a sand-colored Pontiac, almost new. You might have seen him hanging about in the hall outside my office yester-day morning. He had been following me around and before that he might have been following you around."

He looked genuinely surprised. "Why would he do that?"

I lit my cigarette and dropped the match in a jade ashtray that looked as if it had never been used as an ashtray.

"I said he might have. I'm not sure he did. He might have just been watching this house. He picked me up here and I don't think he followed me here." I still had the coin on my hand. I looked down at it, turned it over by tossing it, looked at the initials E. B. stamped into the left wing, and put it away. "He might have been watching the house because he had been hired to peddle a rare coin to an old coin dealer named Morningstar. And the old coin dealer somehow suspected where the coin came from, and told Phillips, or hinted to him, that the coin was stolen. Incidentally, he was wrong about that. If your Brasher Doubloon is really at this moment upstairs, then the coin Phillips was hired to peddle was not a stolen coin. It was a counterfeit."

His shoulders gave a quick little jerk, as if he was cold. Otherwise he didn't move or change position.

"I'm afraid it's getting to be one of those long stories after all," I said, rather gently. "I'm sorry. I'd better organize it a little better. It's not a pretty story, because it has two murders in it, maybe three. A man named Vannier and a man named Teager had an idea. Teager is a dental technician in the Belfont Building, old Morningstar's building. The idea was to counterfeit a rare and valuable gold coin, not too rare to be marketable, but rare enough to be worth a lot of money. The method they thought of was about what a dental technician uses to make a gold inlay. Requiring the same materials, the same apparatus, the same skills. That is, to reproduce a model exactly, in gold, by making a matrix in a hard white fine cement called albastone, then making a replica of the model in that matrix in molding wax, complete in the finest detail, then investing the wax, as they call it, in another kind of cement called crystobolite, which has the property of standing great heat without distortion. A small opening is left from the wax to outside by attaching a steel pin which is withdrawn when the cement sets. Then the crystobolite casting is cooked over a flame until the wax boils out through this small opening, leaving a hollow mold of the original model. This is clamped against a crucible on a centrifuge and molten gold is shot into it by centrifugal force from the crucible. Then the crystobolite, still hot, is held under cold water and it disintegrates, leaving the gold core with a gold pin attached, representing the small opening. That is trimmed off, the casting is cleaned in acid and polished and you have, in this case, a brand new Brasher Doubloon, made of solid gold and exactly the same as the original. You get the idea?"

He nodded and moved a hand wearily across his head.

"The amount of skill this would take," I went on, "would be just what a dental technician would have. The process would be of no use for a current coinage, if we had a gold coinage, because the material and labor would cost more than the coin would be worth. But for a gold coin that was valuable through being rare, it would fit fine. So that's what they did. But they had to have a model. That's where you came in. You took the doubloon all right, but not to give to Morny. You took it to give to Vannier. Right?"

He stared at the floor and didn't speak.

"Loosen up," I said. "In the circumstances it's nothing very awful. I suppose he promised you money, because you needed it to pay off gambling debts and your mother is close. But he had a stronger hold over you than that."

He looked up quickly then, his face very white, a kind of horror in his eyes. "How did you know that?" he almost whispered.

"I found out. Some I was told, some I researched, some I guessed. I'll get to that later. Now Vannier and his pal have made a doubloon and they want to try it out. They wanted to know their merchandise would stand up under inspection by a man supposed to know rare coins. So Vannier had the idea of hiring a sucker and getting him to try to sell the counterfeit to old Morningstar, cheap enough so the old guy would think it was stolen. They picked George Anson Phillips for their sucker, through a silly ad he was running in the paper for business. I think Lois Morny was Vannier's contact with Phillips, at first anyway. I don't think she was in the racket. She was seen to give Phillips a small package. This package may have contained the doubloon Phillips was to try to sell. But when he showed it to old Morningstar he ran into a snag.

The old man knew his coin collections and his rare coins. He probably thought the coin was genuine enough—it would take a lot of testing to show it wasn't—but the way the maker's initials were stamped on the coin was unusual and suggested to him that the coin might be the Murdock Brasher. He called up here and tried to find out. That made your mother suspicious and the coin was found to be missing and she suspected Linda, whom she hates, and hired me to get it back and put the squeeze on Linda for a divorce, without alimony."

"I don't want a divorce," Murdock said hotly. "I never had any such idea. She had no right—" he stopped and made a despairing gesture and a kind of sobbing sound.

"Okay, I know that. Well, old Morningstar threw a scare into Phillips, who wasn't crooked, just dumb. He managed to get Phillips' phone number out of him. I heard the old man call that number, eavesdropping in his office after he thought I had left. I had just offered to buy the doubloon back for a thousand dollars and Morningstar had taken up the offer, thinking he could get the coin from Phillips, make himself some money and everything lovely. Meantime Phillips was watching this house, perhaps to see if any cops were coming and going. He saw me, saw my car, got my name off the registration and it just happened he knew who I was.

"He followed me around trying to make up his mind to ask me for help until I braced him in a downtown hotel and he mumbled about knowing me from a case in Ventura when he was a deputy up there, and about being in a spot he didn't like and about being followed around by a tall guy with a funny eye. That was Eddie Prue, Morny's sidewinder. Morny knew his wife was playing games with Vannier and had her shadowed. Prue saw her make contact with Phillips near where he lived on Court Street, Bunker Hill, and then followed Phillips until he thought Phillips had spotted him, which he had. And Prue, or somebody working for Morny, may have seen me go to Phillips' apartment on Court Street. Because he tried to scare me over the phone and later asked me to come and see Morny."

I got rid of my cigarette stub in the jade ashtray, looked at the bleak unhappy face of the man sitting opposite me, and plowed on. It was heavy going, and the sound of my voice was beginning to sicken me.

"Now we come back to you. When Merle told you your mother had hired a dick, that threw a scare into *you*. You figured she had missed the doubloon and you came steaming up to my office and tried to pump me. Very debonair, very sarcastic at first, very solicitous for your wife, but very worried. I don't know what you think you found out, but you got in touch with Vannier. You now had to get the coin back to your mother in a hurry, with some kind of story. You met Vannier somewhere and he gave you a doubloon. Chances are it's another counterfeit. He would be likely to hang on to the real one. Now Vannier sees his racket in danger of blowing up before it gets started. Morningstar has called your mother and I have been hired. Morningstar has spotted something. Vannier goes down to Phillips' apartment, sneaks in the back way, and has it out with Phillips, trying to find out where he stands.

"Phillips doesn't tell him he has already sent the counterfeit doubloon to me, addressing it in a kind of printing afterwards found in a diary in his office. I infer that from the fact Vannier didn't try to get it back from me. I don't know what Phillips told Vannier, of course, but the chances are he told him the job was crooked, that he knew where the coin came from, and that he was going to the police or to Mrs. Murdock. And Vannier pulled a gun, knocked him on the head and shot him. He searched him and the apartment and didn't find the doubloon. So he went to Morningstar. Morningstar didn't have the counterfeit doubloon either, but Vannier probably thought he had. He cracked the old man's skull with a gun butt and went through his safe, perhaps found some money, perhaps found nothing, at any rate left the appearance of a stickup behind him. Then Mr. Vannier breezed on home, still rather annoyed because he hadn't found the doubloon, but with the satisfaction of a good afternoon's work under his vest. A couple of nice neat murders. That left you."

▪ 34 ▪

MURDOCK FLICKED A STRAINED LOOK AT ME, THEN HIS eyes went to the black cigarette holder he still had clenched in his hand. He tucked it in his shirt pocket, stood up suddenly, ground the heels of his hands together and sat down again. He got a handkerchief out and mopped his face. "Why me?" he asked in a thick strained voice.

"You knew too much. Perhaps you knew about Phillips, perhaps not. Depends how deep you were in it. But you knew about Morningstar. The scheme had gone wrong and Morningstar had been murdered. Vannier couldn't just sit back and hope you wouldn't hear about that. He had to shut your mouth, very, very tight. But he didn't have to kill you to do it. In fact killing you would be a bad move. It would break his hold on your mother. She's a cold ruthless grasping woman, but hurting you would make a wildcat of her. She wouldn't care what happened."

Murdock lifted his eyes. He tried to make them blank with astonishment. He only made them dull and shocked. "My mother—what—?"

"Don't kid me any more than you have to," I said. "I'm tired to death of being kidded by the Murdock family. Merle came to my apartment this evening. She's there now. She had been over to Vannier's house to bring him some money. Blackmail money. Money that had been paid to him off and on for eight years. I know why."

He didn't move. His hands were rigid with strain on his knees. His eyes had almost disappeared into the back of his head. They were doomed eyes.

"Merle found Vannier dead. She came to me and said she had killed him. Let's not go into why she thinks she ought to confess to other people's murders. I went over there and he had been dead since last night. He was as stiff as a wax dummy. There was a gun lying on the floor by his right hand. It was a gun I had heard described, a gun that belonged to a man named Hench, in an apartment across the hall from Phillips' apartment. Somebody ditched the gun that killed Phillips and took Hench's gun. Hench and his girl were drunk and left their apartment open. It's not proved that it was Hench's gun, but it will be. If it is Hench's gun, and Vannier committed suicide, it ties Vannier to the death of Phillips. Lois Morny also ties him to Phillips, in another way. If Vannier didn't commit suicide—and I don't believe he did—it might still tie him to Phillips. Or it might tie somebody else to Phillips, somebody who also killed Vannier. There are reasons why I don't like that idea."

Murdock's head came up. He said "No?" in a suddenly clear voice. There was a new expression on his face, something bright and shining and at the same time just a little silly. The expression of a weak man being proud.

I said: "I think you killed Vannier." He didn't move and the bright shining expression stayed on his face.

"You went over there last night. He sent for you. He told you he was in a jam and that if the law caught up with him, he would see that you were in the jam with him. Didn't he say something like that?"

"Yes," Murdock said quietly. "Something exactly like that. He was drunk and a bit high and he seemed to have a sense of power. He gloated, almost. He said if they got him in the gas chamber, I would be sitting right beside him. But that wasn't all he said."

"No. He didn't want to sit in the gas chamber and he didn't at the time see any very good reason why he should, if you kept your mouth good and tight. So he played his trump card. His first hold on you, what made you take the doubloon and give it to him, even if he did promise you money as well, was something about Merle and your father. I know about it. Your mother told me what little I hadn't put together already. That was his first hold and it was pretty strong. Because it would let you justify yourself. But last night he wanted something still stronger. So he told you the truth and said he had proof."

He shivered, but the light clear proud look managed to stay on his face. "I pulled a gun on him," he said, almost in a happy voice. "After all she is my mother."

"Nobody can take that away from you."

He stood up, very straight, very tall. "I went over to the chair he sat in and reached down and put the gun against his face. He had a gun in the pocket of his robe. He tried to get it, but he didn't get it in time. I took it away from him. I put my gun back in my pocket. I put the muzzle of the other gun against the side of his head and told him I would kill him, if he didn't produce his proof and give it to me. He began to sweat and babble that he was just kidding me. I clicked back the hammer on the gun to scare him some more."

He stopped and held a hand out in front of him. The hand shook but as he stared down at it it got steady. He dropped it to his side and looked me in the eye.

"The gun must have been filed or had a very light action. It went off. I jumped back against the wall and knocked a picture down. I jumped from surprise that the gun went off, but it kept the blood off me. I wiped the gun off and put his fingers around it and then put it down on the floor close to his hand. He was dead at once. He hardly bled except the first spurt. It was an accident."

"Why spoil it?" I half sneered. "Why not make it a nice clean honest murder?"

"That's what happened. I can't prove it, of course. But I think I might have killed him anyway. What about the police?"

I stood up and shrugged my shoulders. I felt tired, spent, drawn out and sapped. My throat was sore from yapping and my brain ached from trying to keep my thoughts orderly. "I don't know about the police," I said. "They and I are not very good friends, on account of they think I am holding out on them. And God knows they are right. They may get to you. If you weren't seen, if you didn't leave any fingerprints around, and even if you did, if they don't have any other reason to suspect you and get your fingerprints to check, then they may never think of you. If they find out about the doubloon and that it was the Murdock Brasher, I don't know where you stand. It all depends on how well you stand up to them."

"Except for Mother's sake," he said. "I don't very much care. I've always been a flop."

"And on the other hand," I said, ignoring the feeble talk, "if the gun has a very light action and you get a good lawyer and tell an honest story and so on, no jury will convict you. Juries don't like blackmailers."

"That's too bad," he said. "Because I am not in a position to use that defense. I don't know anything about blackmail. Vannier showed me where I could make some money, and I needed it badly."

I said: "Uh-huh. If they get you where you need the blackmail dope, you'll use it all right. Your old lady will make you. If it's her neck or yours, she'll spill."

"It's horrible," he said. "Horrible to say that."

"You were lucky about that gun. All the people we know have been playing with it, wiping prints off and putting them on. I even put a set on myself just to be fashionable. It's tricky when the hand is stiff. But I had to do it. Morny was over there having his wife put hers on. He thinks she killed Vannier, so she probably thinks he did."

He just stared at me. I chewed my lip. It felt as stiff as a piece of glass. "Well, I guess I'll just be running along now," I said.

"You mean you are going to let me get away with it?" His voice was getting a little suspicious again.

"I'm not going to turn you in, if that's what you mean. Beyond that I guarantee nothing. If I'm involved in it, I'll have to face up to the situation. There's no question of morality involved. I'm not a cop nor a common informer nor an officer of the court. You say it was an accident. Okay, it was an accident. I wasn't a witness. I haven't any proof either way. I've been working for your mother and whatever right to my silence that gives her, she can have. I don't like her, I don't like you, I don't like this house. I didn't particularly like your wife. But I like Merle. She's kind of silly and morbid, but she's kind of sweet too. And I know what has been done to her in this damn family for the past eight years. And I know she didn't push anybody out of any window. Does that explain matters?"

He gobbled, but nothing came that was coherent.

"I'm taking Merle home," I said. "I asked your mother to send her clothes to my apartment in the morning. In case she kind of forgets, being busy with her solitaire game, would you see that that is done?"

He nodded dumbly. Then he said in a queer small voice: "You are going—just like that? I haven't—I haven't even thanked you. A man I hardly know, taking risks for me—I don't know what to say."

"I'm going the way I always go," I said. "With an airy smile and a quick flip of the wrist. And with a deep and heartfelt hope that I won't be seeing you in the fish bowl. Good night."

I turned my back on him and went to the door and out. I shut the door with a quiet firm click of the lock. A nice smooth exit, in spite of all the nastiness. For the last time I went over and patted the little painted Negro on the head and then walked across the long lawn by the moon-drenched shrubs and the deodar tree to the street and my car.

I drove back to Hollywood, bought a pint of good liquor, checked in at the Plaza, and sat on the side of the bed staring at my feet and lapping the whiskey out of the bottle.

Just like any common bedroom drunk.

When I had enough of it to make my brain fuzzy enough to stop thinking, I undressed and got into bed and after a while, but not soon enough, I went to sleep.

◾ 35 ◾

IT WAS THREE O'CLOCK IN THE AFTERNOON AND THERE were five pieces of luggage inside the apartment door, side by side on the carpet. There was my yellow cowhide, well scraped on both sides from being pushed around in the boots of cars. There were two nice pieces of airplane luggage both marked L.M. There was an old black imitation walrus thing marked M.D. and there was one of these little leatherette overnight cases which you can buy in drugstores for a dollar forty-nine.

Dr. Carl Moss had just gone out of the door cursing me because he had kept his afternoon class of hypochondriacs waiting. The sweetish smell of his Fatima poisoned the air for me. I was turning over in what was left of my mind what he had said when I asked him how long it would take Merle to get well.

"It depends what you mean by well. She'll always be high on nerves and low on animal emotion. She'll always breathe thin air and smell snow. She'd have made a perfect nun. The religious dream, with its narrowness, its stylized emotions and its grim purity, would have been a perfect release for her. As it is she will probably turn out to be one of these acid-faced virgins that sit behind little desks in public libraries and stamp dates in books."

"She's not that bad," I had said, but he had just grinned at me with his wise face and gone out of the door. "And besides how do you know they are virgins?" I added to the closed door, but that didn't get me any farther.

I lit a cigarette and wandered over to the window and after a while she came through the doorway from the bedroom part of the apartment and stood there looking at me with her eyes dark-ringed and a pale composed little face without any makeup except on the lips. "Put some rouge on your cheeks," I told her. "You look like the snow maiden after a hard night with the fishing fleet."

So she went back and put some rouge on her cheeks. When she came back again she looked at the luggage and said softly: "Leslie lent me two of his suitcases."

I said: "Yeah," and looked her over. She looked very nice. She had a pair of long-waisted rust-colored slacks on, and Bata shoes and a brown and white print shirt and an orange scarf. She didn't have her glasses on. Her large clear cobalt eyes had a slightly dopey look, but not more than you would expect. Her hair was dragged down tight, but I couldn't do anything much about that.

"I've been a terrible nuisance," she said. "I'm terribly sorry."

"Nonsense. I talked to your father and mother both. They're tickled to death. They've only seen you twice in over eight years and they feel as if they had almost lost you."

"I'll love seeing them for a while," she said, looking down at the carpet. "It's very kind of Mrs. Murdock to let me go. She's never been able to spare me for long." She moved her legs as if she wondered what to do with them in slacks, although they were her slacks and she must have had to face the problem before. She finally put her knees close together and clasped her hands on top of them.

"Any little talking we might have to do," I said, "or anything you might want to say to me, let's get it over with now. Because I'm not driving halfway across the United States with a nervous breakdown in the seat beside me."

She bit a knuckle and sneaked a couple of quick looks at me around the side of the knuckle. "Last night—" she said, and stopped and colored.

"Let's use a little of the old acid," I said. "Last night you told me you killed Vannier and then you told me you didn't. I know you didn't. That's settled."

She dropped the knuckle, looked at me levelly, quiet,

composed and the hands on her knees now not straining at all.

"Vannier was dead a long time before you got there. You went there to give him some money for Mrs. Murdock."

"No—for me," she said. "Although of course it was Mrs. Murdock's money. I owe her more than I'll ever be able to repay. Of course she doesn't give me much salary, but that would hardly—"

I said roughly: "Her not giving you much salary is a characteristic touch and your owing her more than you can ever repay is more truth than poetry. It would take the Yankee outfield with two bats to give her what she has coming from you. However, that's unimportant now. Vannier committed suicide because he had got caught out in a crooked job. That's flat and final. The way you behaved was more or less an act. You got a severe nervous shock seeing his leering dead face in a mirror and that shock merged into another one a long time ago and you just dramatized it in your screwy little way."

She looked at me shyly and nodded her copper-blond head, as if in agreement.

"And you didn't push Horace Bright out of any window," I said.

Her face jumped then and turned startlingly pale. "I—I—" her hand went to her mouth and stayed there and her shocked eyes looked at me over it.

"I wouldn't be doing this," I said, "if Dr. Moss hadn't said it would be all right and we might as well hand it to you now. I think maybe you think you killed Horace Bright. You had a motive and an opportunity and just for a second I think you might have had the impulse to take advantage of the opportunity. But it wouldn't be in your nature. At the last minute you would hold back. But at that last minute probably something snapped and you pulled a faint. He did actually fall, of course, but you were not the one that pushed him."

I held it a moment and watched the hand drop down again to join the other one and the two of them twine together and pull hard on each other.

"You were made to think you had pushed him," I said. "It was done with care, deliberation and the sort of quiet ruthlessness you only find in a certain kind of woman dealing with another woman. You wouldn't think of jealousy to look at Mrs. Murdock now—but if that was a motive, she had it. She had a better one—fifty thousand dollars' life insurance—all that was left from a ruined fortune. She had the strange wild possessive love for her son such women have. She's cold, bitter, unscrupulous and she used you without mercy, or pity, as insurance, in case Vannier ever blew his top. You were just a scapegoat to her. If you want to come out of this pallid sub-emotional life you have been living, you have got to realize and believe what I am telling you. I know it's tough."

"It's utterly impossible," she said quietly, looking at the bridge of my nose, "Mrs. Murdock has been wonderful to me always. It's true I never remembered very well—but you shouldn't say such awful things about people."

I got out the white envelope that had been in the back of Vannier's picture. Two prints in it and a negative. I stood in front of her and put a print on her lap.

"Okay, look at it. Vannier took it from across the street."

She looked at it. "Why that's Mr. Bright," she said. "It's not a very good picture, is it? And that's Mrs. Murdock—Mrs. Bright she was then—right behind him. Mr. Bright looks mad." She looked up at me with a sort of mild curiosity.

"If he looks mad there," I said, "you ought to have seen him a few seconds later, when he bounced."

"When he what?"

"Look," I said, and there was a kind of desperation in my voice now, "that is a snapshot of Mrs. Elizabeth Bright Murdock giving her first husband the heave out of his office window. He's falling. Look at the position of his hands. He's screaming with fear. She is behind him and her face is hard with rage—or something. Don't you get it at all? This is what Vannier has had for proof all these years. The Murdocks never saw it, never really believed it existed. But it did. I found it last night, by a fluke of the same sort that was involved in the taking of the picture. Which is a fair sort of justice. Do you begin to understand?"

She looked at the photo again and laid it aside. "Mrs. Murdock has always been lovely to me," she said.

"She made you the goat," I said, in the quietly strained voice of a stage manager at a bad rehearsal. "She's a smart tough patient woman. She knows her complexes. She'll even spend a dollar to keep a dollar, which is what few of her type will do. I hand it to her. I'd like to hand it to her with an elephant gun, but my polite breeding restrains me."

"Well," she said, "that's that." And I could see she had heard one word in three and hadn't believed what she had heard. "You must never show this to Mrs. Murdock. It would upset her terribly."

I got up and took the photo out of her hand and tore it into small pieces and dropped them in the wastebasket. "Maybe you'll be sorry I did that," I told her, not telling her I had another and the negative. "Maybe some night— three months—three years from now—you will wake up in the night and realize I have been telling you the truth. And maybe then you will wish you could look at that photograph again. And maybe I am wrong about this too. Maybe you would be very disappointed to find out you hadn't really killed anybody. That's fine. Either way it's fine. Now we are going downstairs and get in my car and we are going to drive to Wichita to visit your parents. And I don't think you are going back to Mrs. Murdock, but it may well be that I am wrong about that too. But we are not going to talk about this any more. Not any more."

"I haven't any money," she said.

"You have five hundred dollars that Mrs. Murdock sent you. I have it in my pocket."

"That's really awfully kind of her," she said.

"Oh hell and fireflies," I said and went out to the kitchen and gobbled a quick drink, before we started. It didn't do me any good. It just made me want to climb up the wall and gnaw my way across the ceiling.

■ **36** ■

I WAS GONE TEN DAYS. MERLE'S PARENTS WERE VAGUE kind patient people living in an old frame house in a quiet shady street. They cried when I told them as much of the story as I thought they should know. They said they were glad to have her back and they would take good care of her and they blamed themselves a lot, and I let them do it.

When I left Merle was wearing a bungalow apron and rolling pie crust. She came to the door wiping her hands on the apron and kissed me on the mouth and began to cry and ran back into the house, leaving the doorway empty until her mother came into the space with a broad homey smile on her face to watch me drive away.

I had a funny feeling as I saw the house disappear, as though I had written a poem and it was very good and I had lost it and would never remember it again.

I called Lieutenant Breeze when I got back and went down to ask him how the Phillips case was coming. They had cracked it very neatly, with the right mixture of brains and luck you always have to have. The Mornys never went to the police after all, but somebody called and told about a shot in Vannier's house and hung up quickly. The fingerprint man didn't like the prints on the gun too well, so they checked Vannier's hand for powder nitrates. When they found them they decided it was suicide after all. Then a dick named Lackey working out of Central Homicide thought to work on the gun a little and he found that a description of it had been distributed, and a gun like it was wanted in connection with the Phillips killing. Hench identified it, but better than that they found a half print of his thumb on the side of the trigger, which, not ordinarily being pulled back, had not been wiped off completely.

With that much in hand and a better set of Vannier's prints than I could make they went over Phillips' apartment again and also over Hench's. They found Vannier's left hand on Hench's bed and one of his fingers on the underside of the toilet flush lever in Phillips' place. Then they got to work in the neighborhood with photographs of Vannier and proved he had been along the alley twice and on a side street at least three times. Curiously, nobody in the apartment house had seen him, or would admit it.

All they lacked now was a motive. Teager obligingly gave them that by getting himself pinched in Salt Lake City trying to peddle a Brasher Doubloon to a coin dealer who thought it was genuine but stolen. He had a dozen of them at his hotel, and one of them turned out to be genuine. He told them the whole story and showed a minute mark that he had used to identify the genuine coin. He didn't know where Vannier got it and they never found out because there was enough in the papers to make the owner come forward, if it had been stolen. And the owner never did. And the police didn't care any more about Vannier once they were convinced he had done murder. They left it at suicide, although they had a few doubts.

They let Teager go after a while, because they didn't think he had any idea of murder being done and all they had on him was attempted fraud. He had bought the gold legally and counterfeiting an obsolete New York State coin didn't come under the federal counterfeiting laws. Utah refused to bother with him.

They never believed Hench's confession. Breeze said he just used it for a squeeze on me, in case I was holding out. He knew I couldn't keep quiet if I had proof that Hench was innocent. It didn't do Hench any good either. They put him in the lineup and pinned five liquor store holdups on him and an Italian named Gaetano Prisco, in one of which a man was shot dead. I never heard whether Prisco was a relative of Palermo's, but they never caught him anyway.

"Like it?" Breeze asked me, when he had told me all this, or all that had then happened.

"Two points not clear," I said. "Why did Teager run away and why did Phillips live on Court Street under a phony name?"

"Teager ran away because the elevator man told him old Morningstar had been murdered and he smelled a hookup. Phillips was using the name of Anson because the finance company was after his car and he was practically broke and getting desperate. That explains why a nice young boob like him could get roped into something that must have looked shady from the start."

I nodded and agreed that could be so.

Breeze walked to his door with me. He put a hard hand on my shoulder and squeezed. "Remember that Cassidy case you were howling about to Spangler and me that night in your apartment?"

"Yes."

"You told Spangler there wasn't any Cassidy case. There was—under another name. I worked on it." He took his hand off my shoulder and opened the door for me and grinned straight into my eyes. "On account of the Cassidy case," he said, "and the way it made me feel, I sometimes give a guy a break he could perhaps not really deserve. A little something paid back out of the dirty millions to a working stiff—like me—or like you. Be good."

It was night. I went home and put my old house clothes on and set the chessmen out and mixed a drink and played over another Capablanca. It went fifty-nine moves. Beautiful cold remorseless chess, almost creepy in its silent implacability.

When it was done I listened at the open window for a while and smelled the night. Then I carried my glass out to the kitchen and rinsed it and filled it with ice water and stood at the sink sipping it and looking at my face in the mirror.

"You and Capablanca," I said.

About the Author

RAYMOND CHANDLER was born in Chicago, Illinois, on July 23, 1888, but spent most of his boyhood and youth in England, where he attended Dulwich College and later worked as a free-lance journalist for *The Westminster Gazette* and *The Spectator*. During World War I, he served in France with the First Division of the Canadian Expeditionary Force, transferring later to the Royal Flying Corps (R.A.F.). In 1919 he returned to the United States, settling in California, where he eventually became director of a number of independent oil companies. The Depression put an end to his business career, and in 1933 at the age of forty-five, he turned to writing, publishing his first stories in *Black Mask*. His first novel, *The Big Sleep,* was published in 1939. Never a prolific writer, he published only one collection of stories and seven novels in his lifetime. In the last year of his life he was elected president of the Mystery Writers of America. He died in La Jolla, California, on March 26, 1959.